Mail Order Ninja Vol. 2
written by Joshua Elder
illustrated by Erich Owen

Lettering - Lucas Rivera
Cover Design - Chris Tjaslma

Editor - Paul Morrissey
Digital Imaging Manager - Chris Buford
Pre-Production Supervisor - Erika Terriquez
Art Director - Anne Marie Horne
Managing Editor - Vy Nguyen
Editorial Directior - Jeremy Ross
Production Manager - Elisabeth Brizzi
VP of Production - Ron Klamert
Editor-in-Chief - Rob Tokar
Publisher - Mike Kiley
President and C.O.O. - John Parker
C.E.O. and Chief Creative Officer - Stuart Levy

A  Manga

TOKYOPOP Inc.
5900 Wilshire Blvd. Suite 2000
Los Angeles, CA 90036

E-mail: info@TOKYOPOP.com
Come visit us online at www.TOKYOPOP.com

ISBN: 1-59816-729-4

First TOKYOPOP printing: December 2006
10 9 8 7 6 5 4 3 2 1
Printed in the USA

VOL. 2

TIMMY STRIKES BACK!

WRITTEN BY JOSHUA ELDER
ILLUSTRATED BY ERICH OWEN

TOKYOPOP®

HAMBURG // LONDON // LOS ANGELES // TOKYO

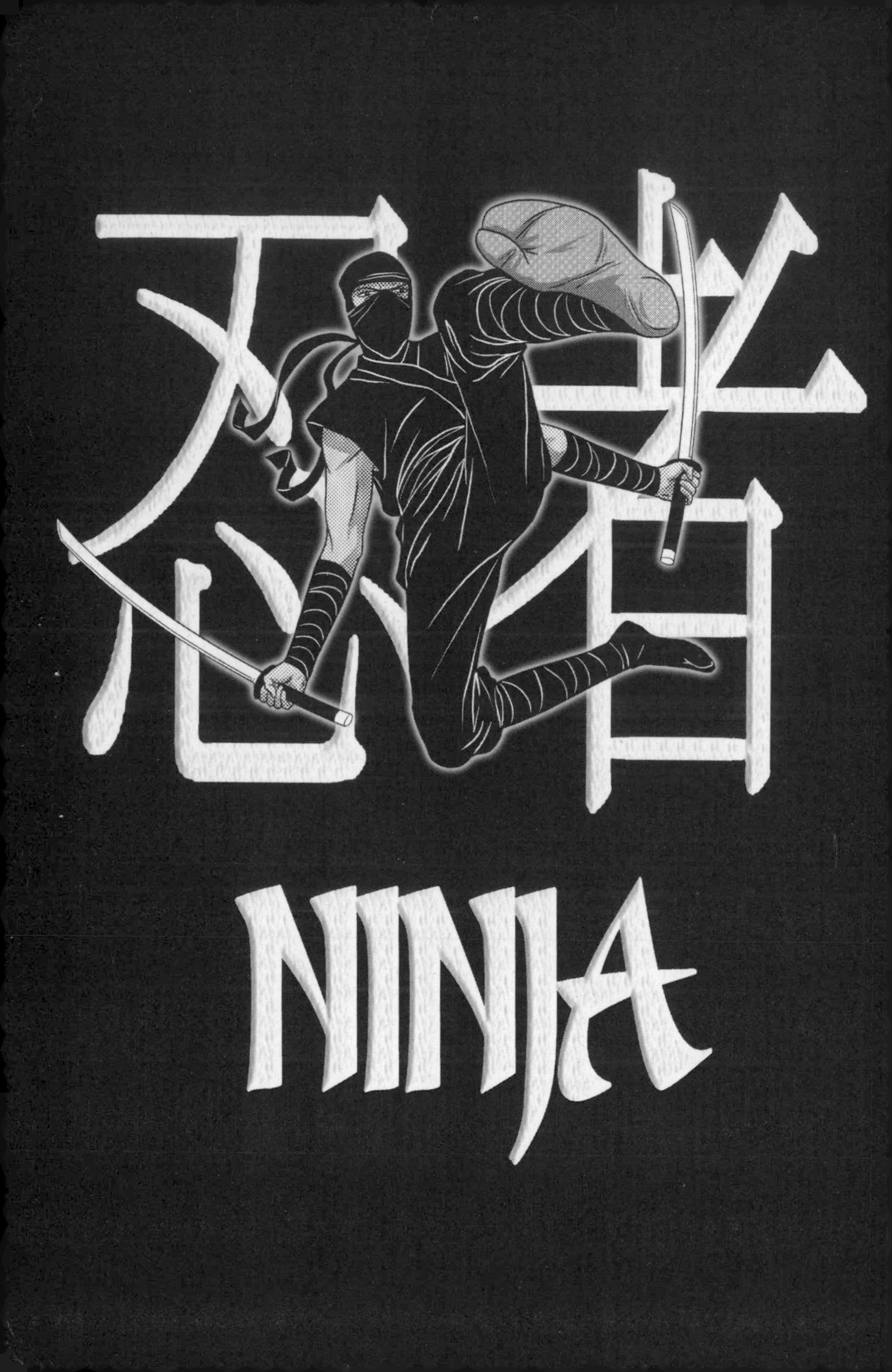
忍者
NINJA

CONTENTS

A few weeks ago in a small town not that far away...

MAIL ORDER NINJA

Episode II

TIMMY STRIKES BACK

NINJA! The balance of power at L. Frank Baum Elementary has shifted in favor of the geeky and downtrodden. The bullies and trust-fund babies have been humbled. Awesomeness is everywhere.

To celebrate, student body president Timmy McAllister (under the watchful eye of his mail order ninja Yoshida Jiro) is throwing the party to end all parties in the school's gymnasium.

But evil rich girl Felicity Huntington, obsessed with getting revenge on young McAllister, has bought a ninja of her own: the dreaded Hakuryuu Nobunaga...

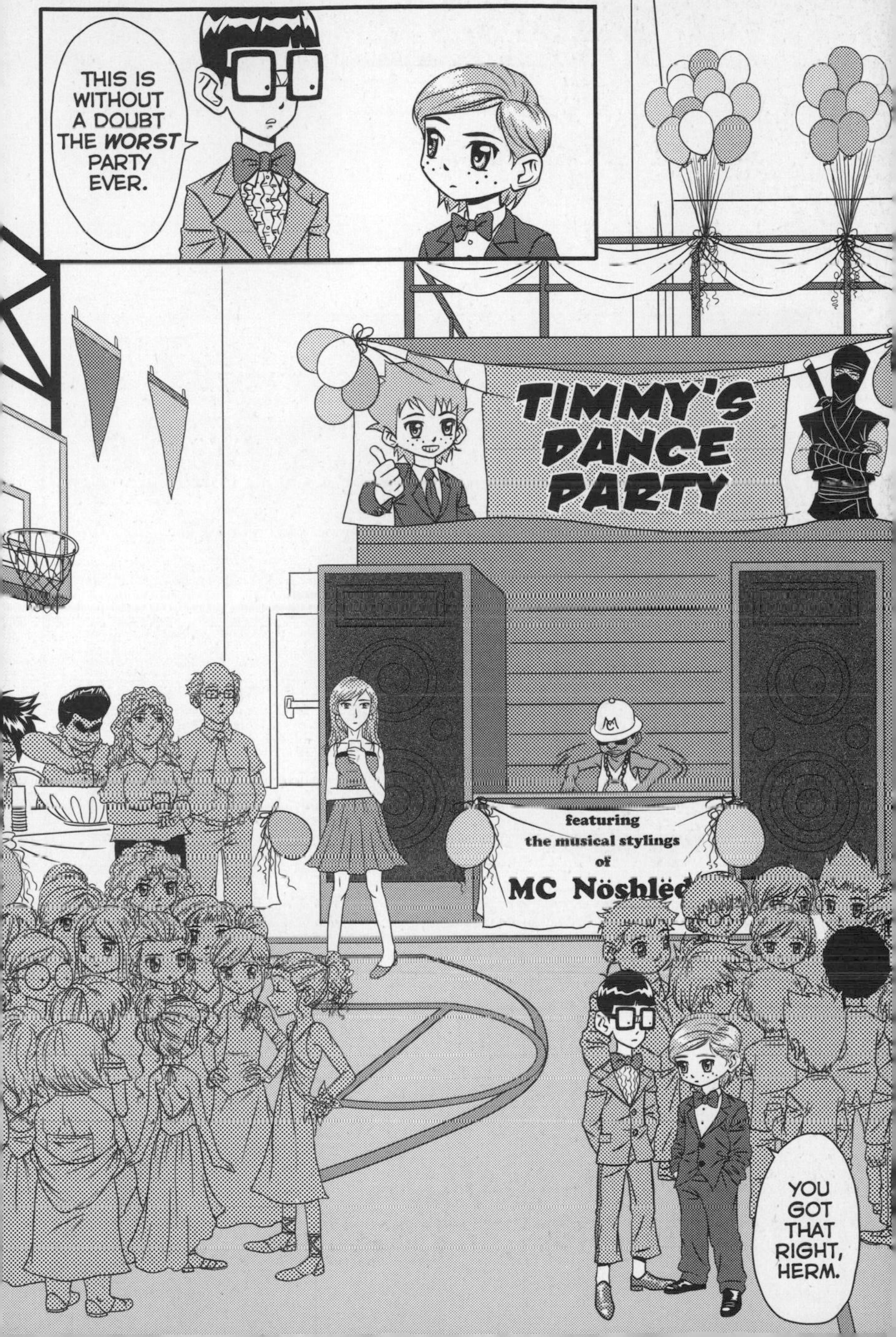
THIS IS WITHOUT A DOUBT THE *WORST* PARTY EVER.
TIMMY'S DANCE PARTY
featuring the musical stylings of
MC Nöshlëd
YOU GOT THAT RIGHT, HERM.

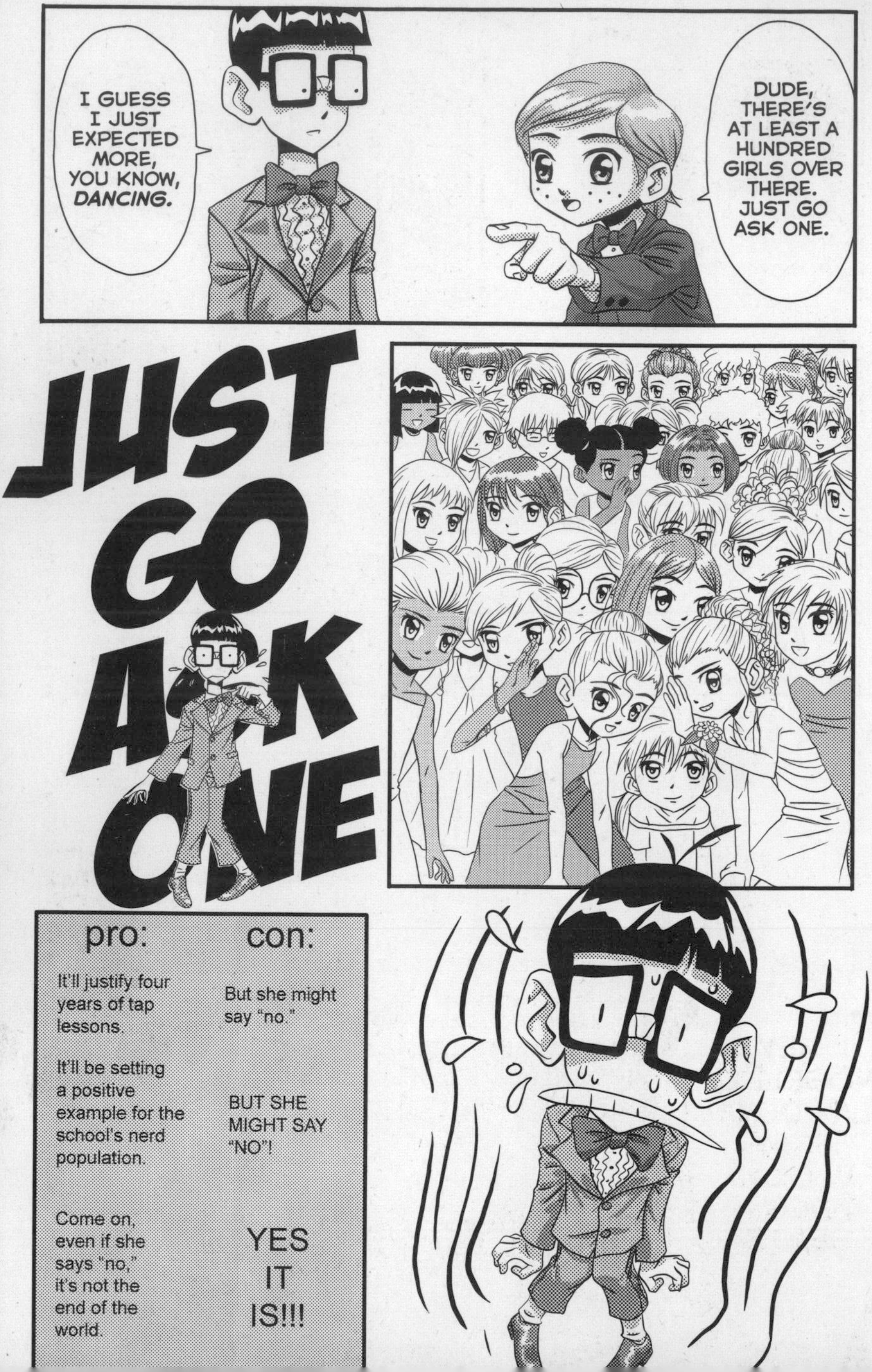
I GUESS I JUST EXPECTED MORE, YOU KNOW, *DANCING.*
DUDE, THERE'S AT LEAST A HUNDRED GIRLS OVER THERE. JUST GO ASK ONE.
JUST GO ASK ONE
pro:
con:
It'll justify four years of tap lessons.
But she might say "no."
It'll be setting a positive example for the school's nerd population.
BUT SHE MIGHT SAY "NO"!
Come on, even if she says "no," it's not the end of the world.
YES IT IS!!!

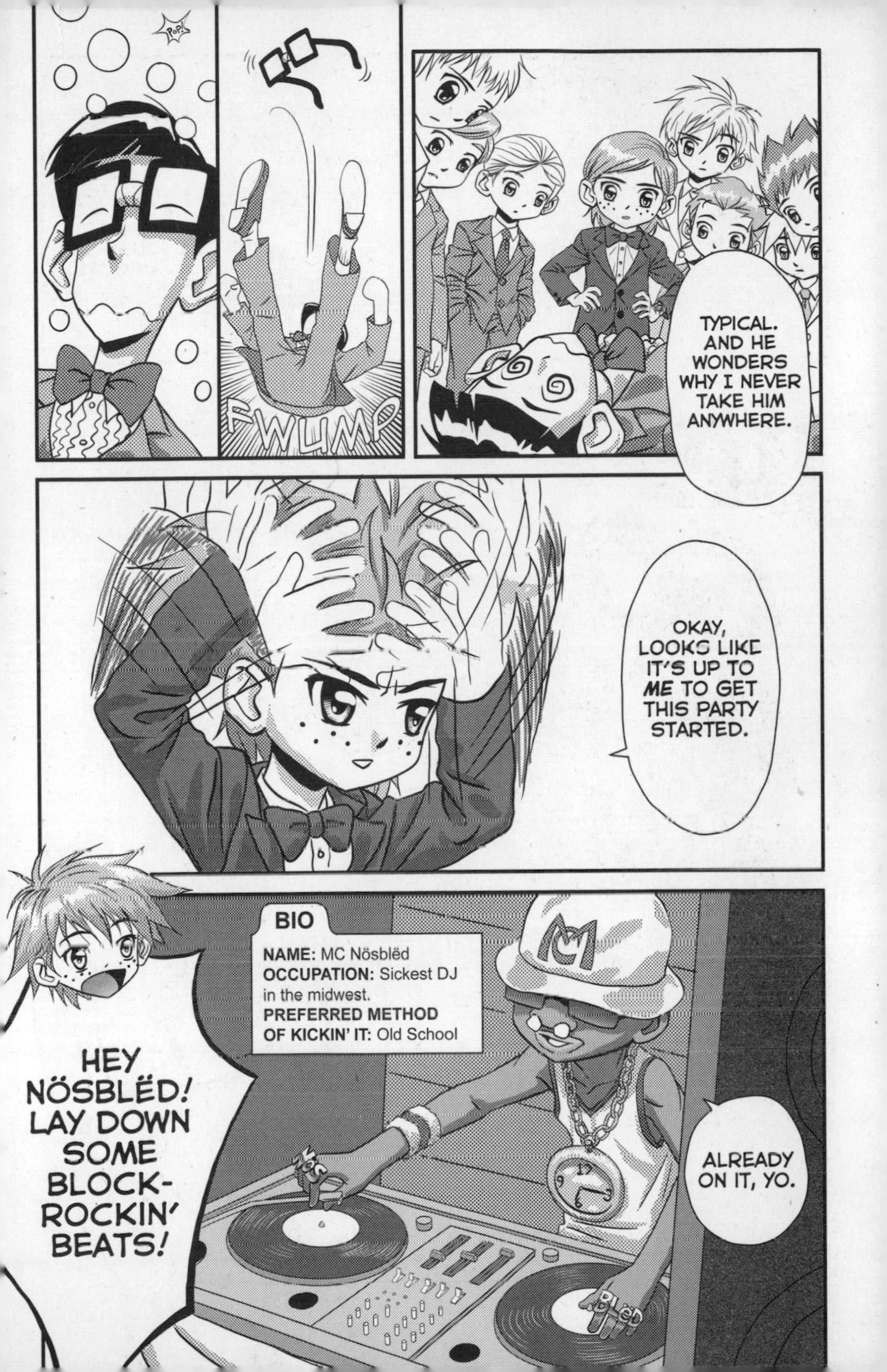
POP!
FWUMP
TYPICAL. AND HE WONDERS WHY I NEVER TAKE HIM ANYWHERE.
OKAY, LOOKS LIKE IT'S UP TO *ME* TO GET THIS PARTY STARTED.
BIO
NAME: MC Nösblëd
OCCUPATION: Sickest DJ in the midwest.
PREFERRED METHOD OF KICKIN' IT: Old School
HEY NÖSBLËD! LAY DOWN SOME BLOCK-ROCKIN' BEATS!
ALREADY ON IT, YO.

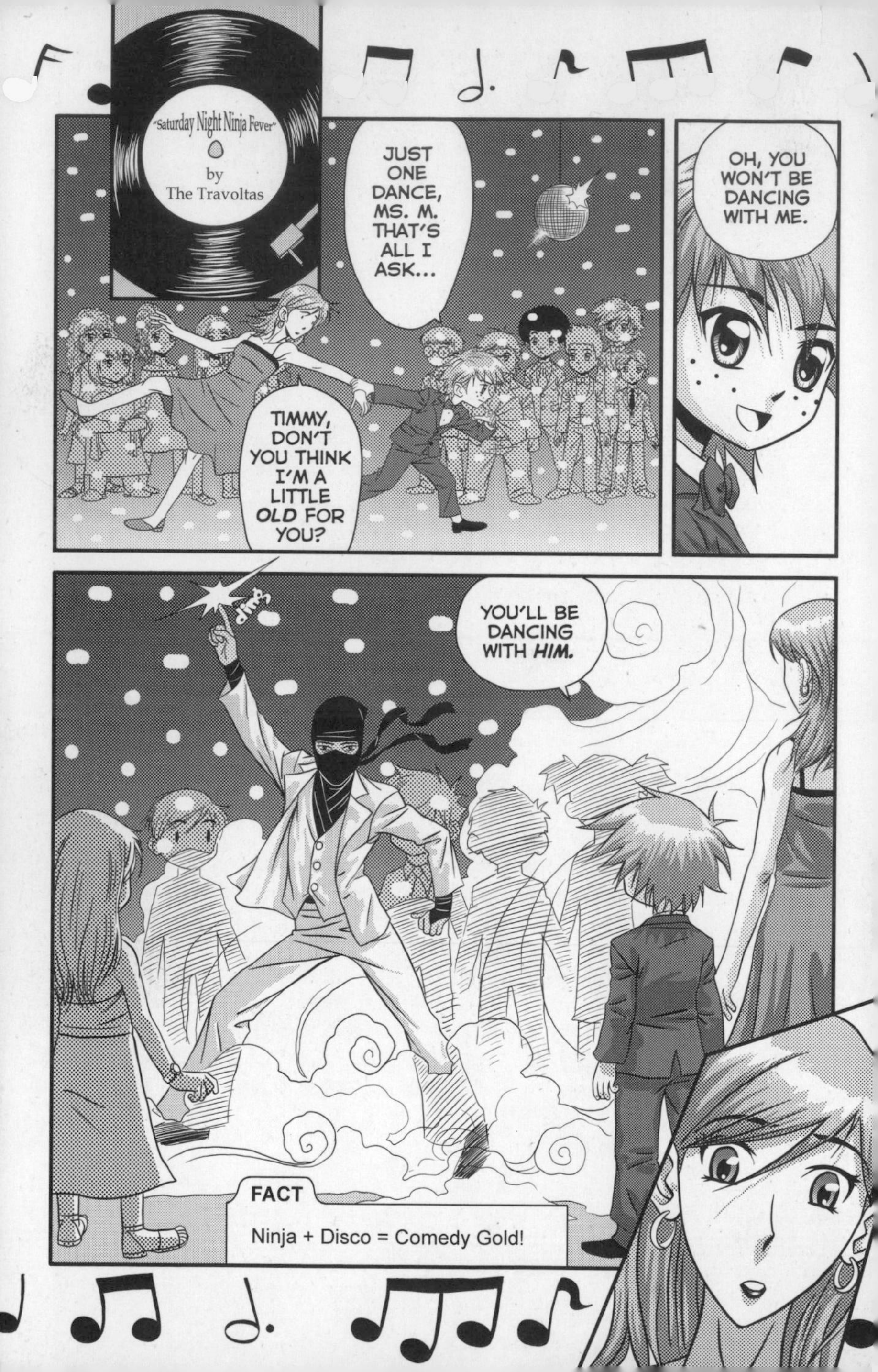
"Saturday Night Ninja Fever"
by
The Travoltas
JUST ONE DANCE, MS. M. THAT'S ALL I ASK...
TIMMY, DON'T YOU THINK I'M A LITTLE *OLD* FOR YOU?
OH, YOU WON'T BE DANCING WITH ME.
YOU'LL BE DANCING WITH *HIM.*
FACT
Ninja + Disco = Comedy Gold!

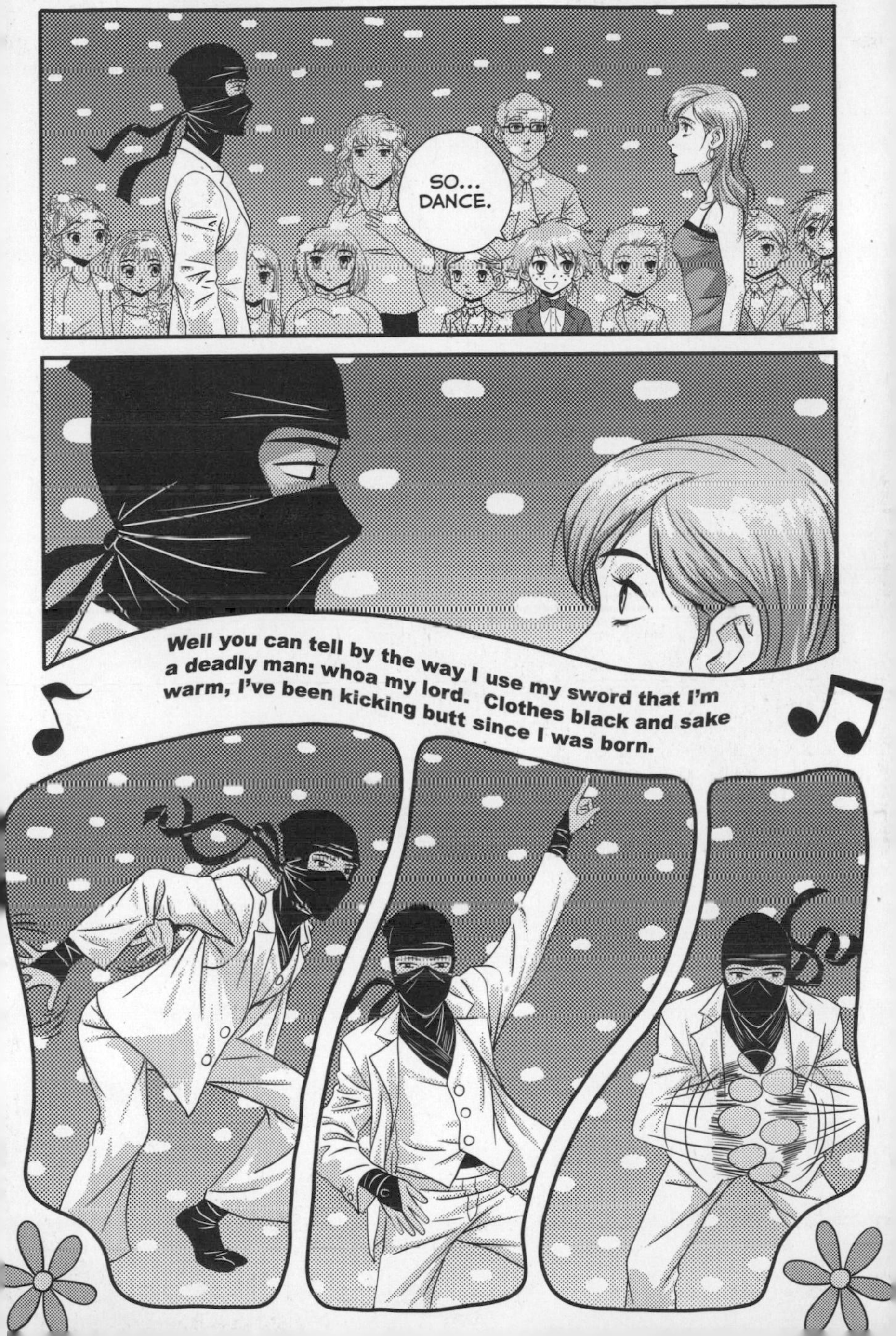
SO... DANCE.
Well you can tell by the way I use my sword that I'm a deadly man: whoa my lord. Clothes black and sake warm, I've been kicking butt since I was born.

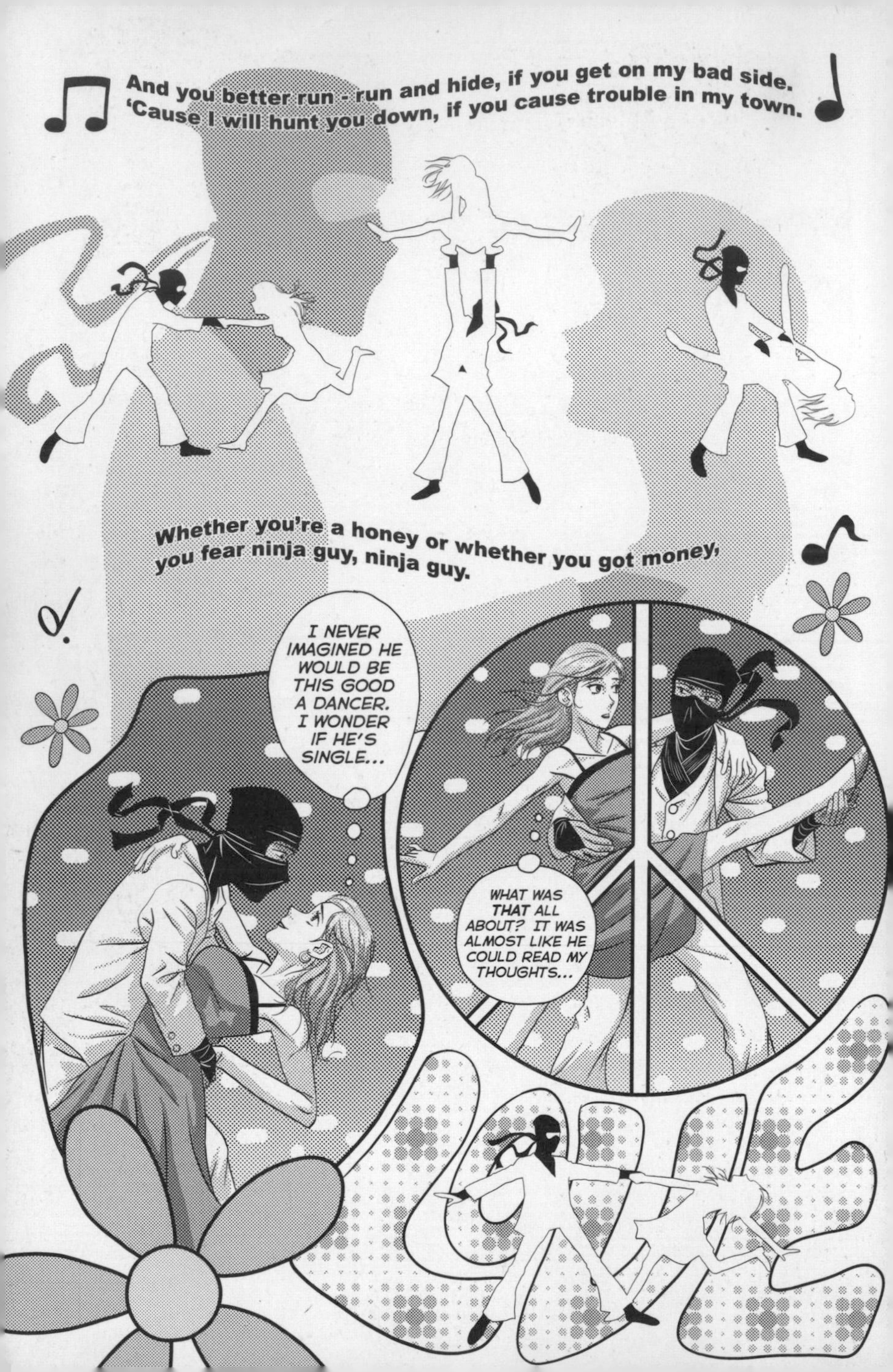
And you better run - run and hide, if you get on my bad side.
'Cause I will hunt you down, if you cause trouble in my town.
Whether you're a honey or whether you got money, you fear ninja guy, ninja guy.
I NEVER IMAGINED HE WOULD BE THIS GOOD A DANCER. I WONDER IF HE'S SINGLE...
WHAT WAS THAT ALL ABOUT? IT WAS ALMOST LIKE HE COULD READ MY THOUGHTS...

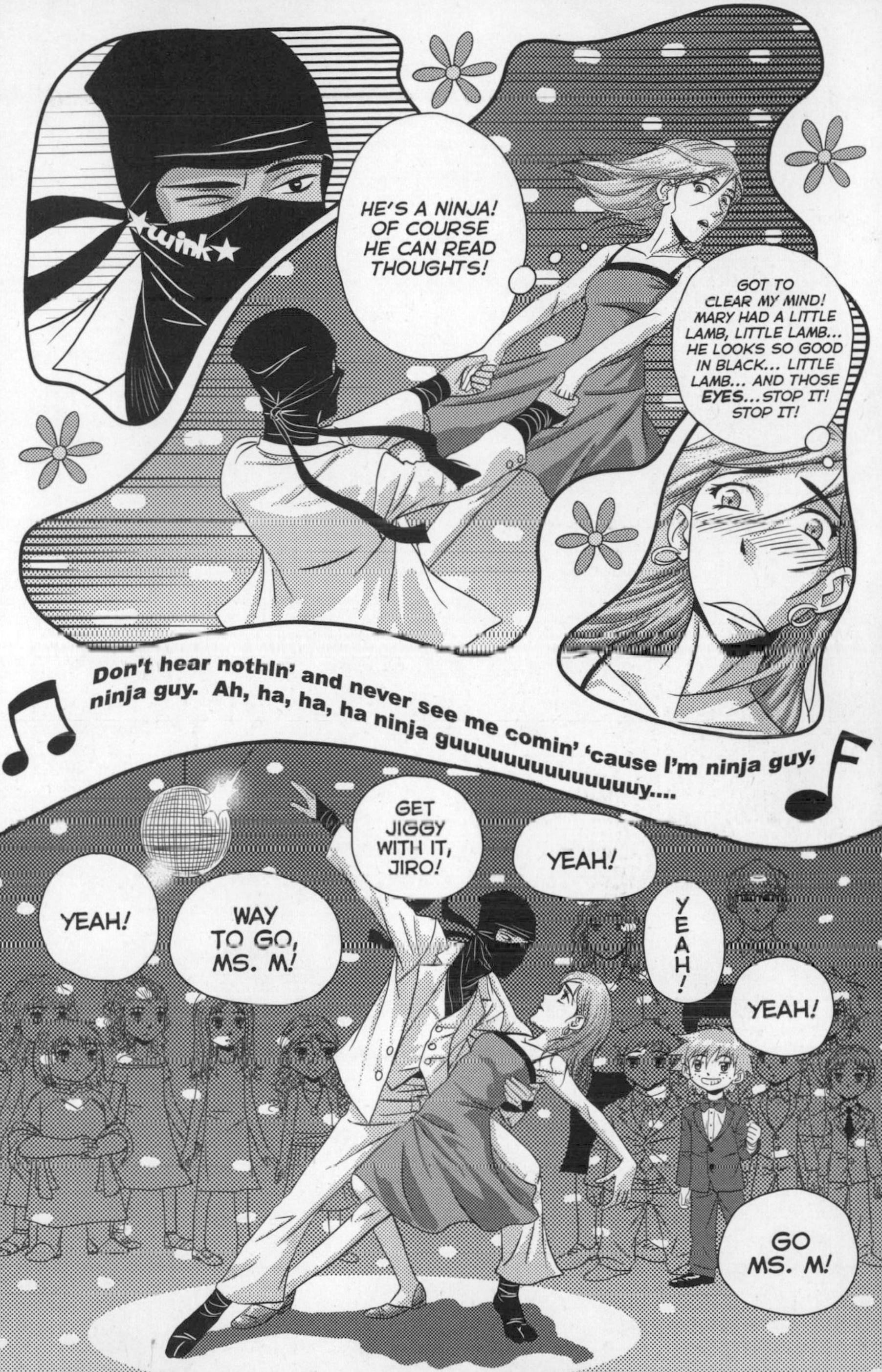
★wink★
HE'S A NINJA! OF COURSE HE CAN READ THOUGHTS!
GOT TO CLEAR MY MIND! MARY HAD A LITTLE LAMB, LITTLE LAMB... HE LOOKS SO GOOD IN BLACK... LITTLE LAMB... AND THOSE EYES... STOP IT! STOP IT!
Don't hear nothin' and never see me comin' 'cause I'm ninja guy, ninja guy. Ah, ha, ha, ha ninja guuuuuuuuuuuuuy....
GET JIGGY WITH IT, JIRO!
YEAH!
YEAH!
WAY TO GO, MS. M!
YEAH!
YEAH!
GO MS. M!

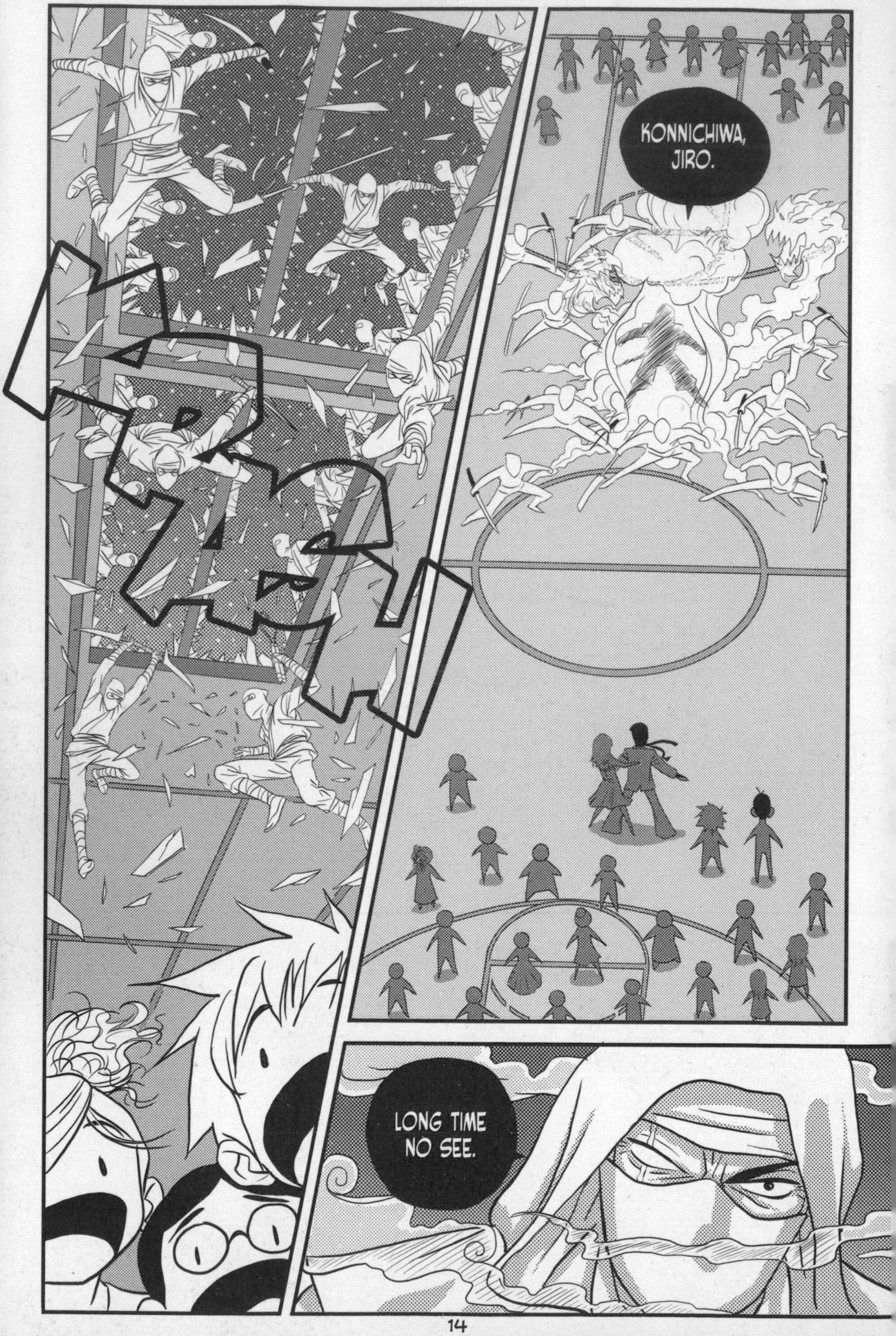
KONNICHIWA, JIRO.
LONG TIME NO SEE.

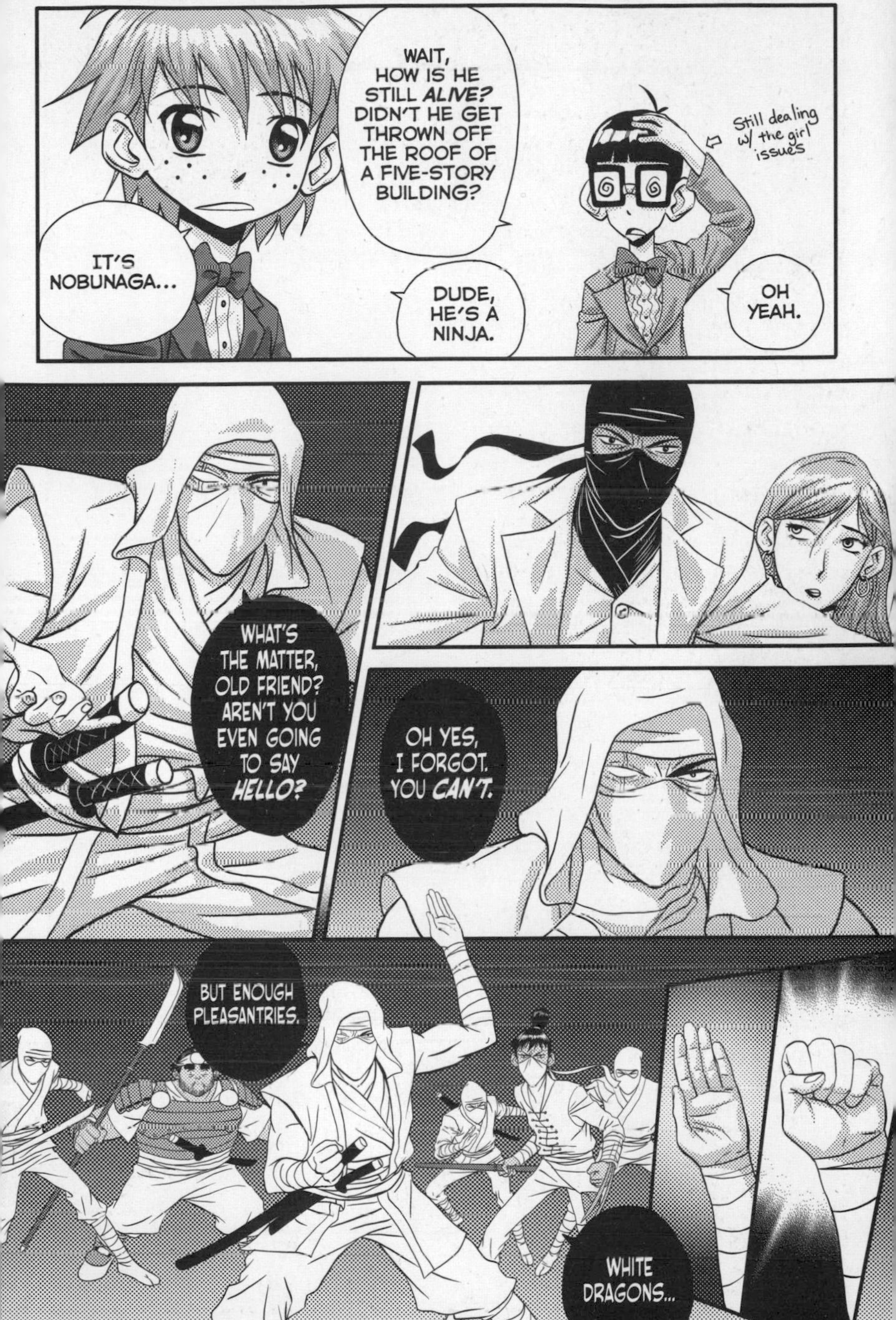
IT'S NOBUNAGA...
WAIT, HOW IS HE STILL *ALIVE?* DIDN'T HE GET THROWN OFF THE ROOF OF A FIVE-STORY BUILDING?
Still dealing w/ the girl issues
DUDE, HE'S A NINJA.
OH YEAH.
WHAT'S THE MATTER, OLD FRIEND? AREN'T YOU EVEN GOING TO SAY *HELLO?*
OH YES, I FORGOT. YOU *CAN'T.*
BUT ENOUGH PLEASANTRIES.
WHITE DRAGONS...

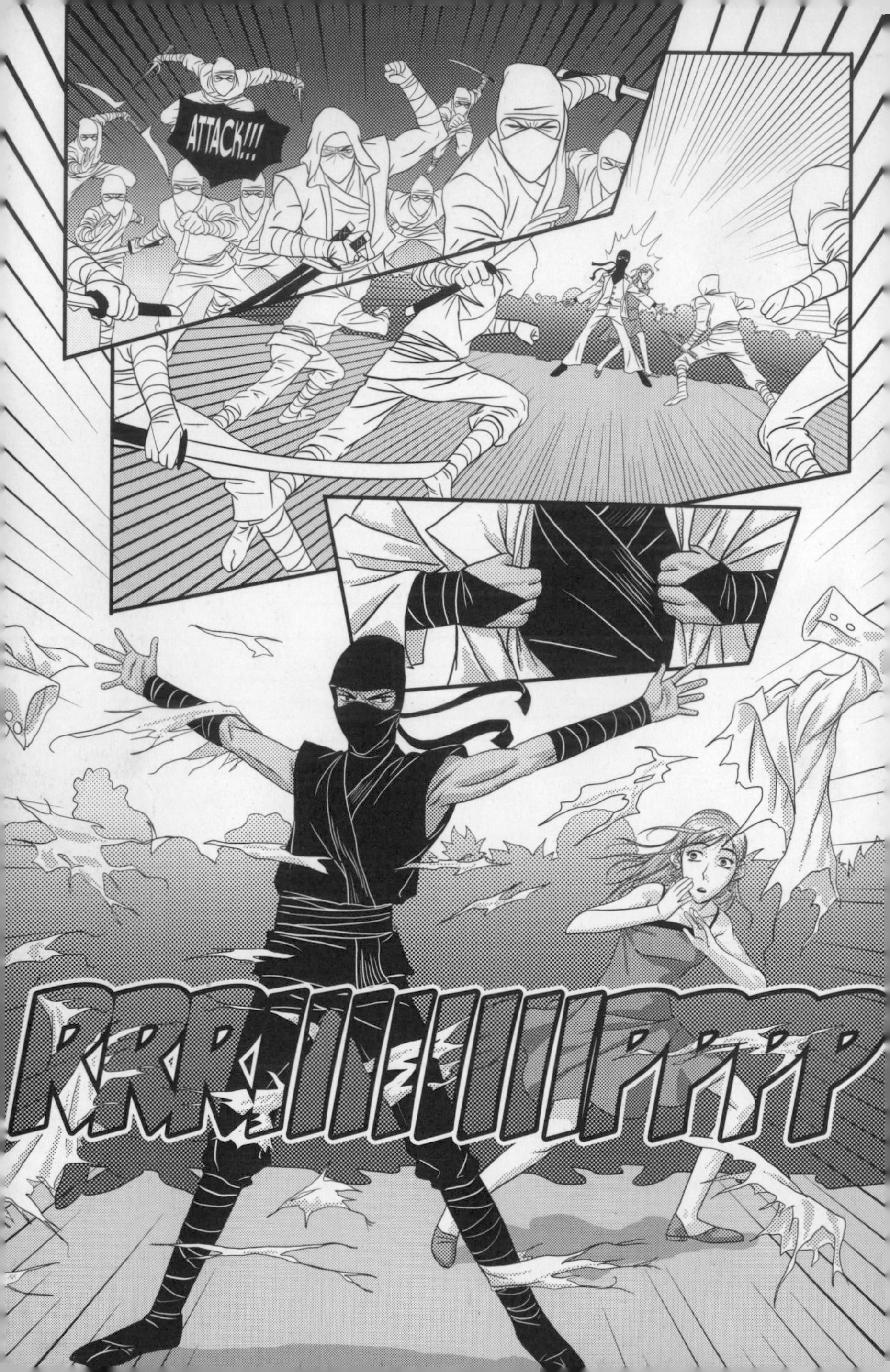
ATTACK!!!
RRRIIIIIIIPPPP

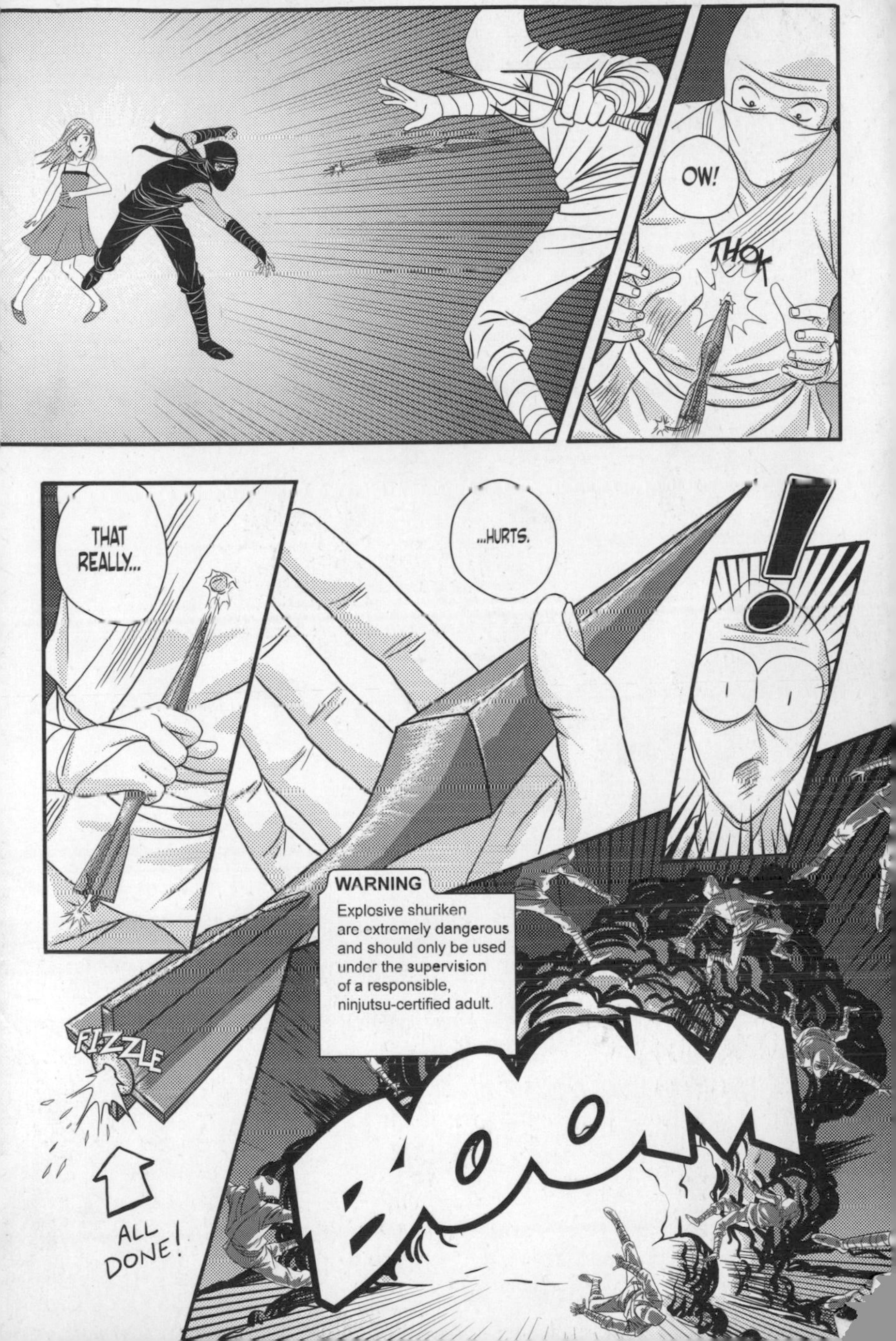
OW!
THOK
THAT REALLY...
...HURTS.
!
WARNING
Explosive shuriken are extremely dangerous and should only be used under the supervision of a responsible, ninjutsu-certified adult.
FIZZLE
ALL DONE!
BOOM

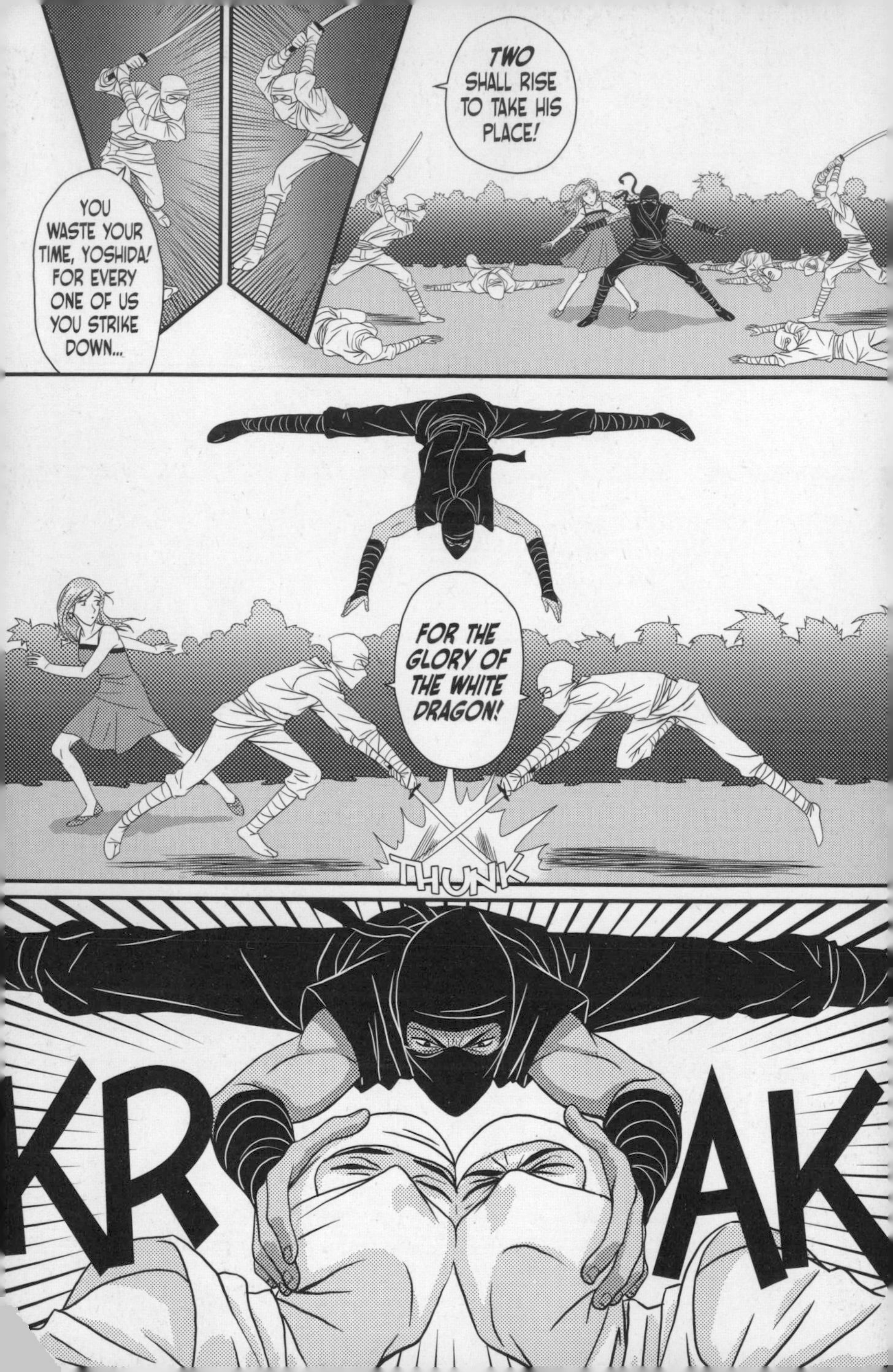
YOU WASTE YOUR TIME, YOSHIDA! FOR EVERY ONE OF US YOU STRIKE DOWN...
TWO SHALL RISE TO TAKE HIS PLACE!
FOR THE GLORY OF THE WHITE DRAGON!
THUNK
KR AK

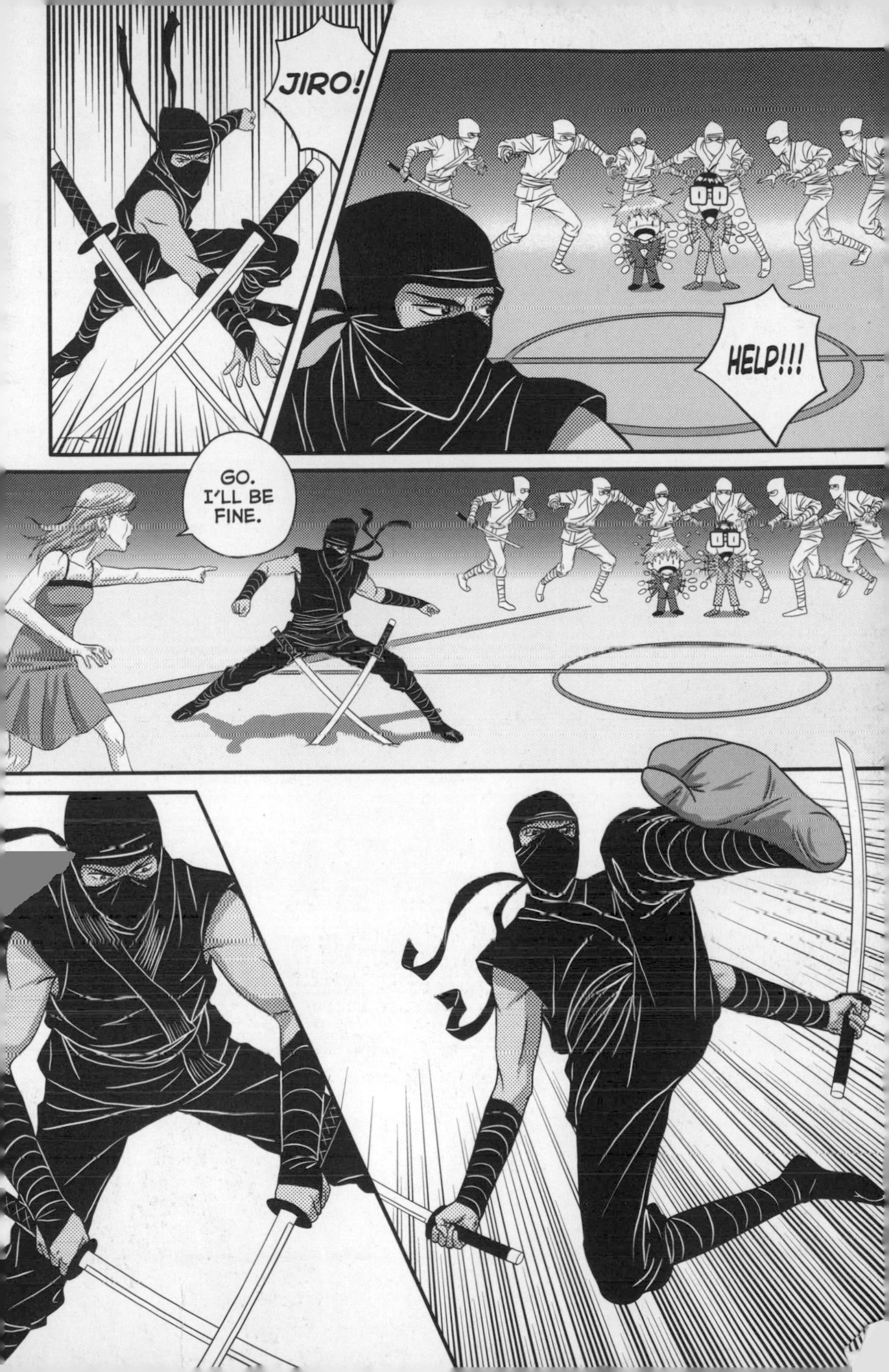
JIRO!
HELP!!!
GO. I'LL BE FINE.

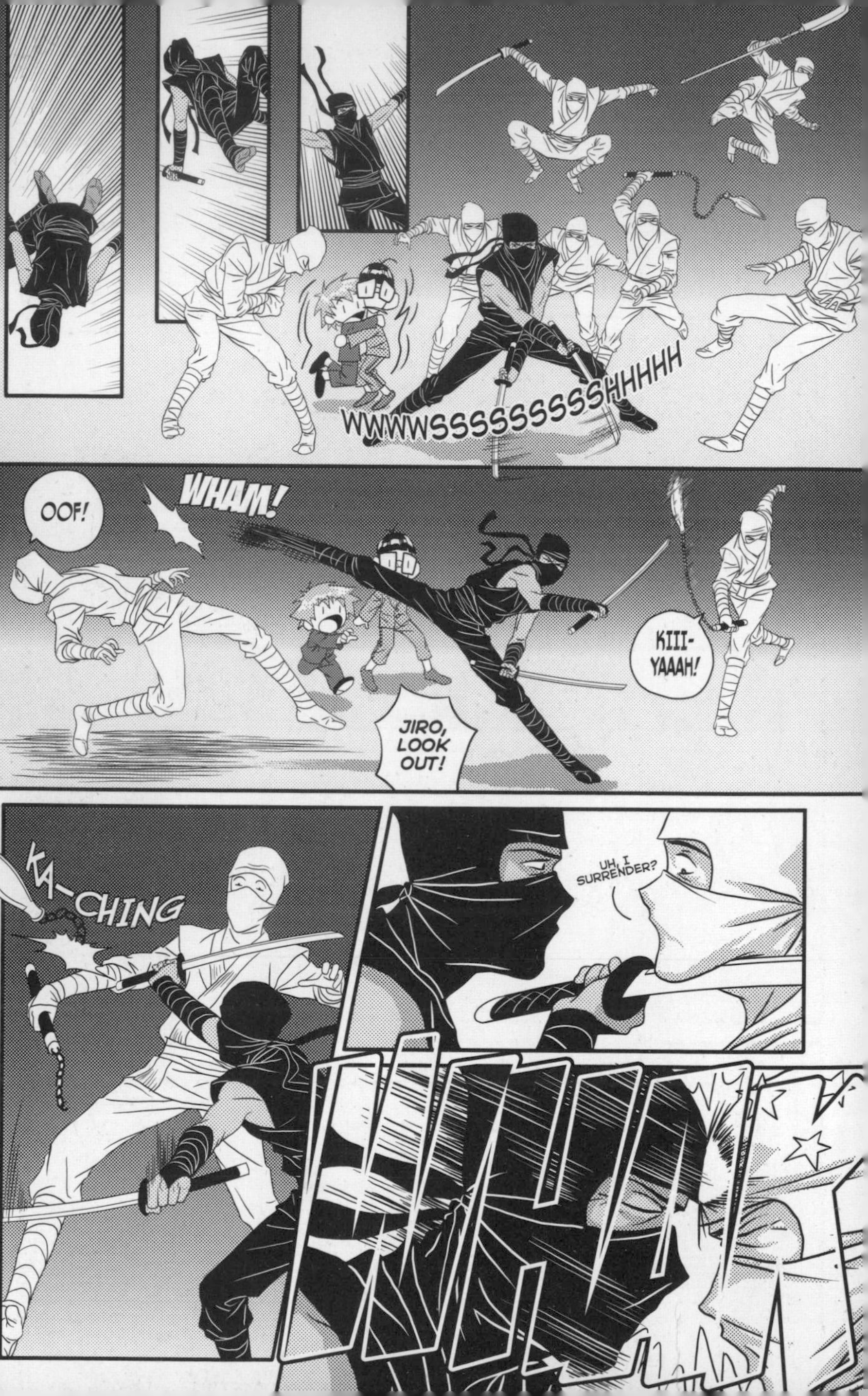
WWWWSSSSSSSSSHHHHH
OOF!
WHAM!
JIRO, LOOK OUT!
KIII-YAAAH!
KA-CHING
UH, I SURRENDER?

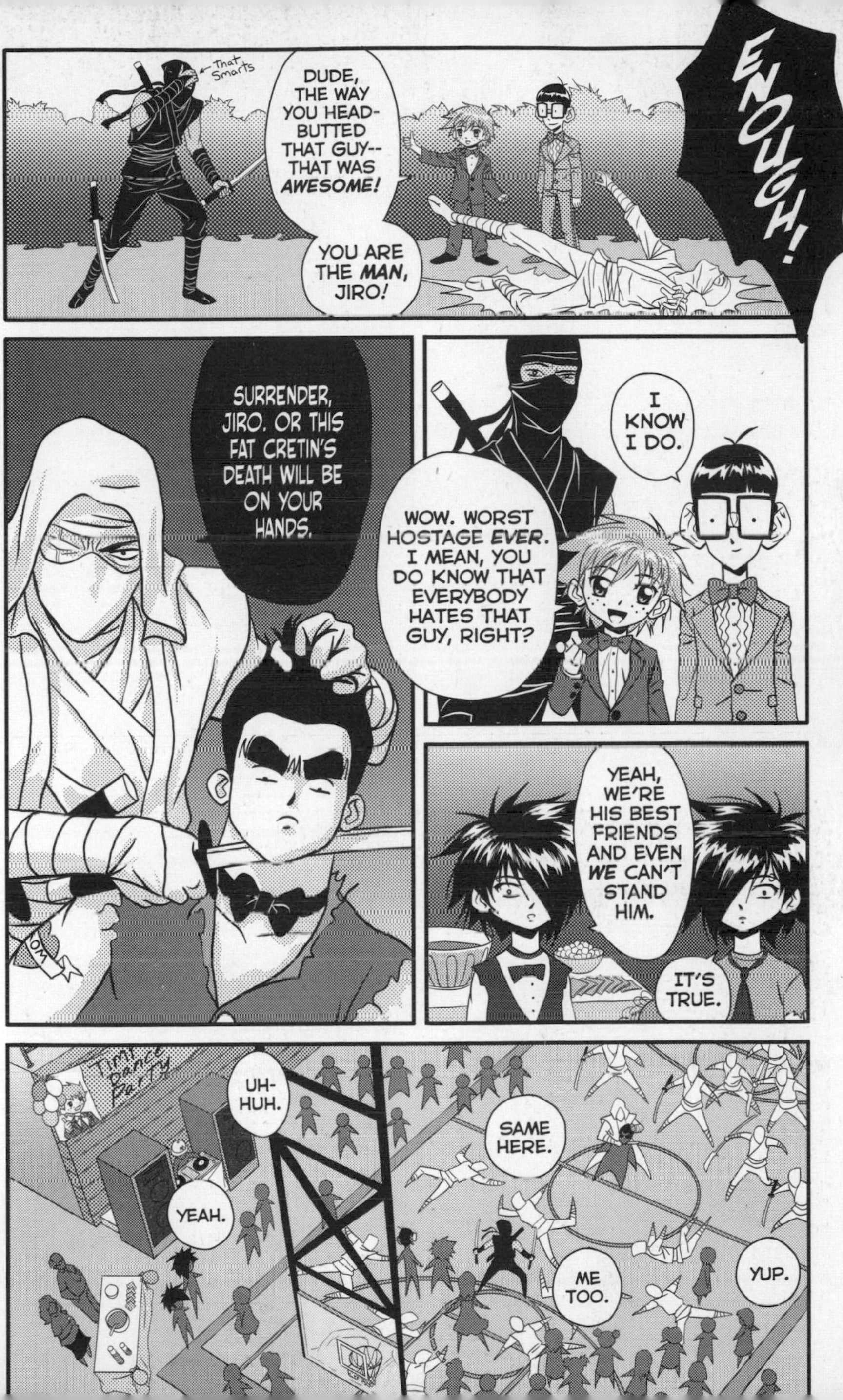
That Smarts
DUDE, THE WAY YOU HEAD-BUTTED THAT GUY-- THAT WAS *AWESOME!*
YOU ARE THE *MAN*, JIRO!
ENOUGH!
SURRENDER, JIRO. OR THIS FAT CRETIN'S DEATH WILL BE ON YOUR HANDS.
WOW. WORST HOSTAGE *EVER*. I MEAN, YOU DO KNOW THAT EVERYBODY HATES THAT GUY, RIGHT?
I KNOW I DO.
YEAH, WE'RE HIS BEST FRIENDS AND EVEN *WE* CAN'T STAND HIM.
IT'S TRUE.
Dance Party
UH-HUH.
SAME HERE.
YEAH.
YUP.
ME TOO.

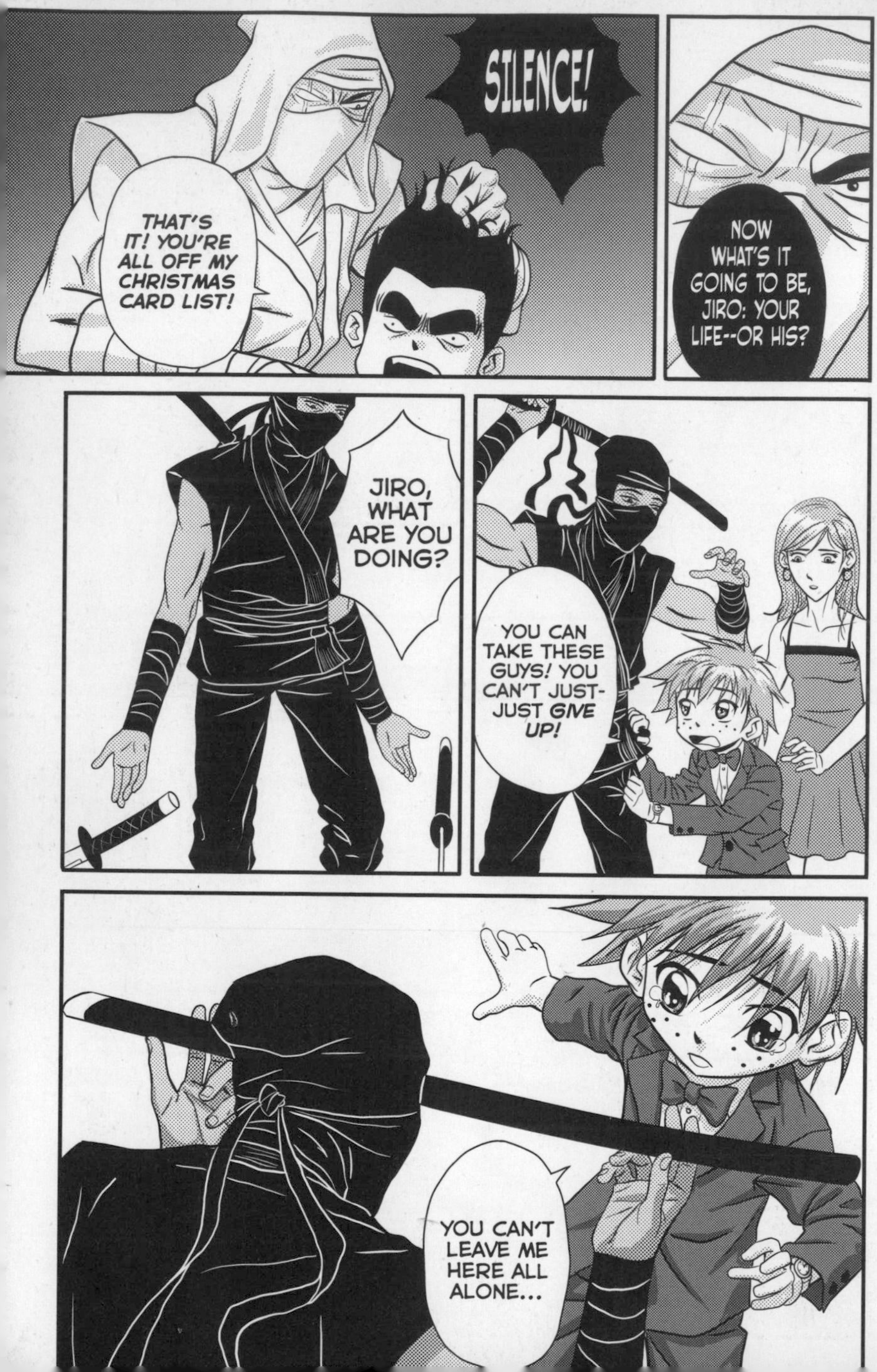
THAT'S IT! YOU'RE ALL OFF MY CHRISTMAS CARD LIST!
SILENCE!
NOW WHAT'S IT GOING TO BE, JIRO: YOUR LIFE--OR HIS?
JIRO, WHAT ARE YOU DOING?
YOU CAN TAKE THESE GUYS! YOU CAN'T JUST-JUST GIVE UP!
YOU CAN'T LEAVE ME HERE ALL ALONE...

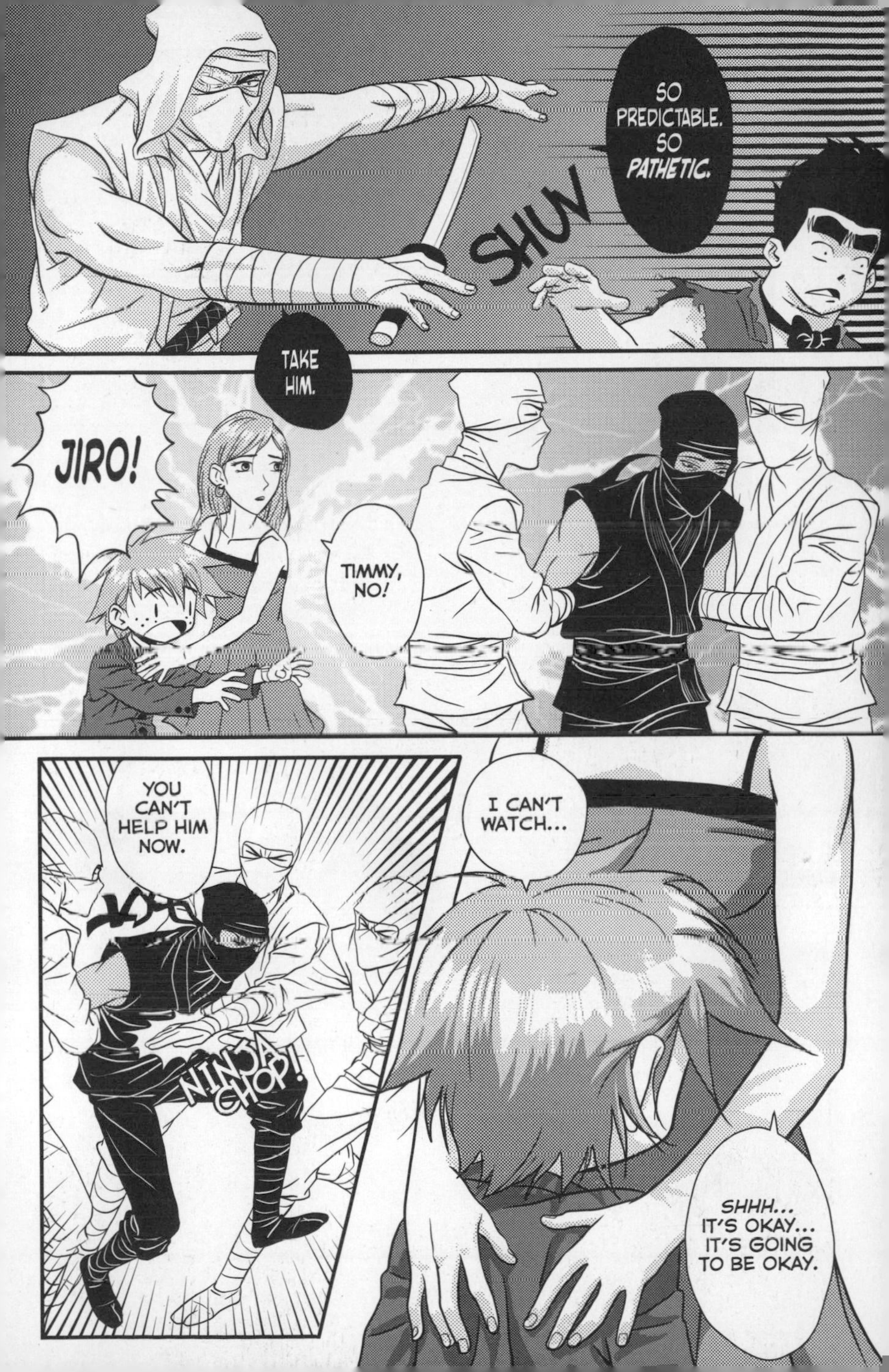
SHW
SO PREDICTABLE. SO *PATHETIC.*
TAKE HIM.
JIRO!
TIMMY, NO!
YOU CAN'T HELP HIM NOW.
NINJA CHOP!
I CAN'T WATCH...
SHHH... IT'S OKAY... IT'S GOING TO BE OKAY.

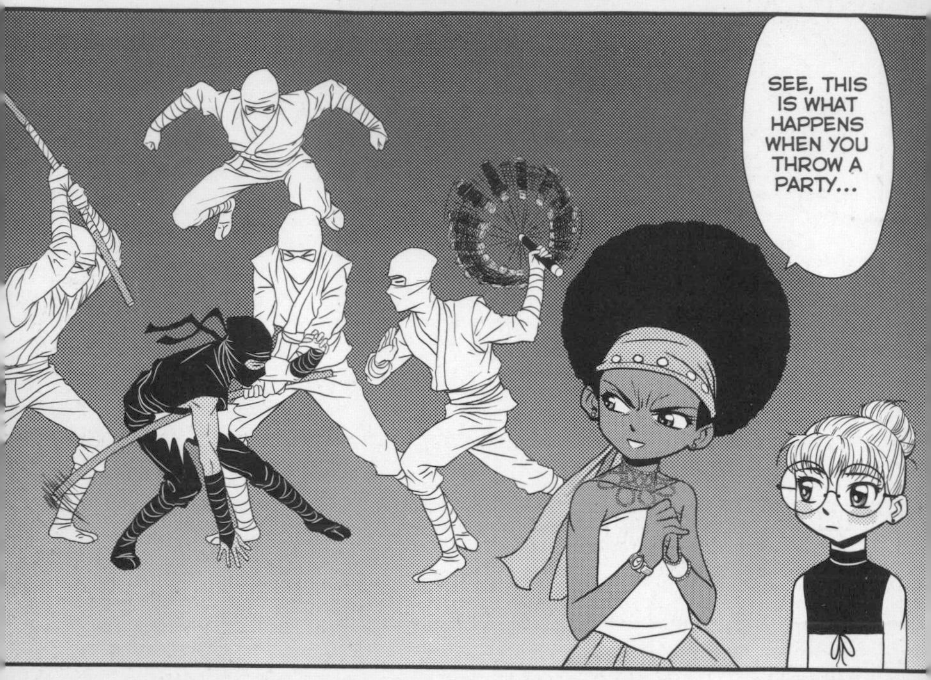
SEE, THIS IS WHAT HAPPENS WHEN YOU THROW A PARTY...

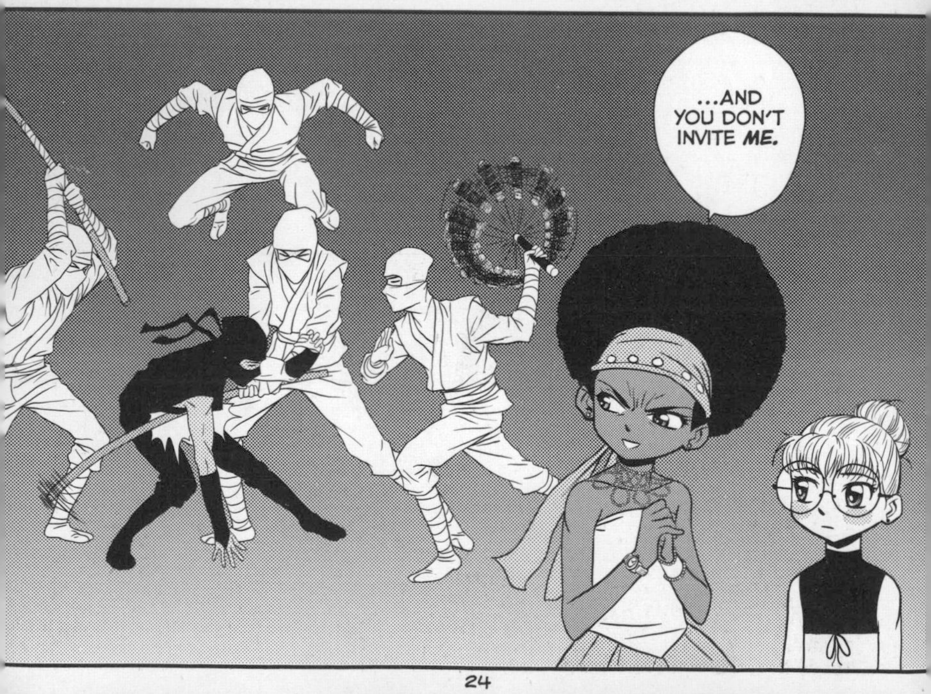
...AND YOU DON'T INVITE *ME.*

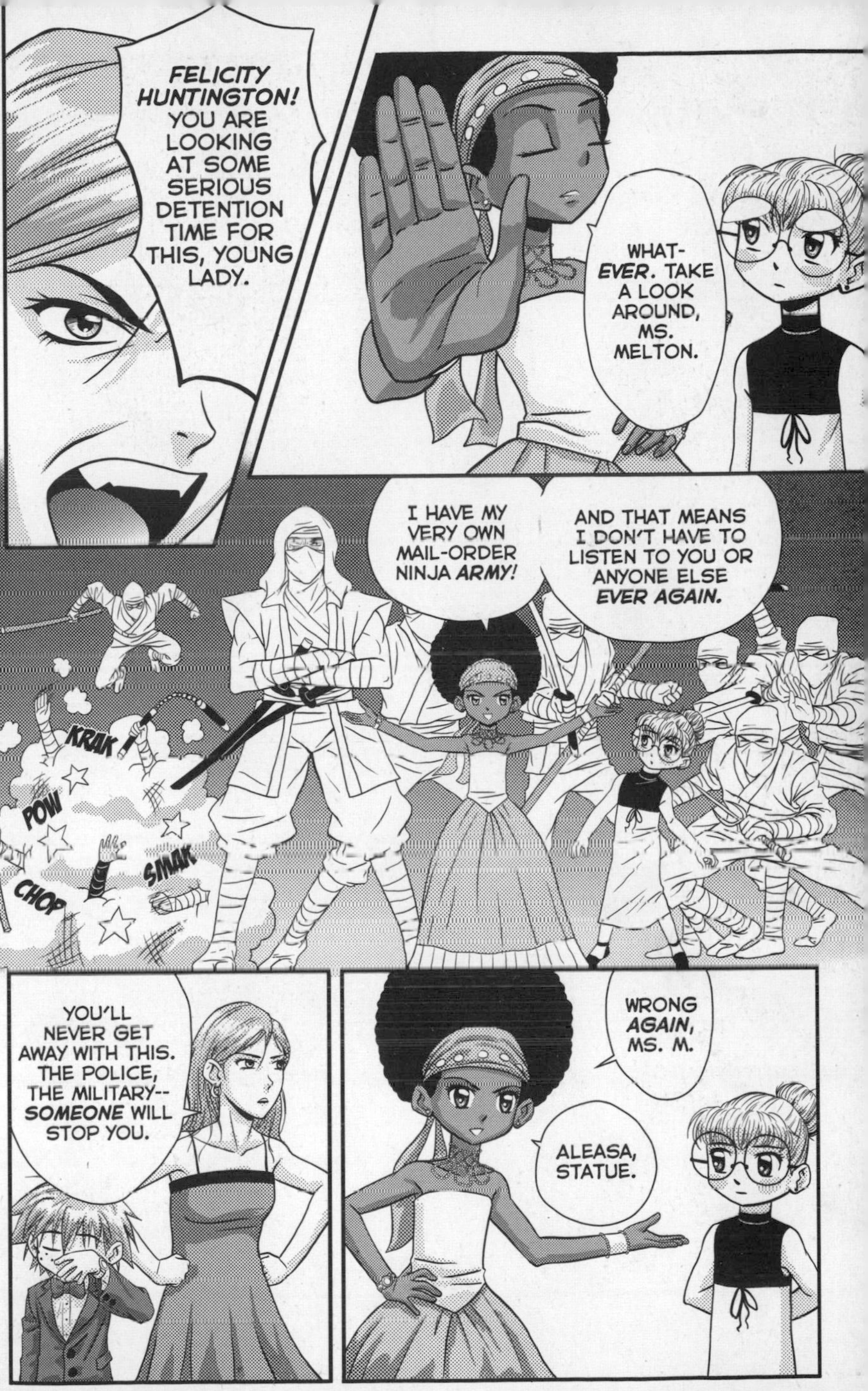
FELICITY HUNTINGTON! YOU ARE LOOKING AT SOME SERIOUS DETENTION TIME FOR THIS, YOUNG LADY.
WHAT-EVER. TAKE A LOOK AROUND, MS. MELTON.
I HAVE MY VERY OWN MAIL-ORDER NINJA ARMY!
AND THAT MEANS I DON'T HAVE TO LISTEN TO YOU OR ANYONE ELSE EVER AGAIN.
KRAK
POW
SMAK
CHOP
YOU'LL NEVER GET AWAY WITH THIS. THE POLICE, THE MILITARY-- SOMEONE WILL STOP YOU.
WRONG AGAIN, MS. M.
ALEASA, STATUE.

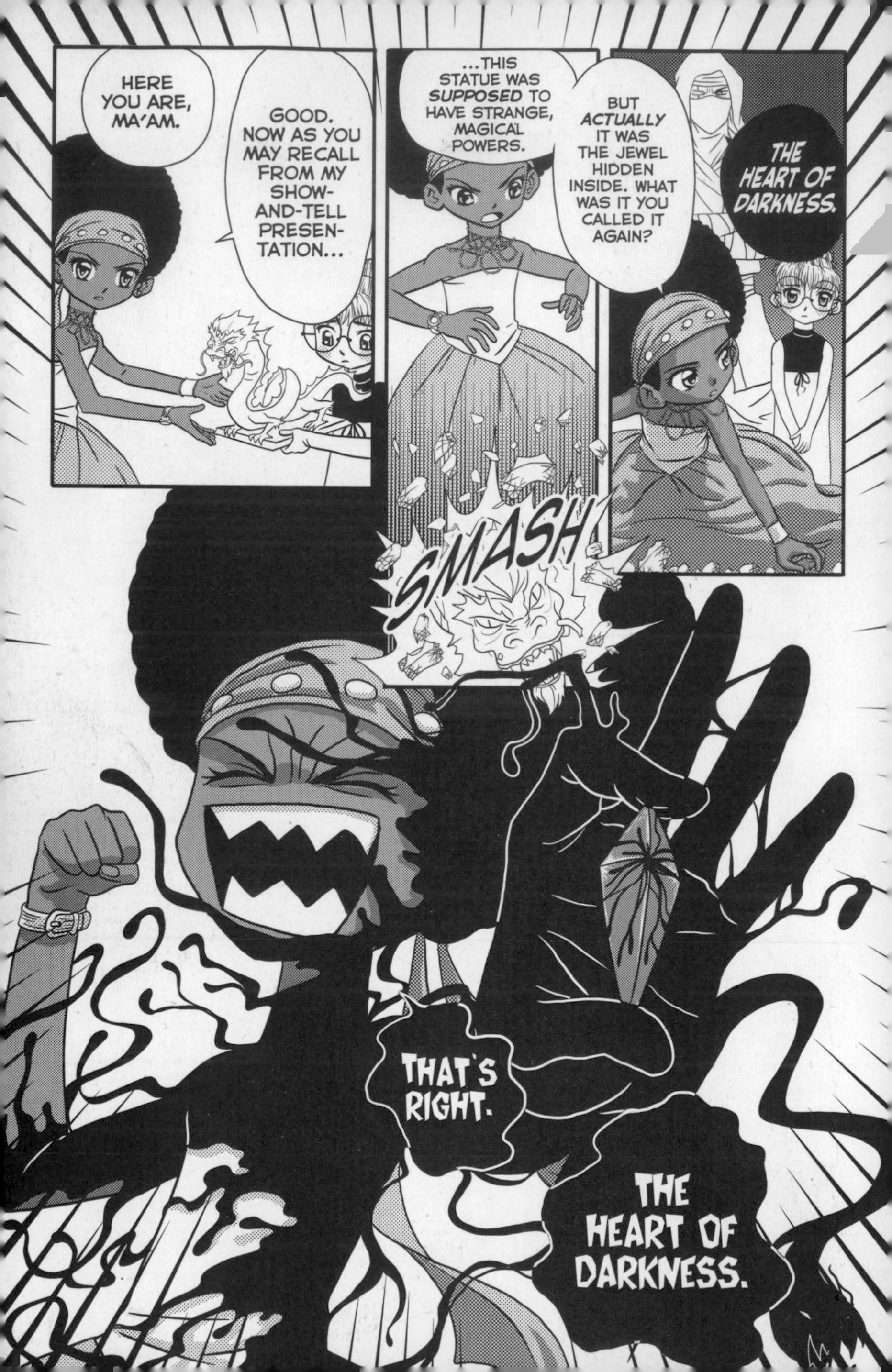
HERE YOU ARE, MA'AM.
GOOD. NOW AS YOU MAY RECALL FROM MY SHOW-AND-TELL PRESEN-TATION...
...THIS STATUE WAS *SUPPOSED* TO HAVE STRANGE, MAGICAL POWERS.
SMASH
BUT *ACTUALLY* IT WAS THE JEWEL HIDDEN INSIDE. WHAT WAS IT YOU CALLED IT AGAIN?
THE HEART OF DARKNESS.
THAT'S RIGHT.
THE HEART OF DARKNESS.

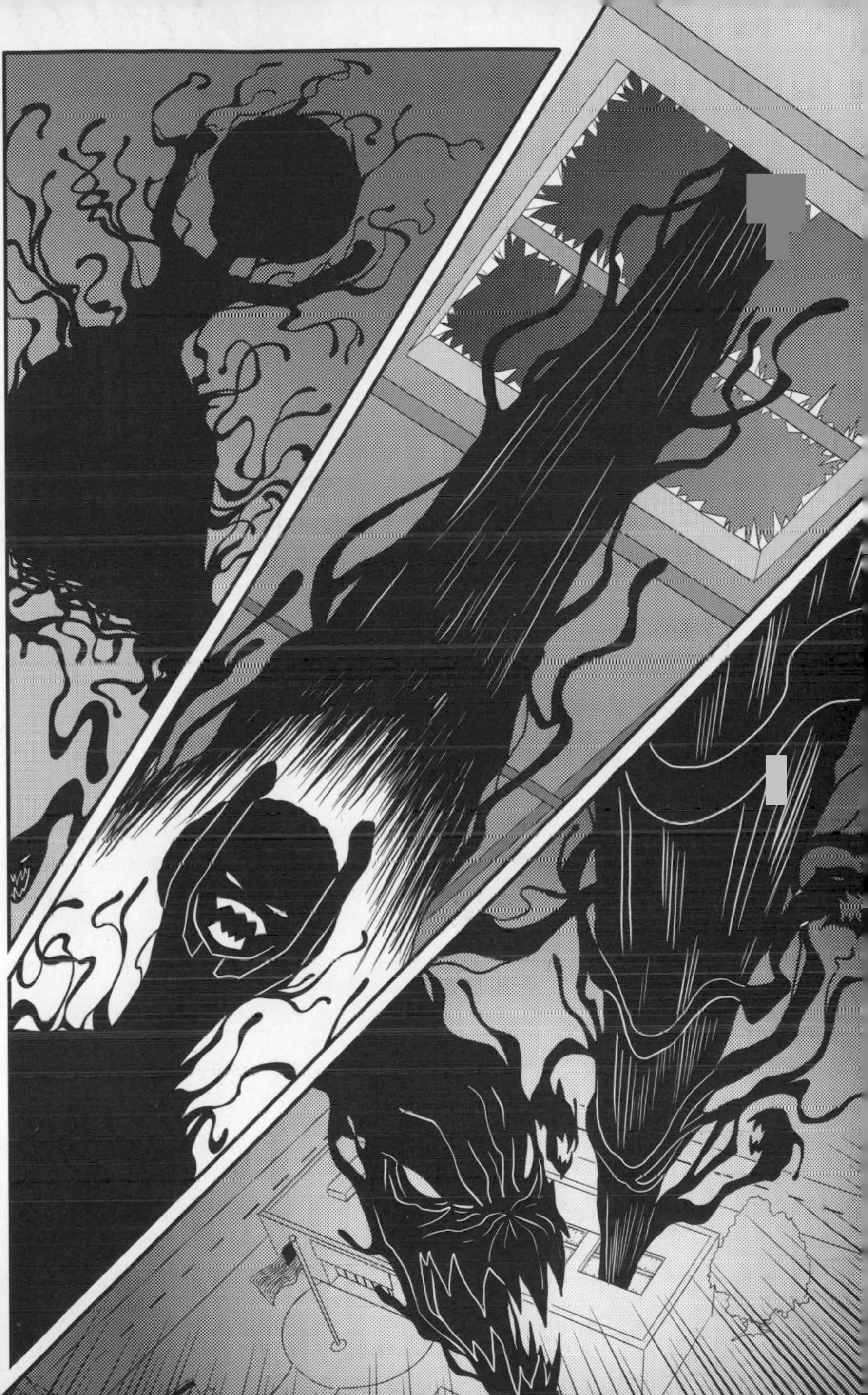

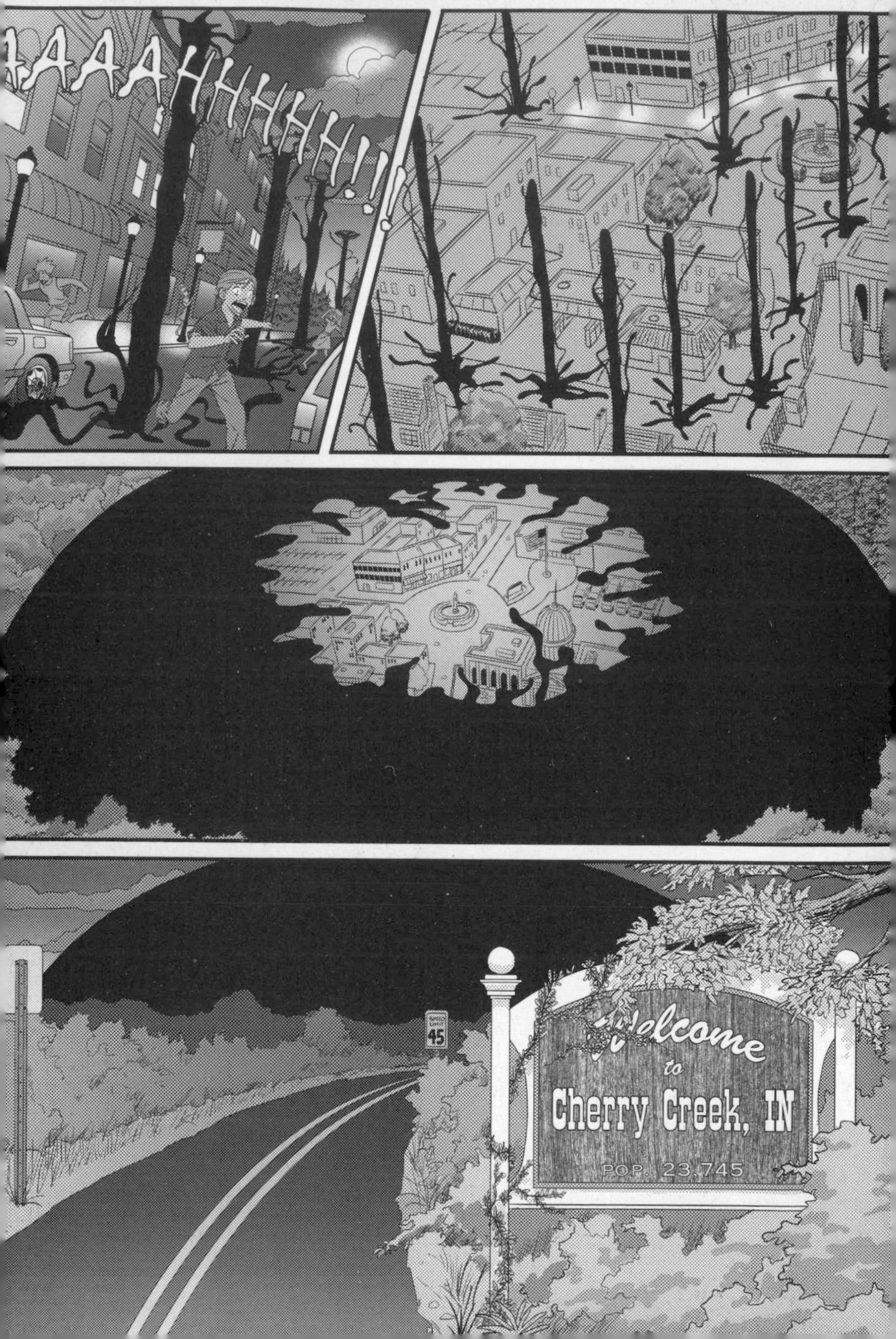
AAAAHHHHHHHH!!!
45
Welcome
to
Cherry Creek, IN
POP. 23,745

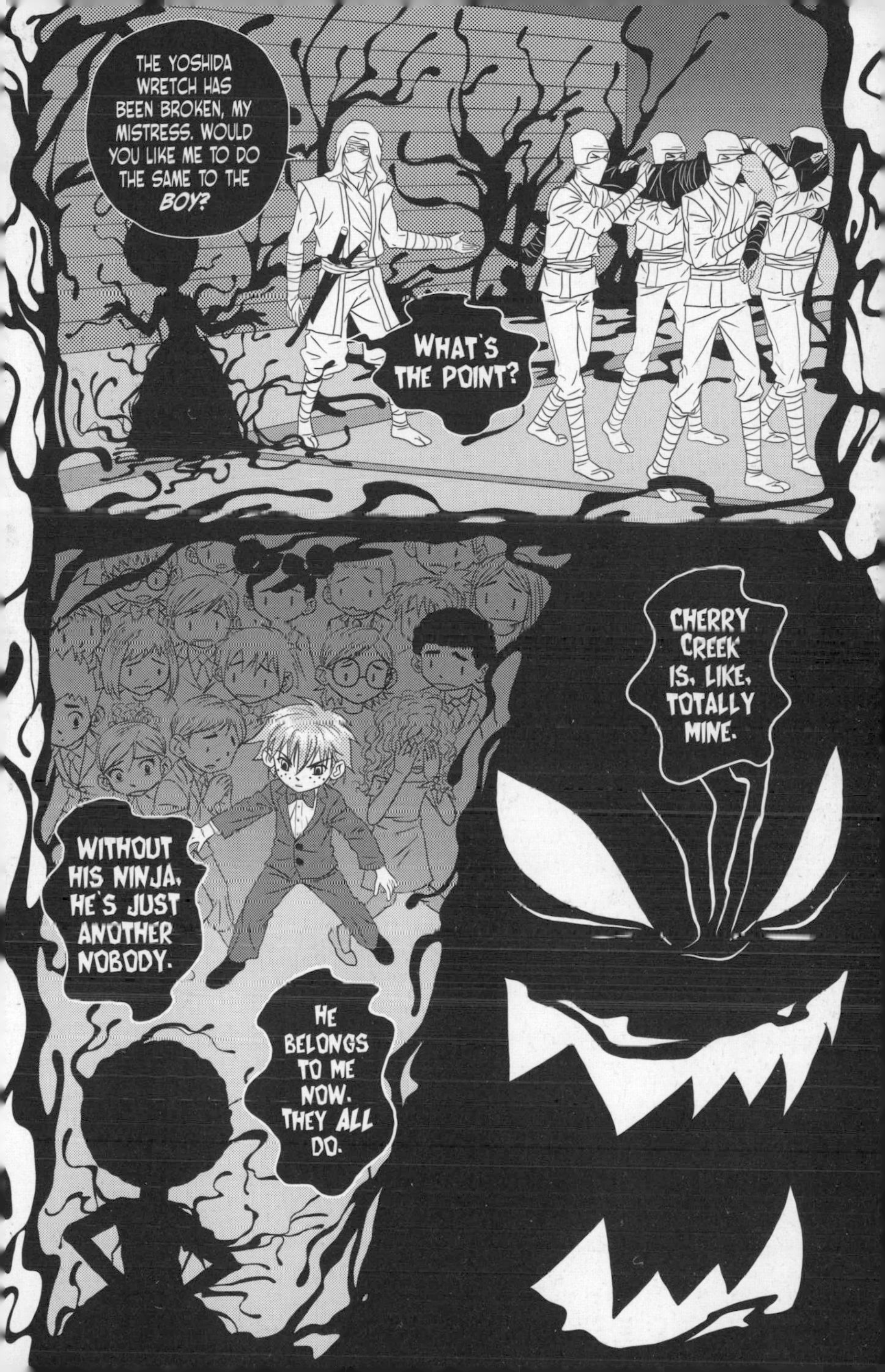
THE YOSHIDA WRETCH HAS BEEN BROKEN, MY MISTRESS. WOULD YOU LIKE ME TO DO THE SAME TO THE *BOY?*
WHAT'S THE POINT?
WITHOUT HIS NINJA, HE'S JUST ANOTHER NOBODY.
HE BELONGS TO ME NOW. THEY *ALL* DO.
CHERRY CREEK IS, LIKE, TOTALLY MINE.

CHAPTER 2

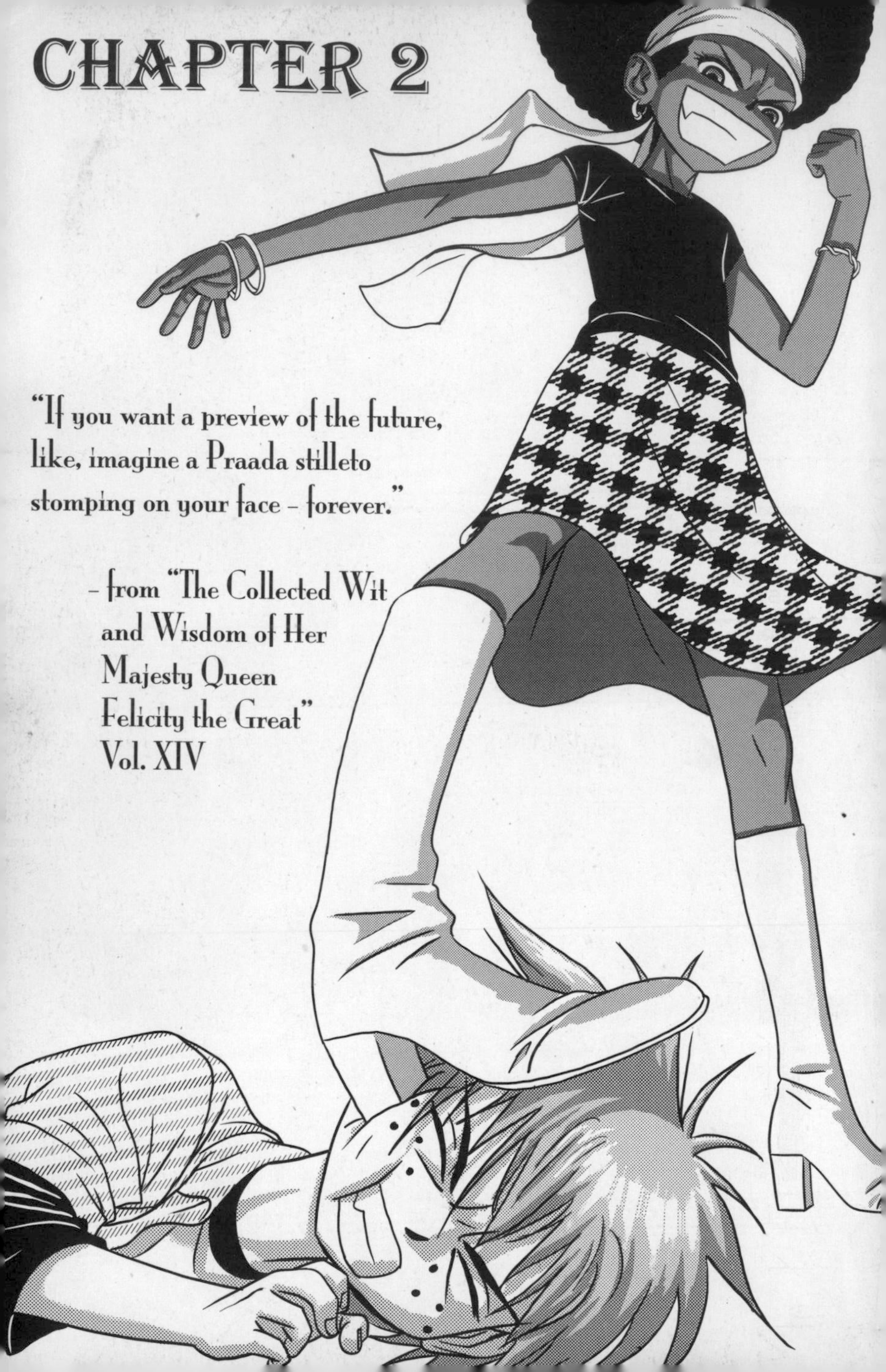

"If you want a preview of the future, like, imagine a Praada stilleto stomping on your face - forever."

- from "The Collected Wit and Wisdom of Her Majesty Queen Felicity the Great" Vol. XIV

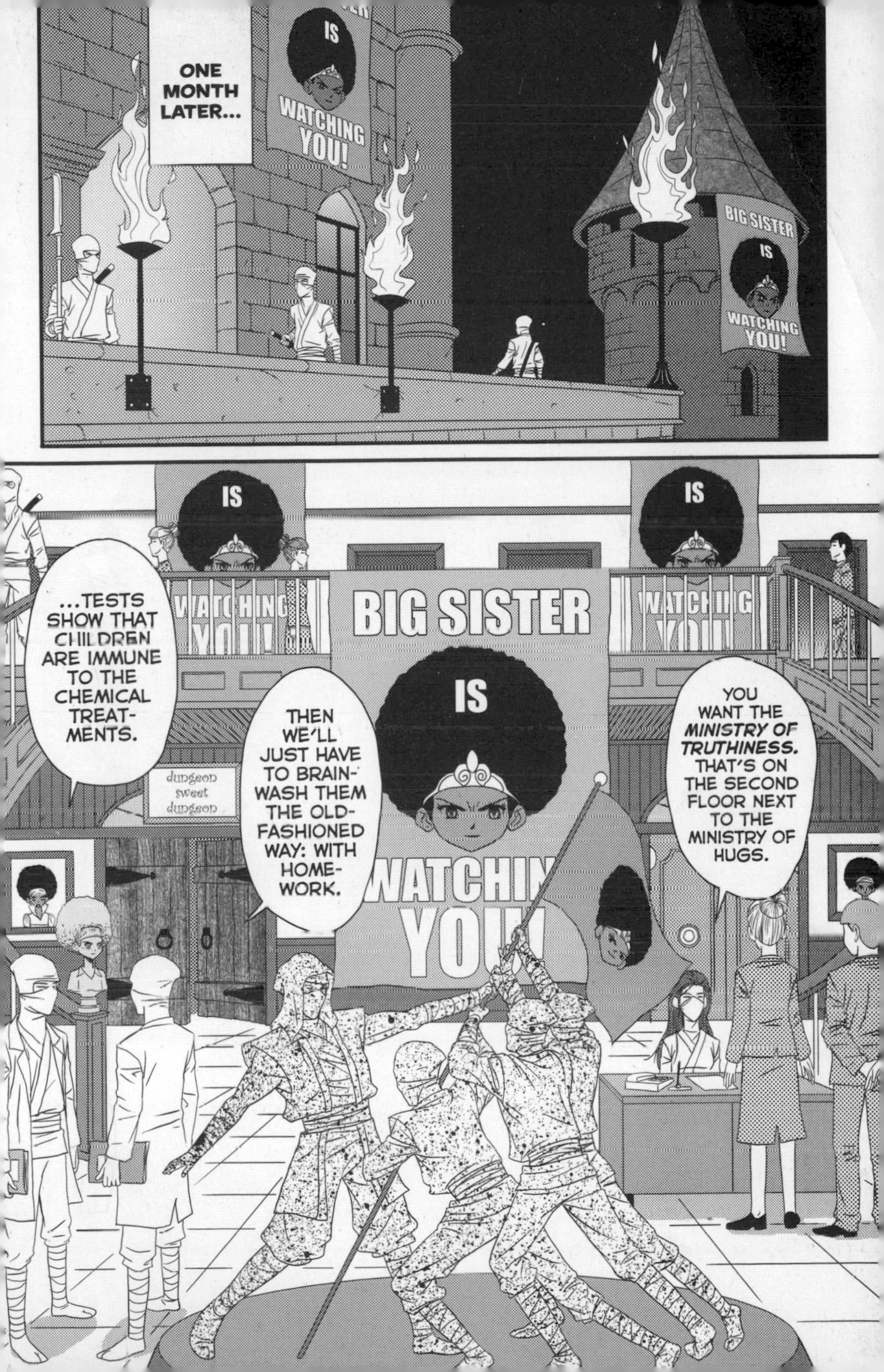

ONE MONTH LATER...
IS WATCHING YOU!
BIG SISTER IS WATCHING YOU!
...TESTS SHOW THAT CHILDREN ARE IMMUNE TO THE CHEMICAL TREAT- MENTS.
dungeon sweet dungeon
THEN WE'LL JUST HAVE TO BRAIN- WASH THEM THE OLD- FASHIONED WAY: WITH HOME- WORK.
BIG SISTER IS WATCHIN YOU
YOU WANT THE *MINISTRY OF TRUTHINESS.* THAT'S ON THE SECOND FLOOR NEXT TO THE MINISTRY OF HUGS.

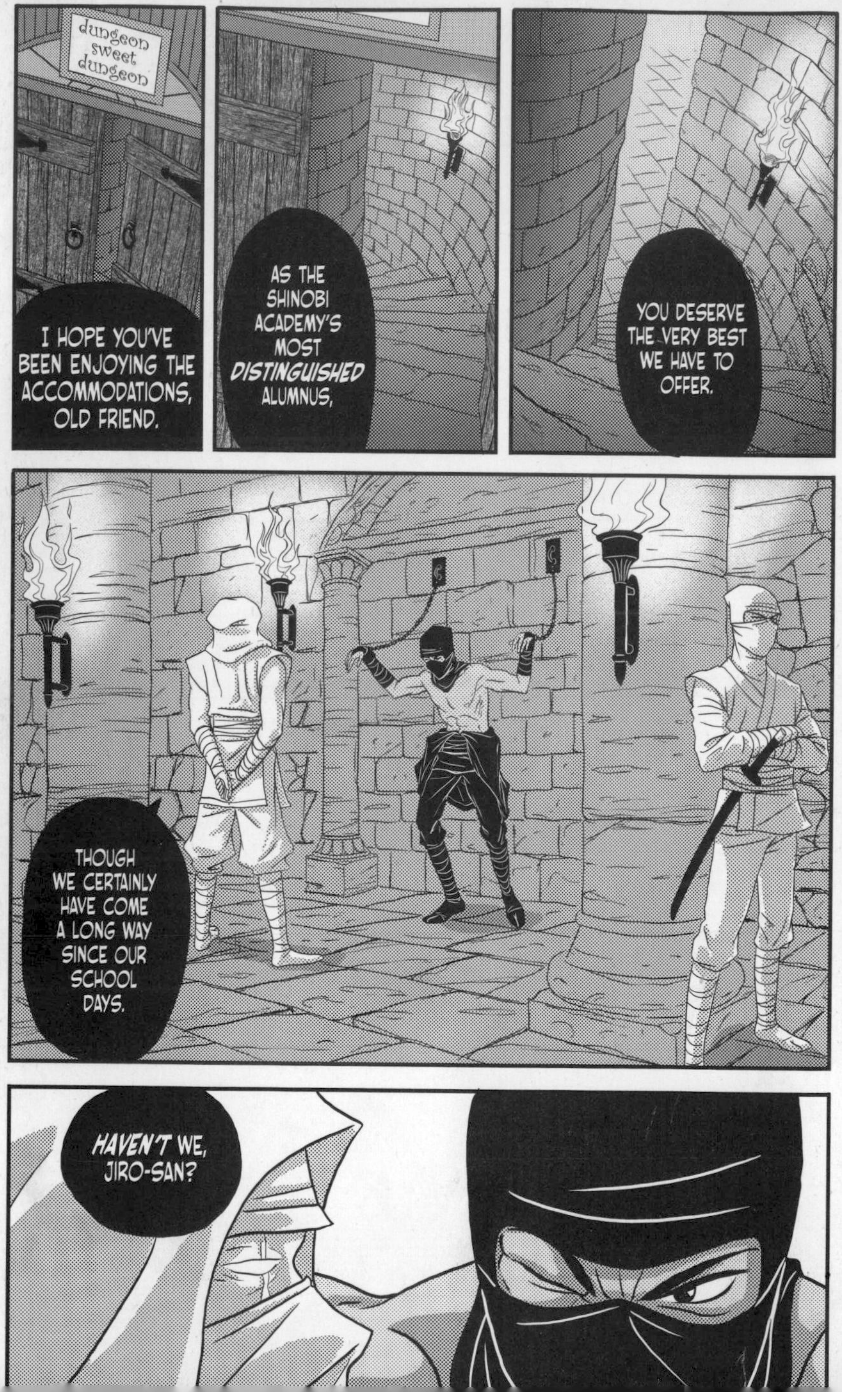
dungeon sweet dungeon
I HOPE YOU'VE BEEN ENJOYING THE ACCOMMODATIONS, OLD FRIEND.
AS THE SHINOBI ACADEMY'S MOST *DISTINGUISHED* ALUMNUS,
YOU DESERVE THE VERY BEST WE HAVE TO OFFER.
THOUGH WE CERTAINLY HAVE COME A LONG WAY SINCE OUR SCHOOL DAYS.
HAVEN'T WE, JIRO-SAN?

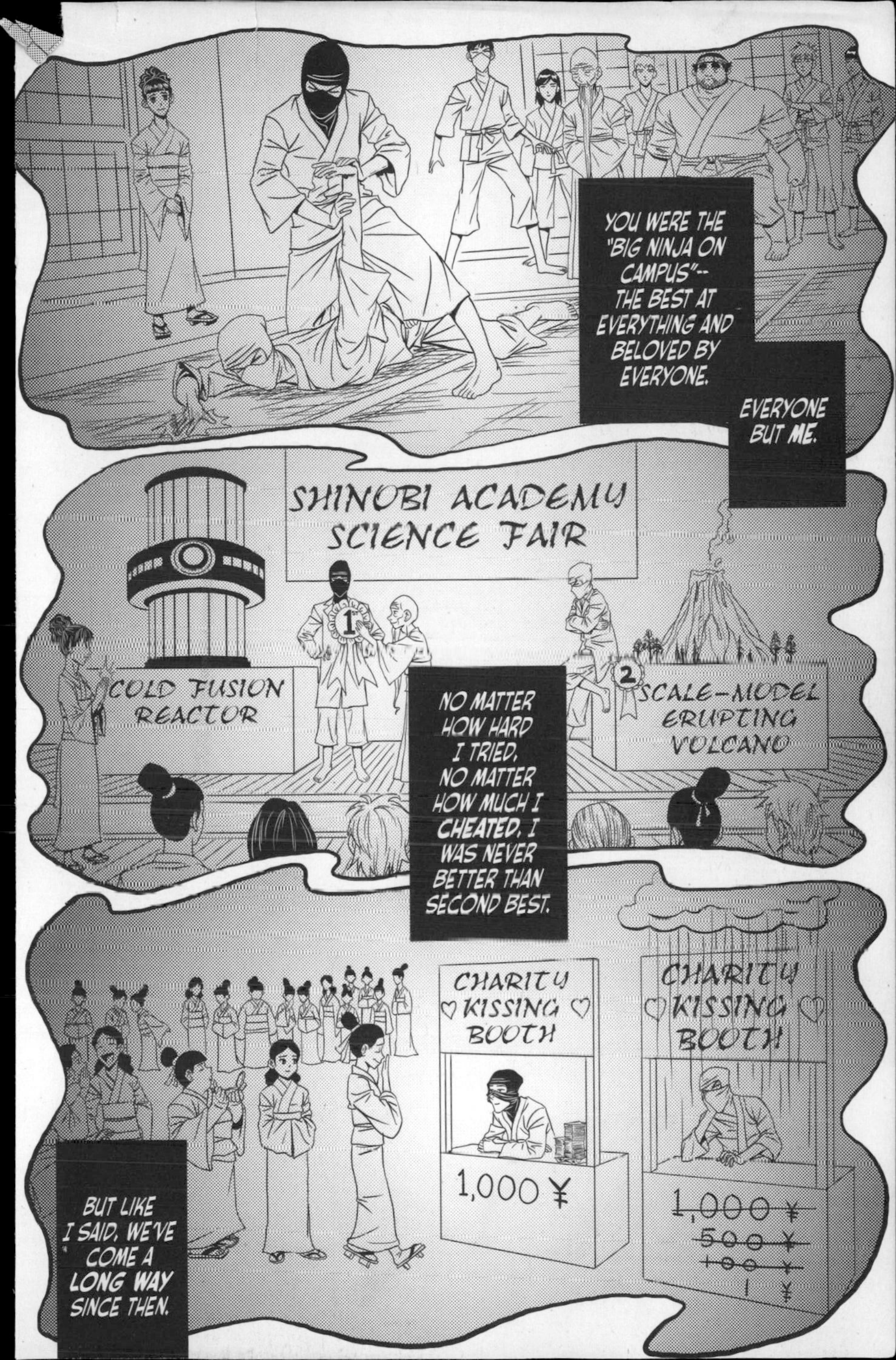
YOU WERE THE "BIG NINJA ON CAMPUS"-- THE BEST AT EVERYTHING AND BELOVED BY EVERYONE.
EVERYONE BUT ME.
SHINOBI ACADEMY SCIENCE FAIR
COLD FUSION REACTOR
NO MATTER HOW HARD I TRIED, NO MATTER HOW MUCH I CHEATED, I WAS NEVER BETTER THAN SECOND BEST.
2
SCALE-MODEL ERUPTING VOLCANO
BUT LIKE I SAID, WE'VE COME A LONG WAY SINCE THEN.
CHARITY ♡ KISSING ♡ BOOTH
1,000 ¥
CHARITY ♡ KISSING ♡ BOOTH
1,000 ¥
500 ¥
100 ¥
1 ¥

HAKURYUU NOBUNAGA, PLEASE REPORT TO THE THRONE ROOM AT ONCE.

≡SIGH≡

AN EVIL NINJA'S WORK IS NEVER DONE.

BUT NOT TO WORRY. YOU'LL HAVE *PLENTY* TO KEEP YOU OCCUPIED UNTIL I RETURN.

SAYONARA.

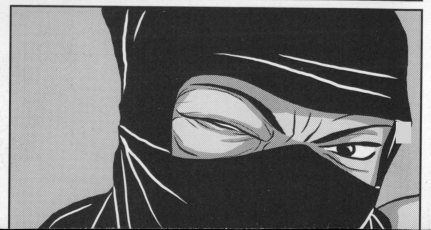

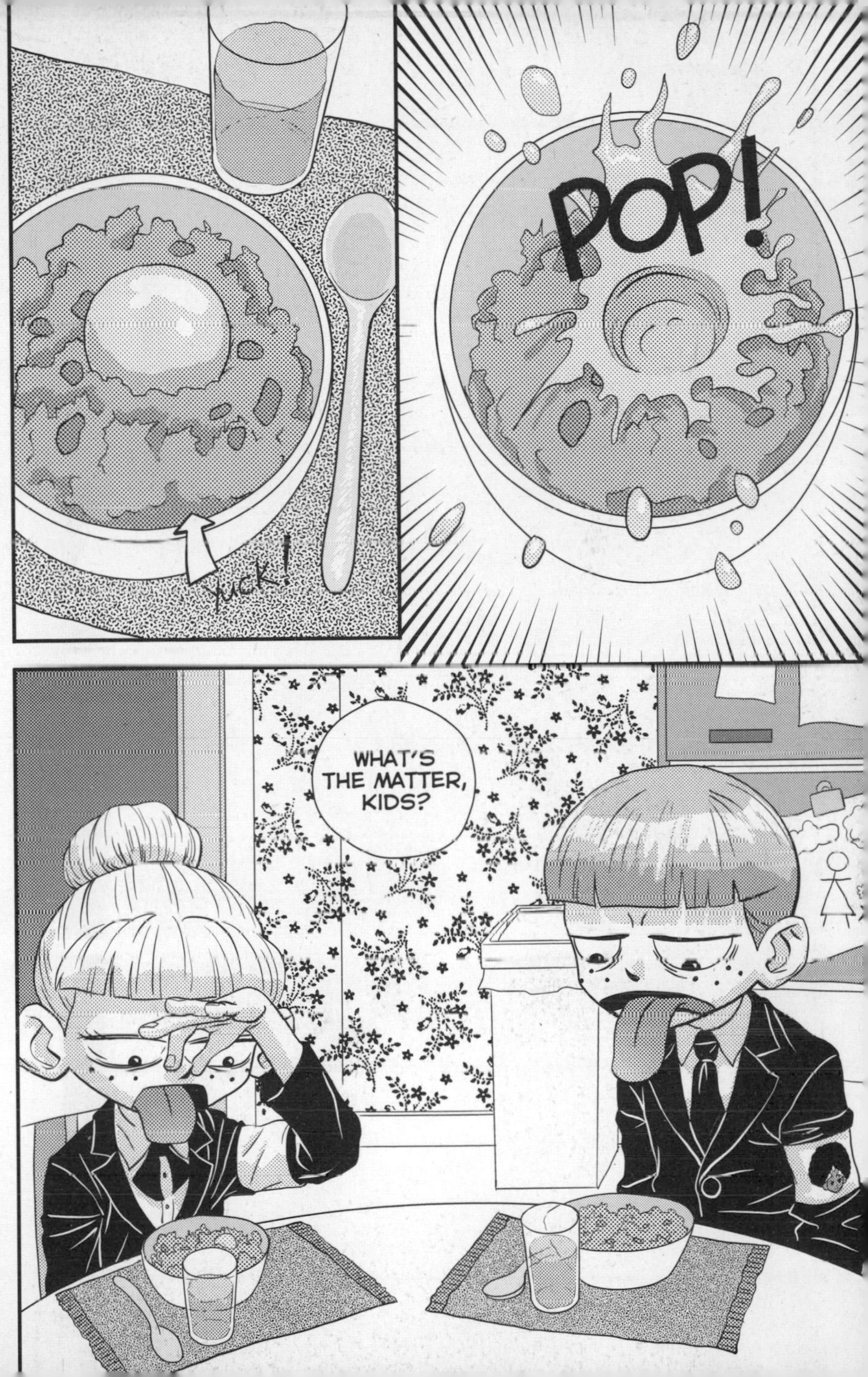
YUCK!
POP!
WHAT'S THE MATTER, KIDS?

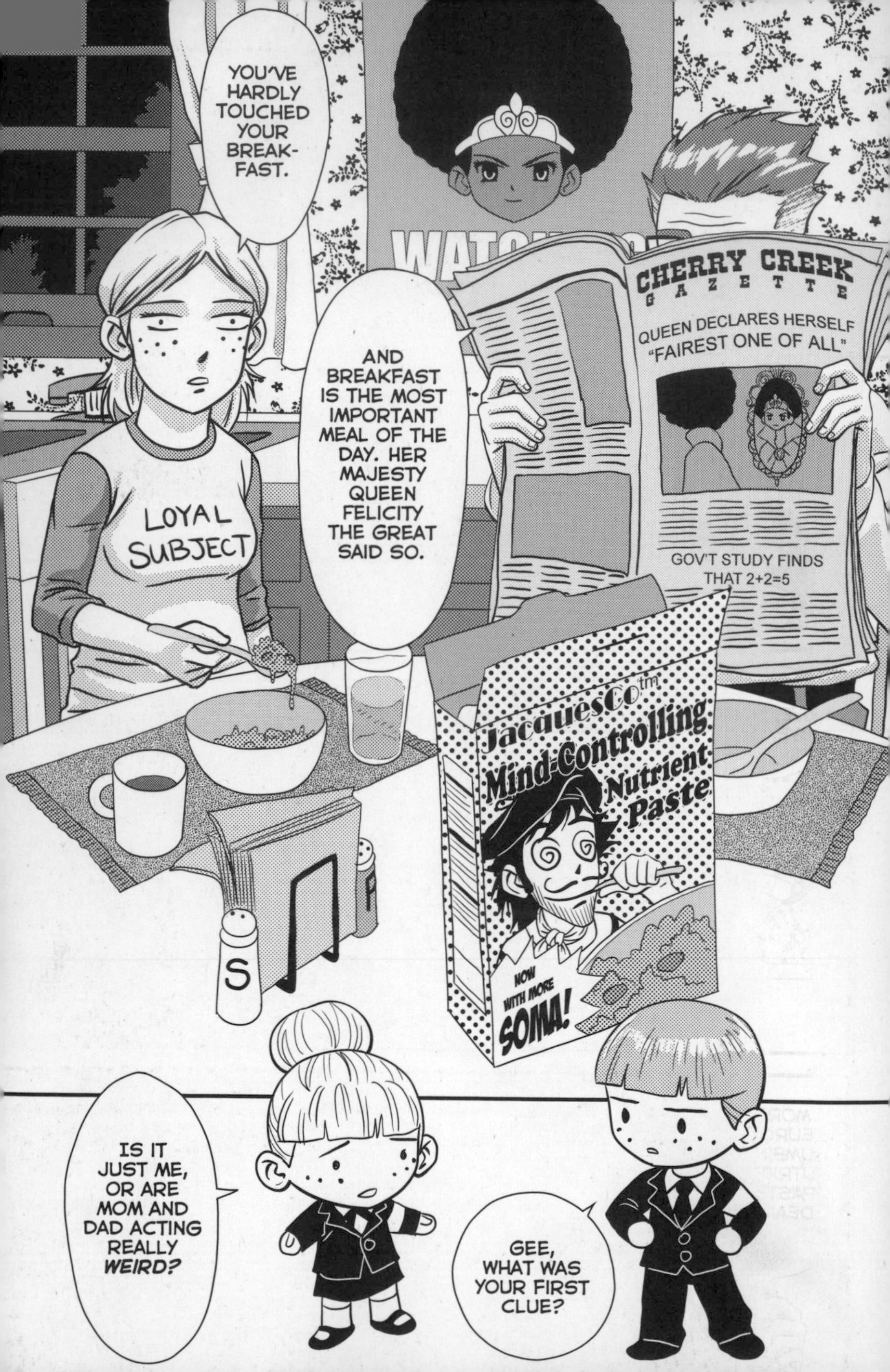
YOU'VE HARDLY TOUCHED YOUR BREAK-FAST.
AND BREAKFAST IS THE MOST IMPORTANT MEAL OF THE DAY. HER MAJESTY QUEEN FELICITY THE GREAT SAID SO.
LOYAL SUBJECT
CHERRY CREEK GAZETTE
QUEEN DECLARES HERSELF "FAIREST ONE OF ALL"
GOV'T STUDY FINDS THAT 2+2=5
JacquesCo™ Mind-Controlling Nutrient Paste
NOW WITH MORE SOMA!
S
IS IT JUST ME, OR ARE MOM AND DAD ACTING REALLY *WEIRD?*
GEE, WHAT WAS YOUR FIRST CLUE?

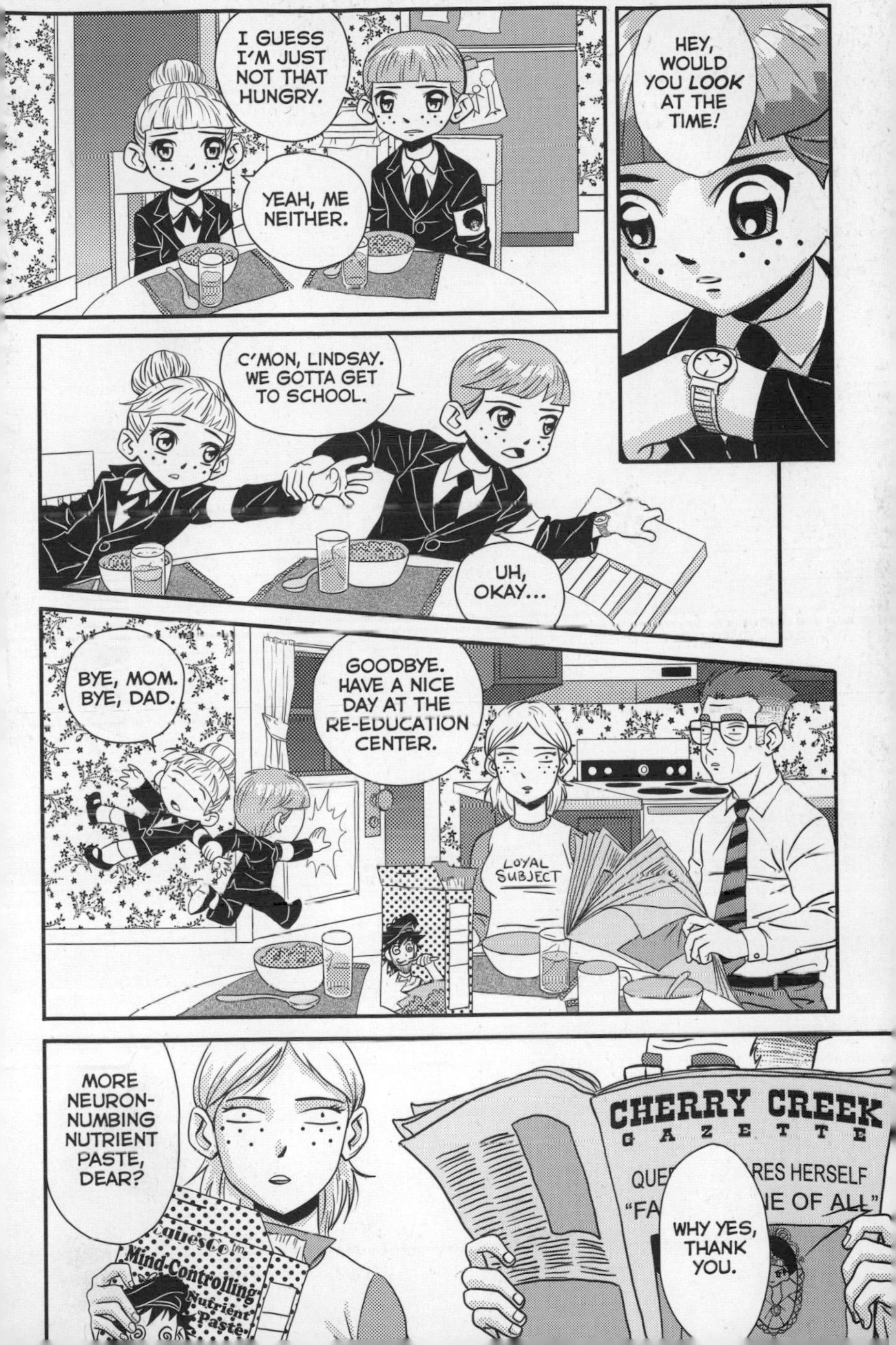
I GUESS I'M JUST NOT THAT HUNGRY.
YEAH, ME NEITHER.
C'MON, LINDSAY. WE GOTTA GET TO SCHOOL.
UH, OKAY...
HEY, WOULD YOU *LOOK* AT THE TIME!
BYE, MOM. BYE, DAD.
GOODBYE. HAVE A NICE DAY AT THE RE-EDUCATION CENTER.
LOYAL SUBJECT
MORE NEURON-NUMBING NUTRIENT PASTE, DEAR?
Mind-Controlling Nutrient Paste
CHERRY CREEK
GAZETTE
WHY YES, THANK YOU.

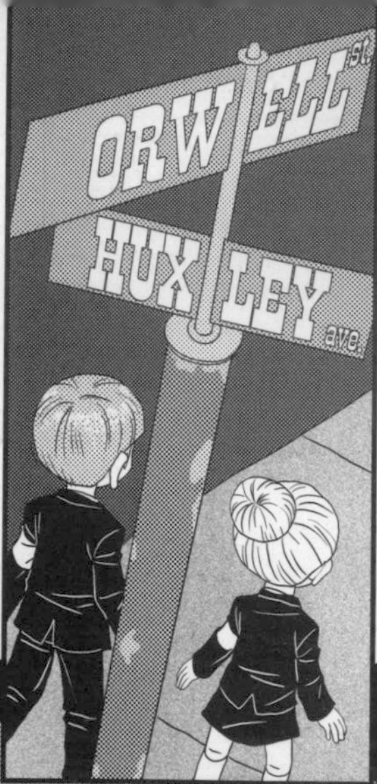
ORWELL st.
HUXLEY ave.

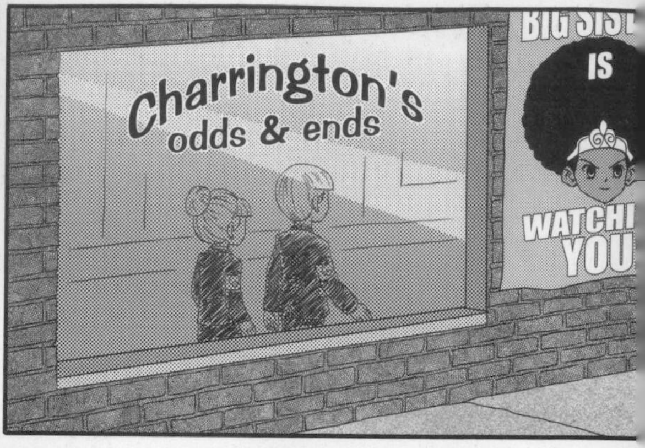
Charrington's
odds & ends
IS
YOU

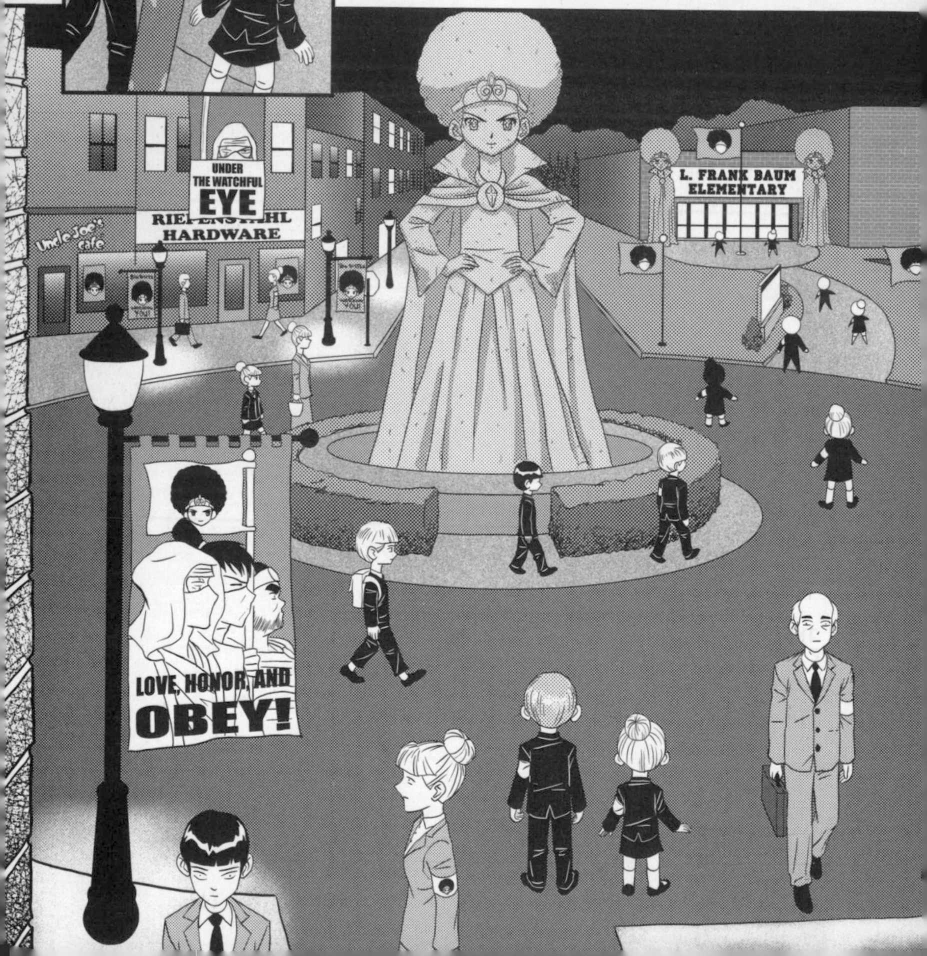
UNDER THE WATCHFUL EYE
HARDWARE
Uncle Joe's cafe
L. FRANK BAUM ELEMENTARY
LOVE, HONOR, AND OBEY!

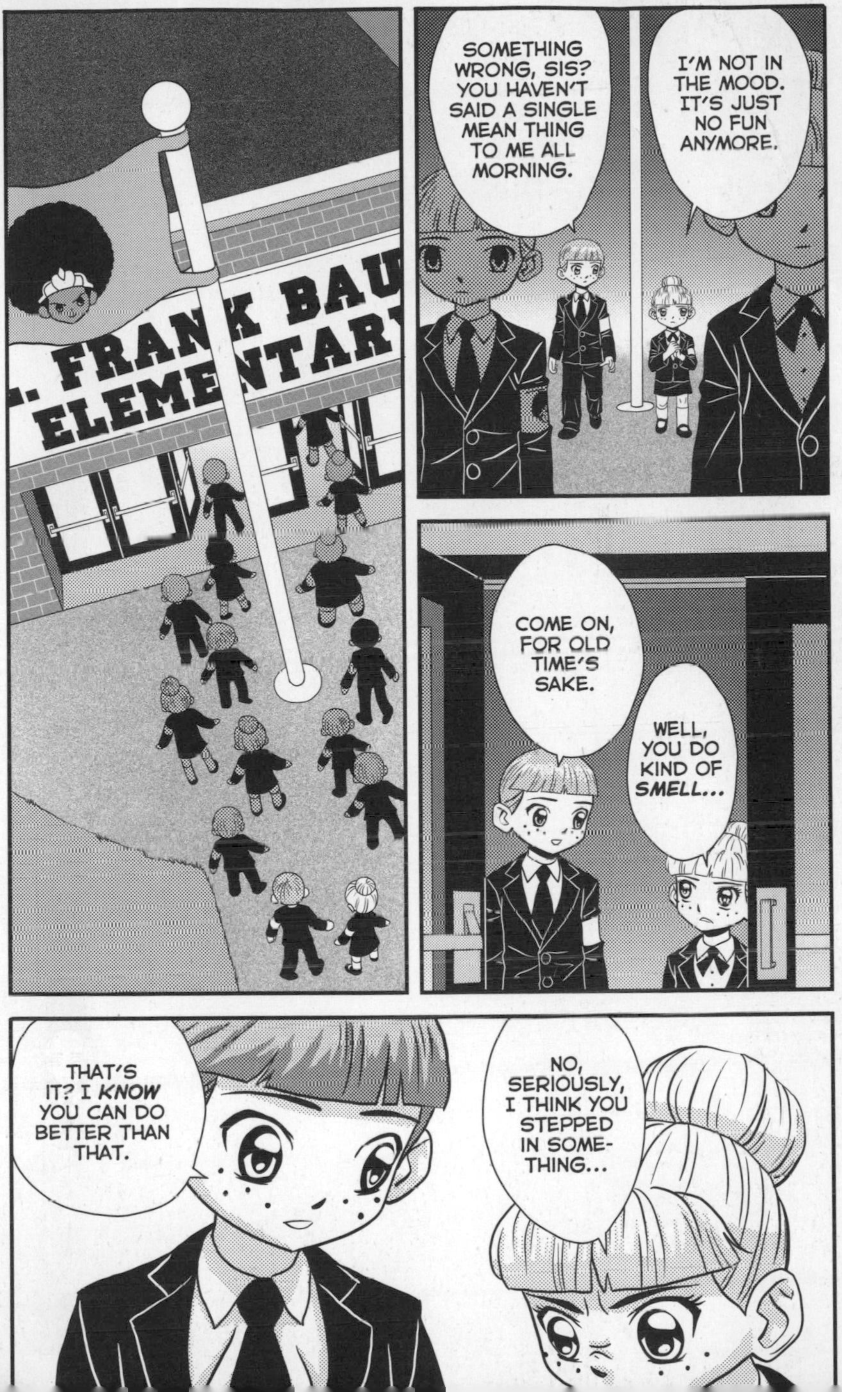
FRANK BAU
ELEMENTAR
SOMETHING WRONG, SIS? YOU HAVEN'T SAID A SINGLE MEAN THING TO ME ALL MORNING.
I'M NOT IN THE MOOD. IT'S JUST NO FUN ANYMORE.
COME ON, FOR OLD TIME'S SAKE.
WELL, YOU DO KIND OF *SMELL*...
THAT'S IT? I *KNOW* YOU CAN DO BETTER THAN THAT.
NO, SERIOUSLY, I THINK YOU STEPPED IN SOME-THING...

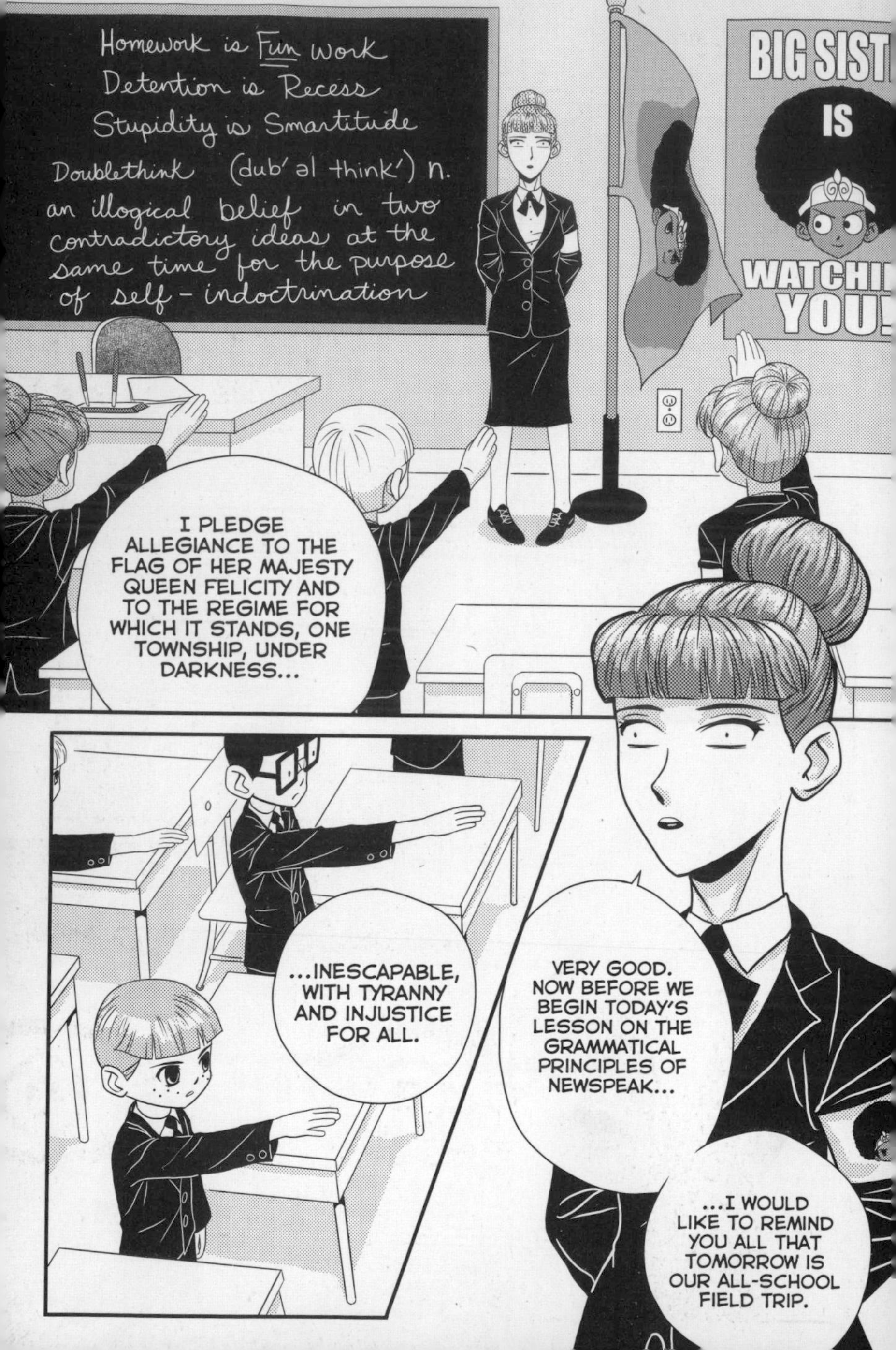

Homework is Fun work
Detention is Recess
Stupidity is Smartitude
Doublethink (dub' əl think') n.
an illogical belief in two contradictory ideas at the same time for the purpose of self-indoctrination
BIG SIST
IS
WATCHI
YOU!
I PLEDGE ALLEGIANCE TO THE FLAG OF HER MAJESTY QUEEN FELICITY AND TO THE REGIME FOR WHICH IT STANDS, ONE TOWNSHIP, UNDER DARKNESS...
...INESCAPABLE, WITH TYRANNY AND INJUSTICE FOR ALL.
VERY GOOD. NOW BEFORE WE BEGIN TODAY'S LESSON ON THE GRAMMATICAL PRINCIPLES OF NEWSPEAK...
...I WOULD LIKE TO REMIND YOU ALL THAT TOMORROW IS OUR ALL-SCHOOL FIELD TRIP.

WE WILL BE JOINING THE REST OF THE TOWN IN HUNTINGTON SQUARE TO CELEBRATE THE ONE-MONTH ANNIVERSARY OF HER MAJESTY QUEEN FELICITY'S BENEVOLENT RULE.

THERE WILL BE CAKE AND ICE CREAM, FOLLOWED BY THE TRIAL AND EXECUTION OF THE CITY'S MOST NOTORIOUS CRIMINAL, YOSHIDA JIRO.

NO, THAT CAN'T BE RIGHT. JIRO ISN'T A CRIMINAL.

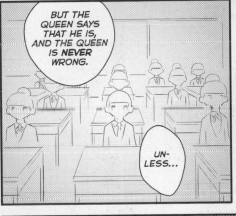

BUT THE QUEEN SAYS THAT HE IS, AND THE QUEEN IS *NEVER* WRONG.

UN-LESS...

UNLESS THIS BRAVE NEW WORLD IS JUST ONE BIG *LIE!*

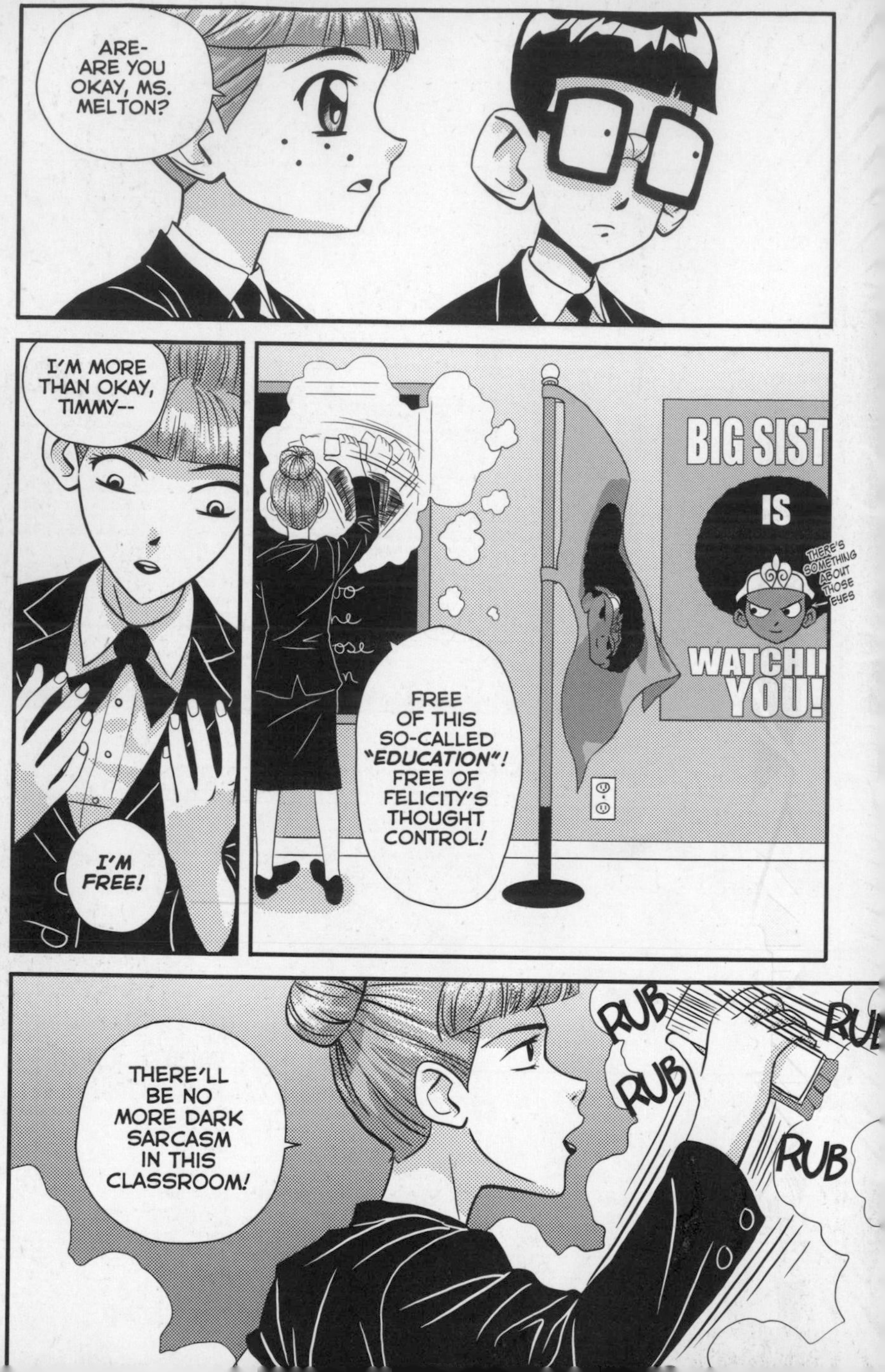
ARE- ARE YOU OKAY, MS. MELTON?
I'M MORE THAN OKAY, TIMMY--
I'M FREE!
BIG SIST
IS
THERE'S SOMETHING ABOUT THOSE EYES
WATCHI
YOU!
FREE OF THIS SO-CALLED "EDUCATION"! FREE OF FELICITY'S THOUGHT CONTROL!
THERE'LL BE NO MORE DARK SARCASM IN THIS CLASSROOM!
RUB
RUB
RUB
RUB

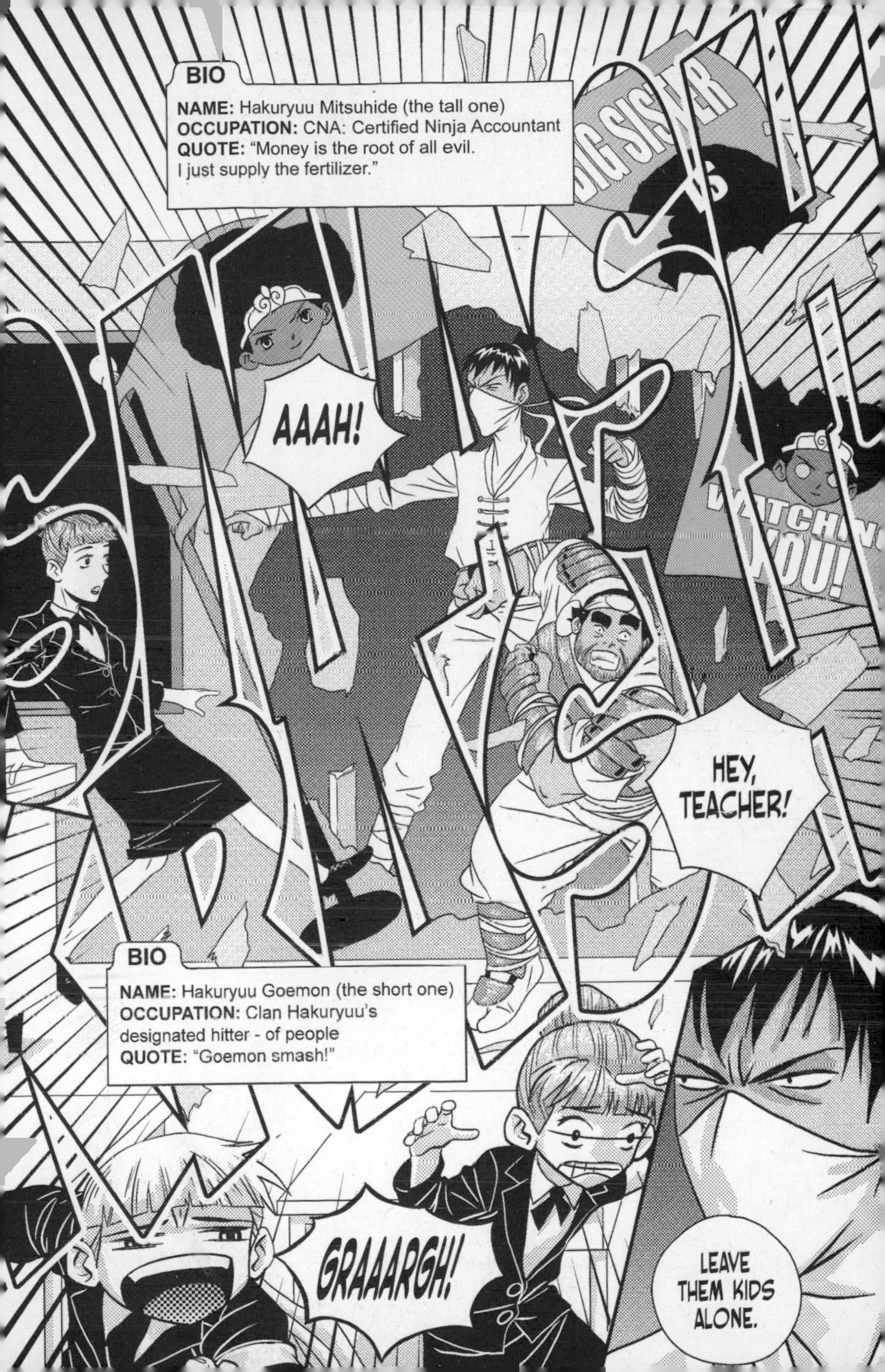
BIO
NAME: Hakuryuu Mitsuhide (the tall one)
OCCUPATION: CNA: Certified Ninja Accountant
QUOTE: "Money is the root of all evil. I just supply the fertilizer."
AAAH!
HEY, TEACHER!
BIO
NAME: Hakuryuu Goemon (the short one)
OCCUPATION: Clan Hakuryuu's designated hitter - of people
QUOTE: "Goemon smash!"
GRAAARGH!
LEAVE THEM KIDS ALONE.

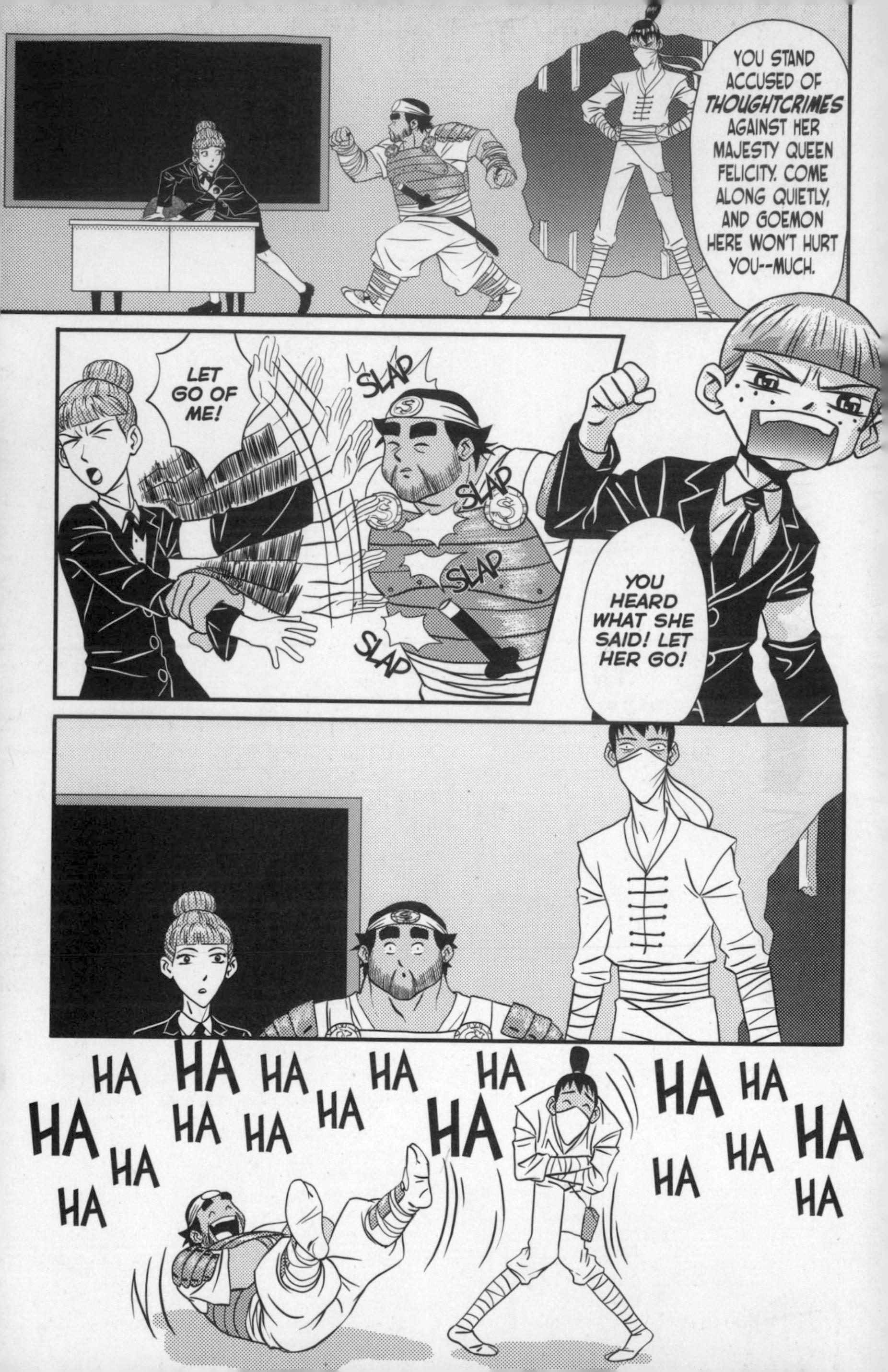
YOU STAND ACCUSED OF *THOUGHTCRIMES* AGAINST HER MAJESTY QUEEN FELICITY. COME ALONG QUIETLY, AND GOEMON HERE WON'T HURT YOU--MUCH.
LET GO OF ME!
SLAP
SLAP
SLAP
SLAP
YOU HEARD WHAT SHE SAID! LET HER GO!
HA HA HA HA HA HA HA
HA HA HA HA HA HA
HA HA HA HA
HA HA

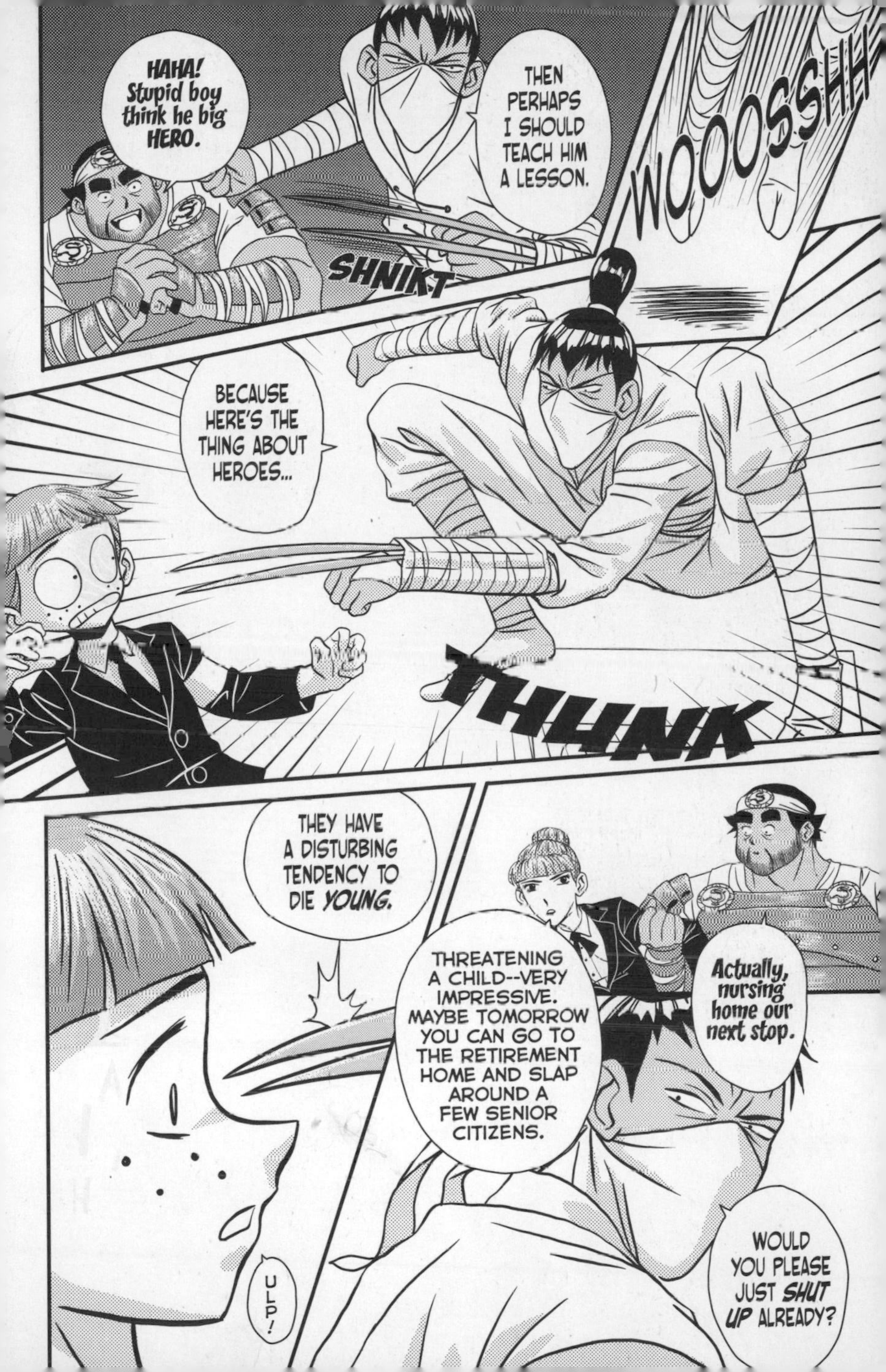
HAHA! Stupid boy think he big HERO.
THEN PERHAPS I SHOULD TEACH HIM A LESSON.
WOOOSSHH
SHNIKT
BECAUSE HERE'S THE THING ABOUT HEROES...
THUNK
THEY HAVE A DISTURBING TENDENCY TO DIE YOUNG.
ULP!
THREATENING A CHILD--VERY IMPRESSIVE. MAYBE TOMORROW YOU CAN GO TO THE RETIREMENT HOME AND SLAP AROUND A FEW SENIOR CITIZENS.
Actually, nursing home our next stop.
WOULD YOU PLEASE JUST SHUT UP ALREADY?

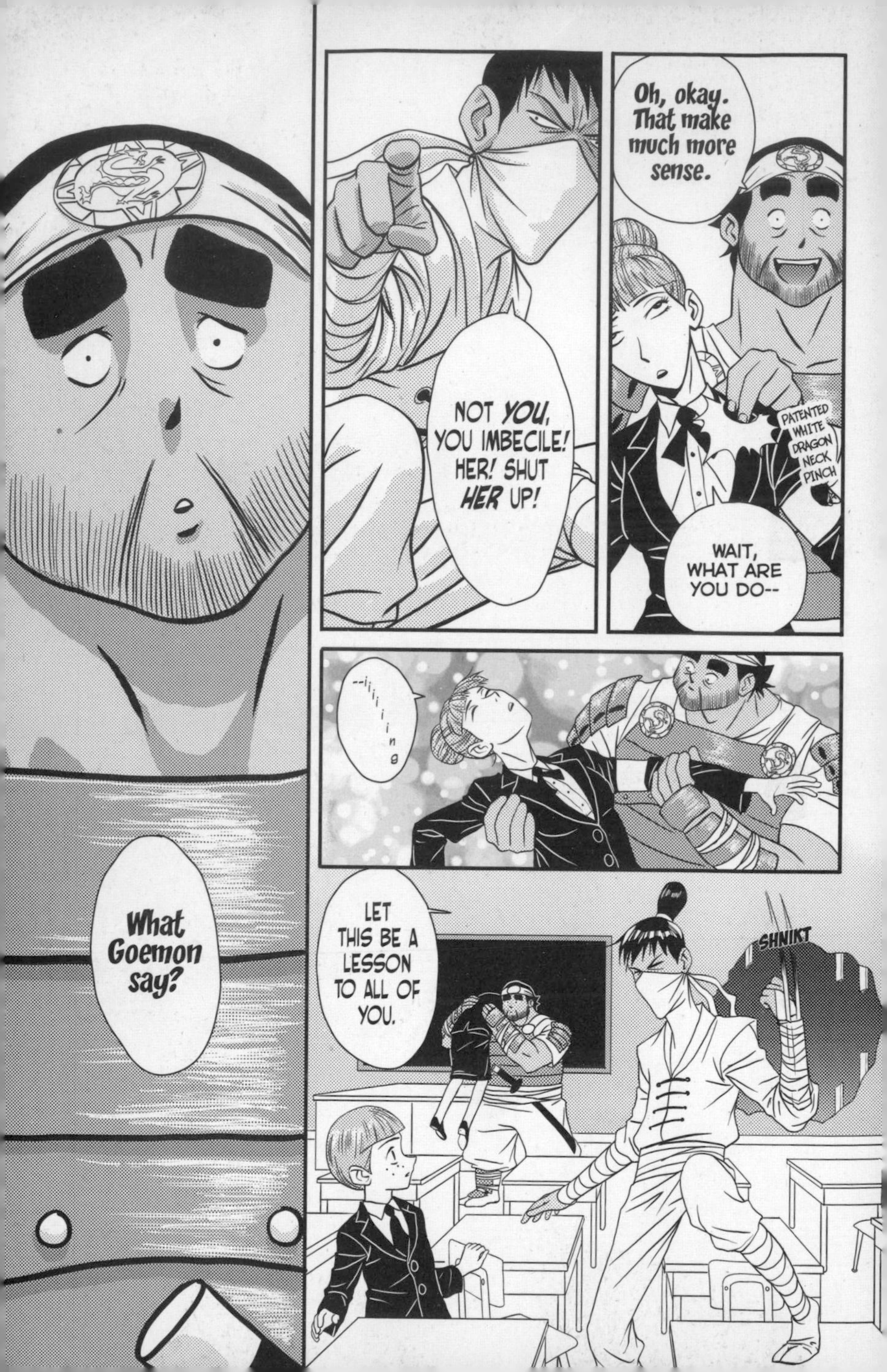
What Goemon say?
NOT YOU, YOU IMBECILE! HER! SHUT HER UP!
Oh, okay. That make much more sense.
PATENTED WHITE DRAGON NECK PINCH
WAIT, WHAT ARE YOU DO--
--iiiiiing
LET THIS BE A LESSON TO ALL OF YOU.
SHNIKT

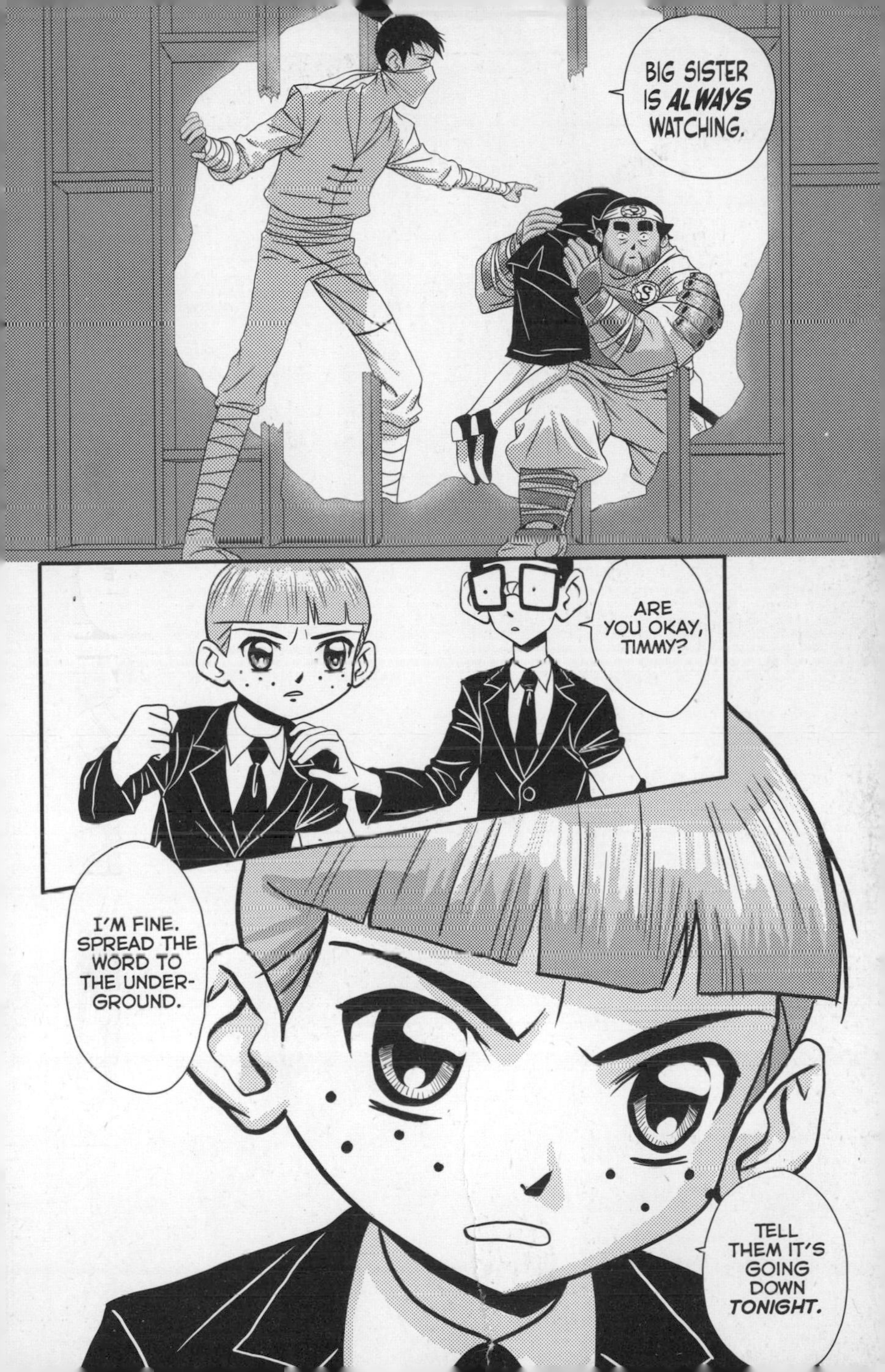
BIG SISTER IS ALWAYS WATCHING.
ARE YOU OKAY, TIMMY?
I'M FINE. SPREAD THE WORD TO THE UNDER-GROUND.
TELL THEM IT'S GOING DOWN TONIGHT.

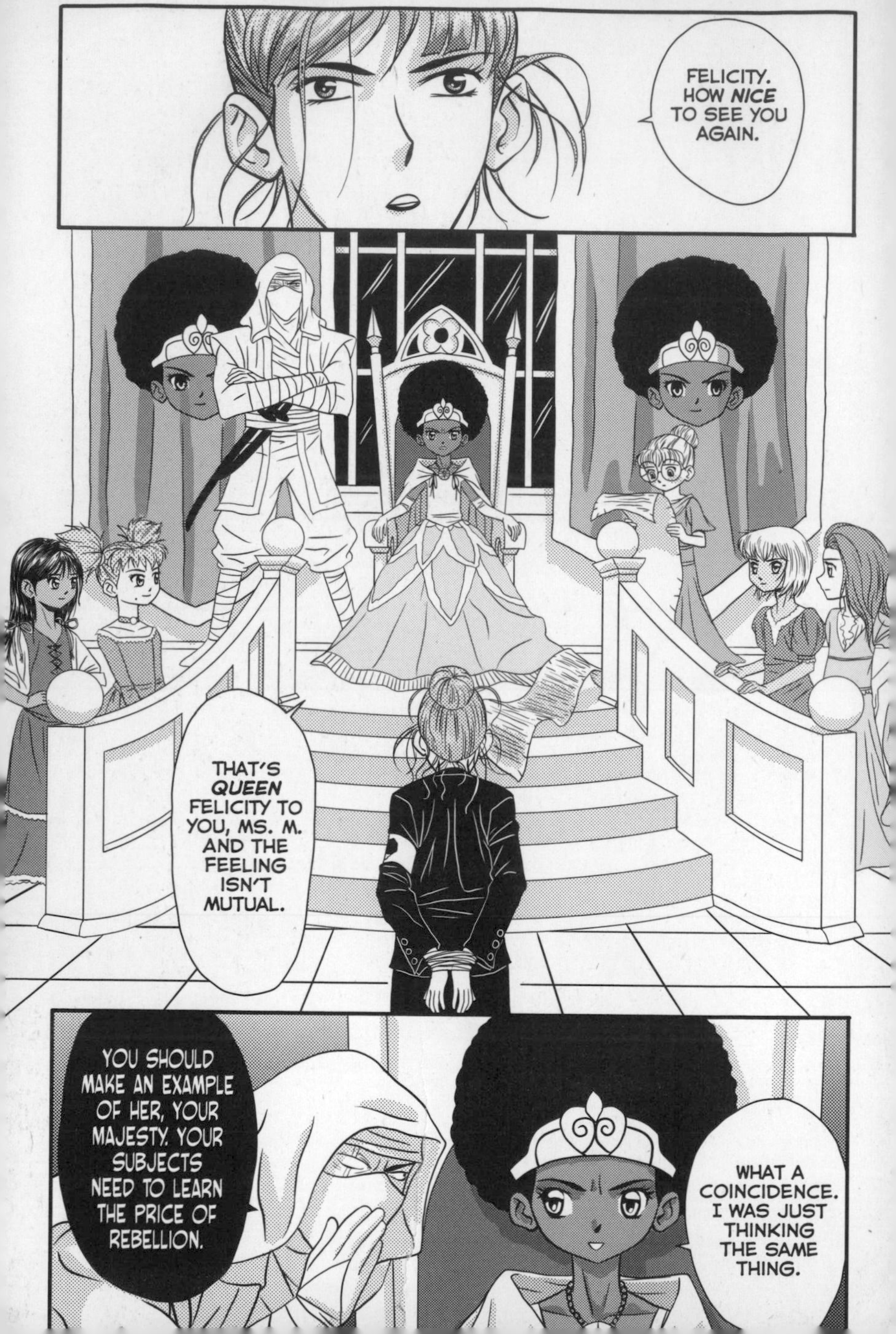
FELICITY. HOW *NICE* TO SEE YOU AGAIN.
THAT'S *QUEEN* FELICITY TO YOU, MS. M. AND THE FEELING ISN'T MUTUAL.
YOU SHOULD MAKE AN EXAMPLE OF HER, YOUR MAJESTY. YOUR SUBJECTS NEED TO LEARN THE PRICE OF REBELLION.
WHAT A COINCIDENCE. I WAS JUST THINKING THE SAME THING.

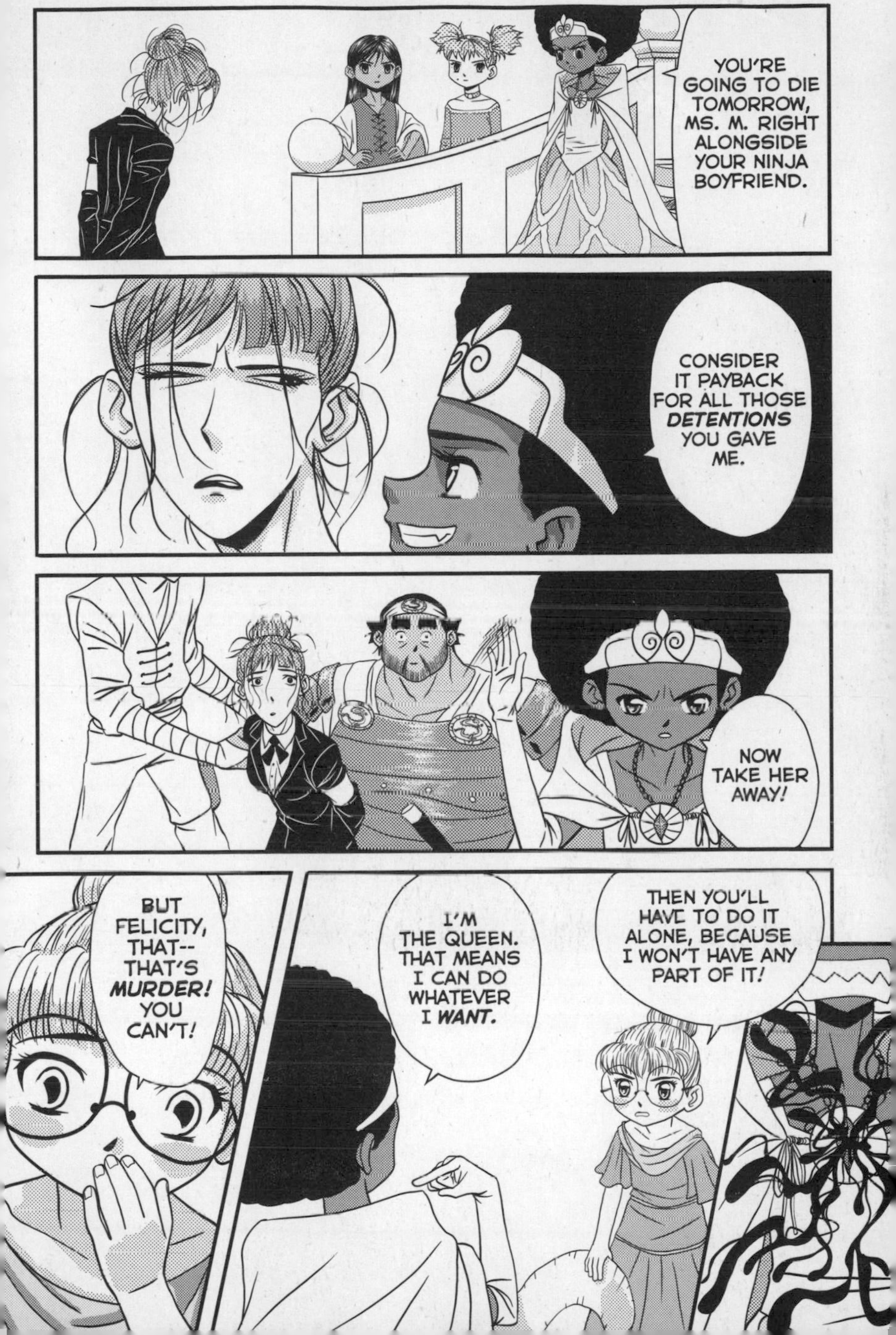

YOU'RE GOING TO DIE TOMORROW, MS. M. RIGHT ALONGSIDE YOUR NINJA BOYFRIEND.
CONSIDER IT PAYBACK FOR ALL THOSE *DETENTIONS* YOU GAVE ME.
NOW TAKE HER AWAY!
BUT FELICITY, THAT-- THAT'S *MURDER!* YOU CAN'T!
I'M THE QUEEN. THAT MEANS I CAN DO WHATEVER I *WANT.*
THEN YOU'LL HAVE TO DO IT ALONE, BECAUSE I WON'T HAVE ANY PART OF IT!

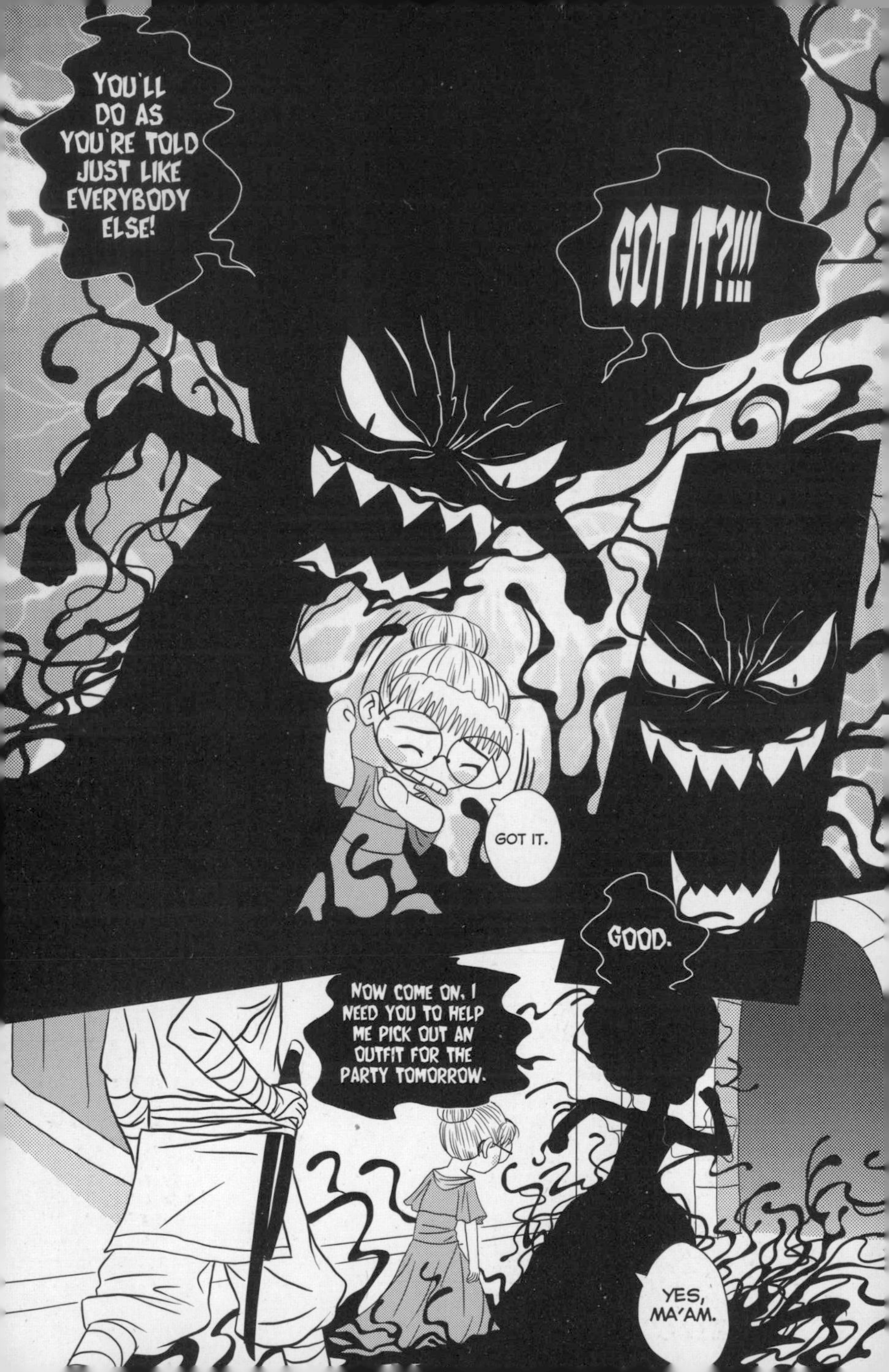
YOU'LL DO AS YOU'RE TOLD JUST LIKE EVERYBODY ELSE!
GOT IT?!!!
GOT IT.
GOOD.
NOW COME ON, I NEED YOU TO HELP ME PICK OUT AN OUTFIT FOR THE PARTY TOMORROW.
YES, MA'AM.

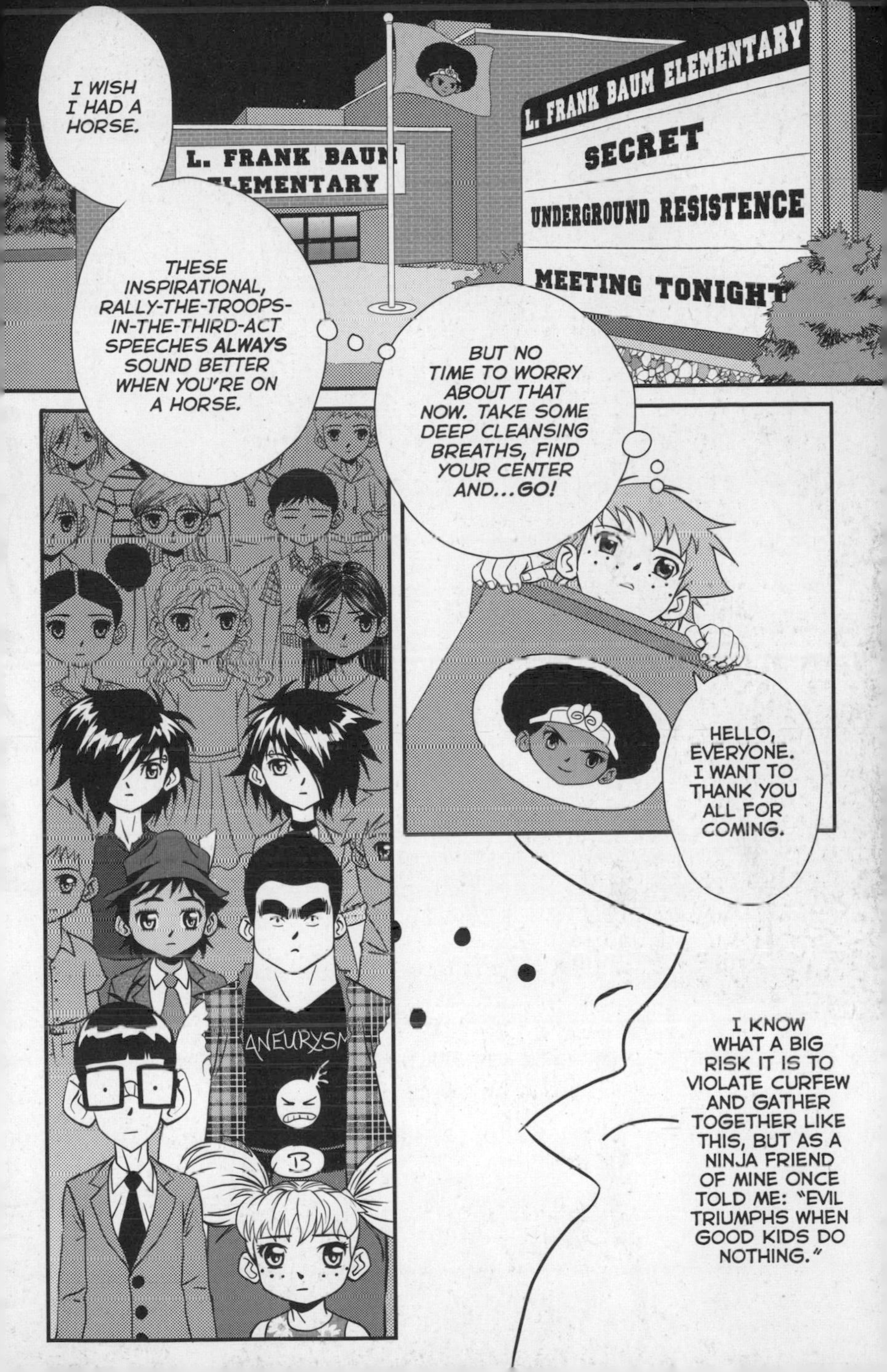
I WISH I HAD A HORSE.
L. FRANK BAUM ELEMENTARY
SECRET
UNDERGROUND RESISTENCE
MEETING TONIGHT
THESE INSPIRATIONAL, RALLY-THE-TROOPS-IN-THE-THIRD-ACT SPEECHES ALWAYS SOUND BETTER WHEN YOU'RE ON A HORSE.
BUT NO TIME TO WORRY ABOUT THAT NOW. TAKE SOME DEEP CLEANSING BREATHS, FIND YOUR CENTER AND...GO!
ANEURYSM
HELLO, EVERYONE. I WANT TO THANK YOU ALL FOR COMING.
I KNOW WHAT A BIG RISK IT IS TO VIOLATE CURFEW AND GATHER TOGETHER LIKE THIS, BUT AS A NINJA FRIEND OF MINE ONCE TOLD ME: "EVIL TRIUMPHS WHEN GOOD KIDS DO NOTHING."

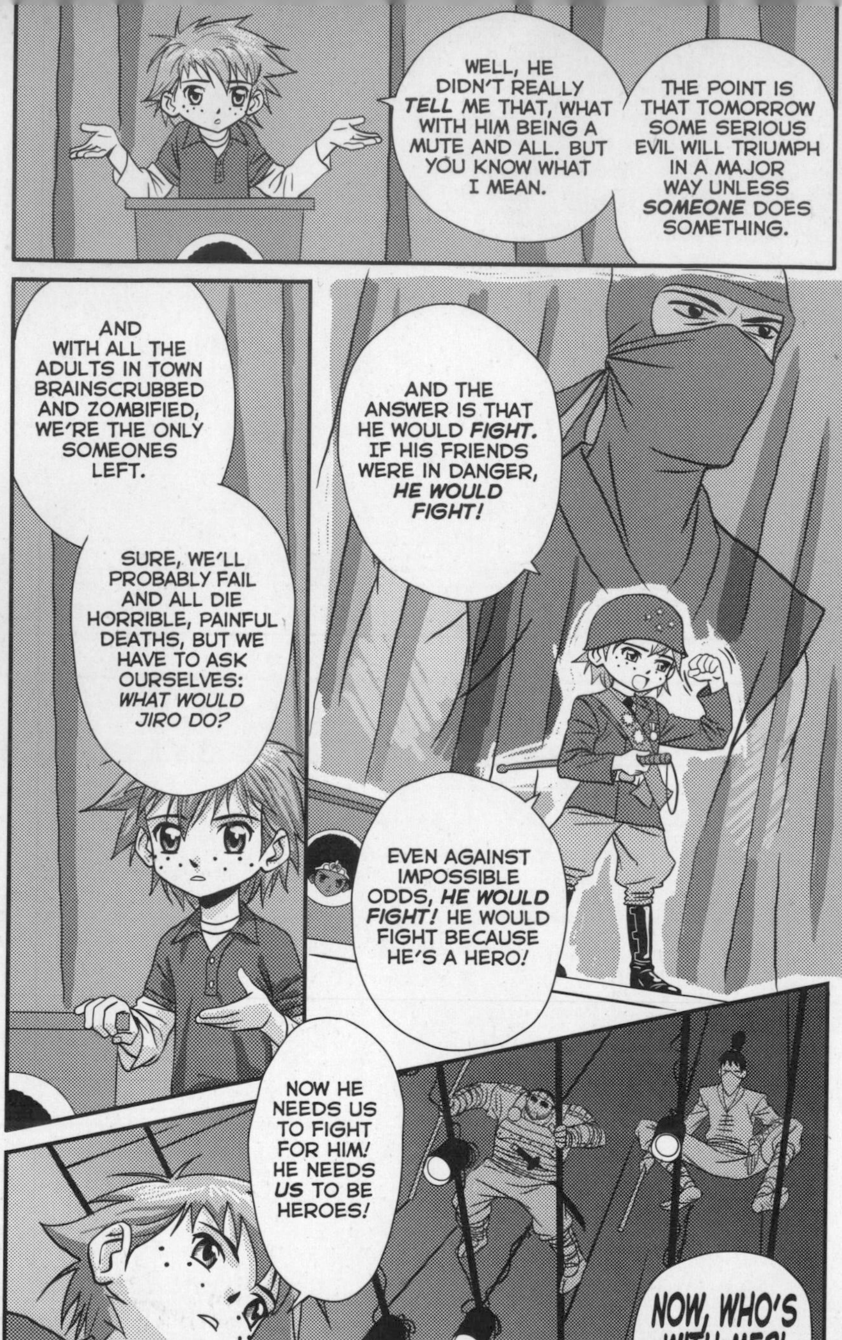
WELL, HE DIDN'T REALLY TELL ME THAT, WHAT WITH HIM BEING A MUTE AND ALL. BUT YOU KNOW WHAT I MEAN.
THE POINT IS THAT TOMORROW SOME SERIOUS EVIL WILL TRIUMPH IN A MAJOR WAY UNLESS SOMEONE DOES SOMETHING.
AND WITH ALL THE ADULTS IN TOWN BRAINSCRUBBED AND ZOMBIFIED, WE'RE THE ONLY SOMEONES LEFT.
SURE, WE'LL PROBABLY FAIL AND ALL DIE HORRIBLE, PAINFUL DEATHS, BUT WE HAVE TO ASK OURSELVES: WHAT WOULD JIRO DO?
AND THE ANSWER IS THAT HE WOULD FIGHT. IF HIS FRIENDS WERE IN DANGER, HE WOULD FIGHT!
EVEN AGAINST IMPOSSIBLE ODDS, HE WOULD FIGHT! HE WOULD FIGHT BECAUSE HE'S A HERO!
NOW HE NEEDS US TO FIGHT FOR HIM! HE NEEDS US TO BE HEROES!
NOW, WHO'S WITH ME?!

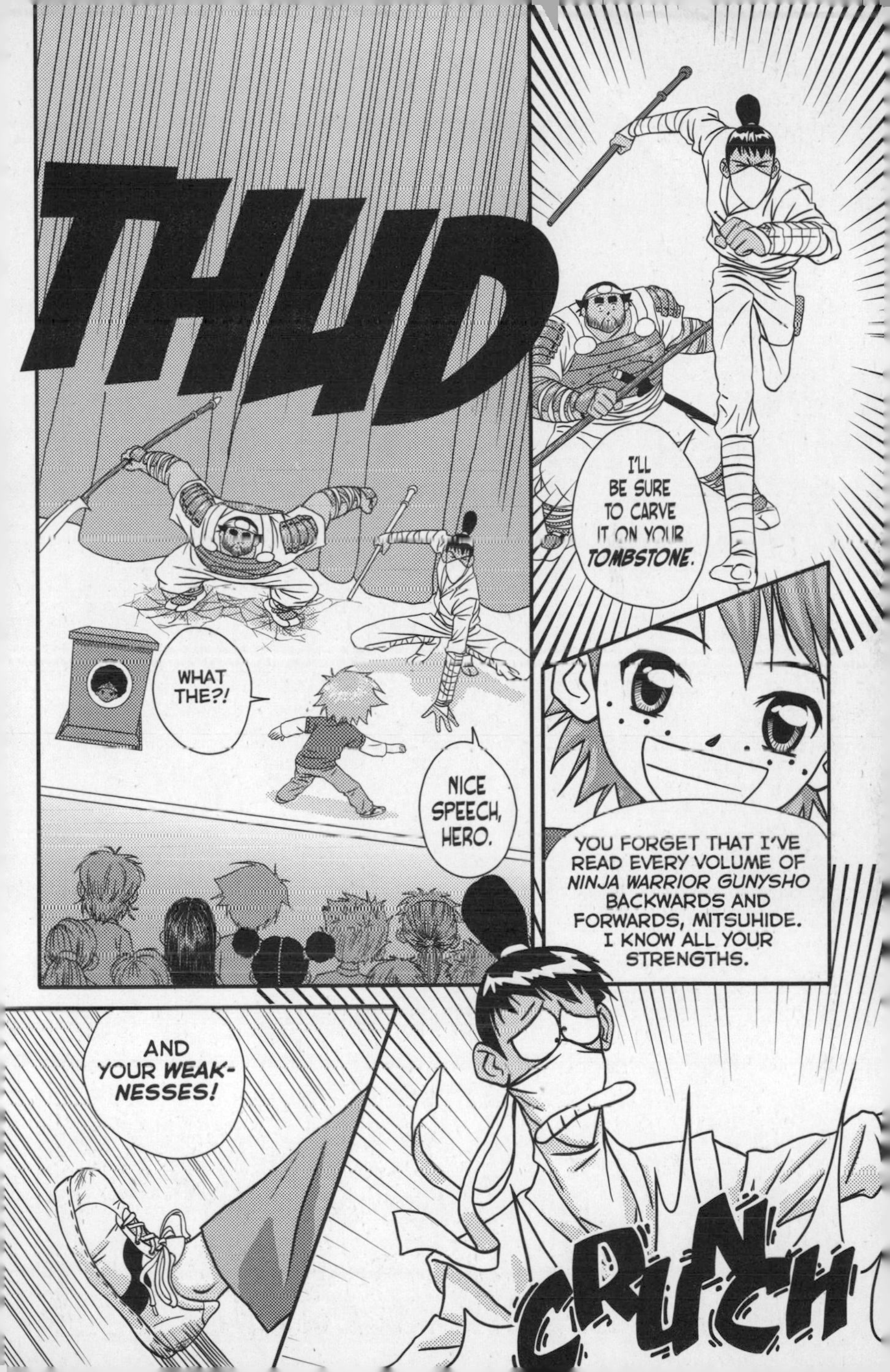
THUD
WHAT THE?!
NICE SPEECH, HERO.
I'LL BE SURE TO CARVE IT ON YOUR TOMBSTONE.
YOU FORGET THAT I'VE READ EVERY VOLUME OF NINJA WARRIOR GUNYSHO BACKWARDS AND FORWARDS, MITSUHIDE. I KNOW ALL YOUR STRENGTHS.
AND YOUR WEAK-NESSES!
CRUNCH

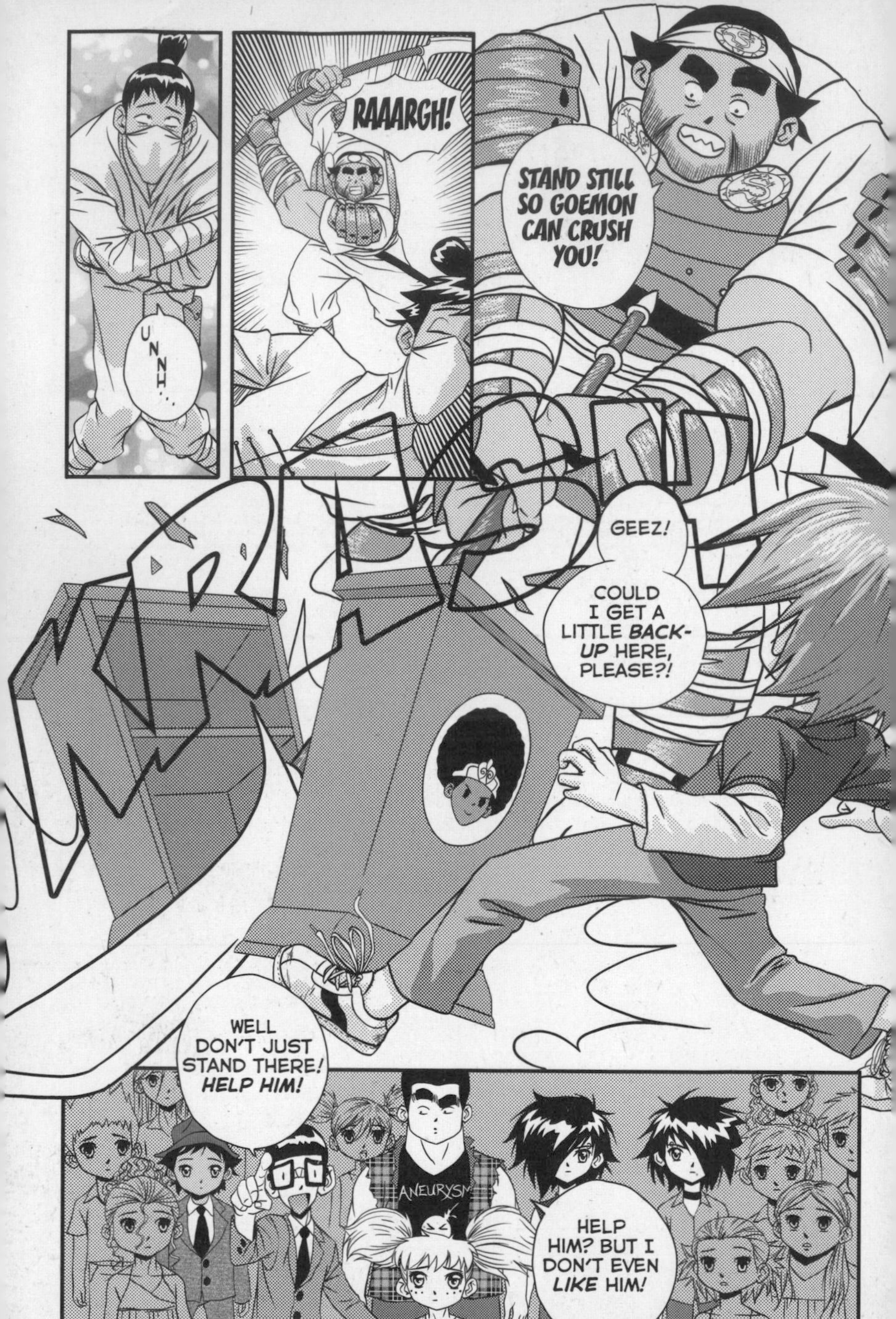
UNNH...
RAAARGH!
STAND STILL SO GOEMON CAN CRUSH YOU!
GEEZ!
COULD I GET A LITTLE BACK-UP HERE, PLEASE?!
WELL DON'T JUST STAND THERE! HELP HIM!
ANEURYSM
HELP HIM? BUT I DON'T EVEN LIKE HIM!

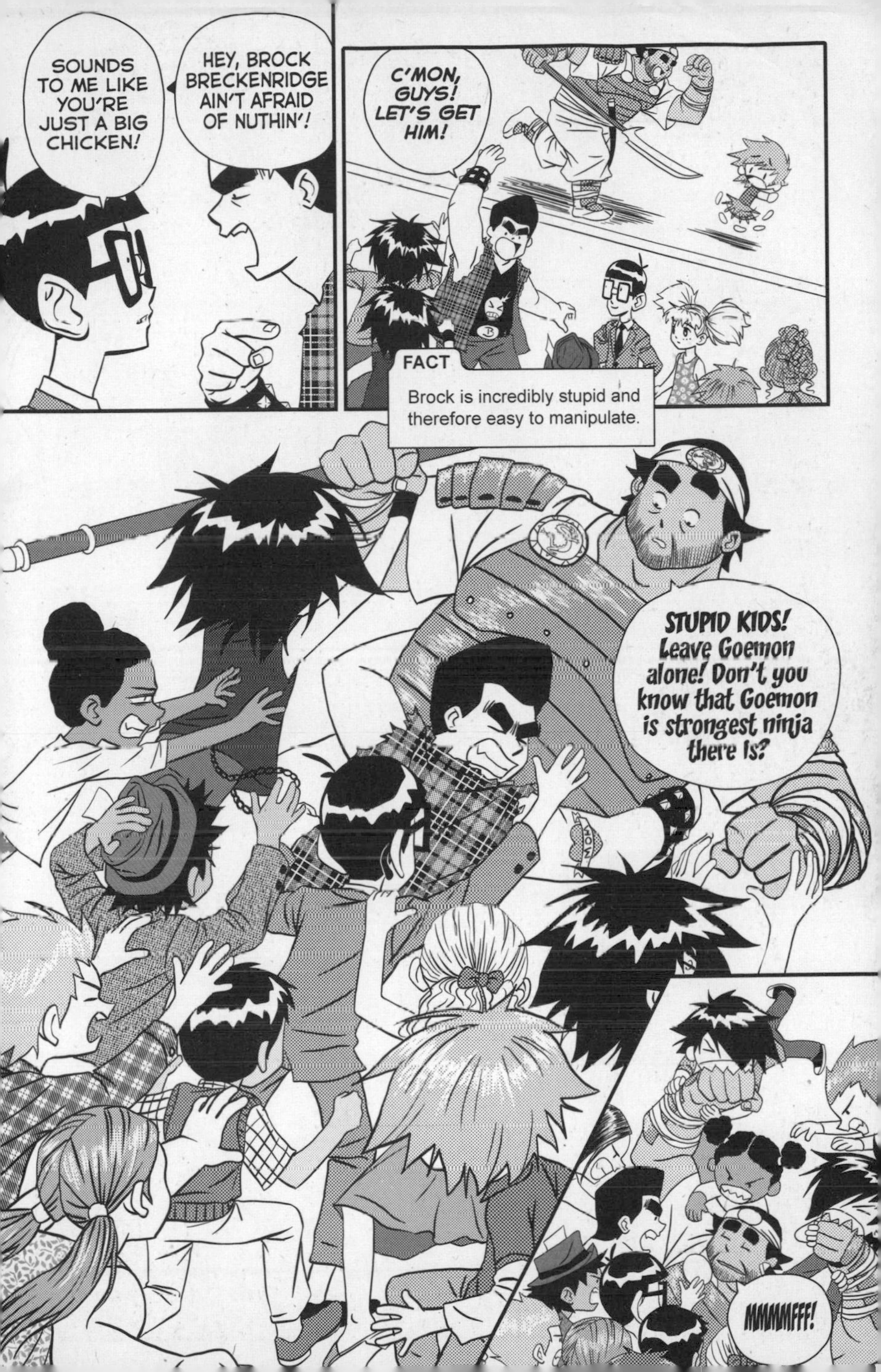
SOUNDS TO ME LIKE YOU'RE JUST A BIG CHICKEN!
HEY, BROCK BRECKENRIDGE AIN'T AFRAID OF NUTHIN'!
C'MON, GUYS! LET'S GET HIM!
FACT
Brock is incredibly stupid and therefore easy to manipulate.
STUPID KIDS! Leave Goemon alone! Don't you know that Goemon is strongest ninja there is?
MMMMFFF!

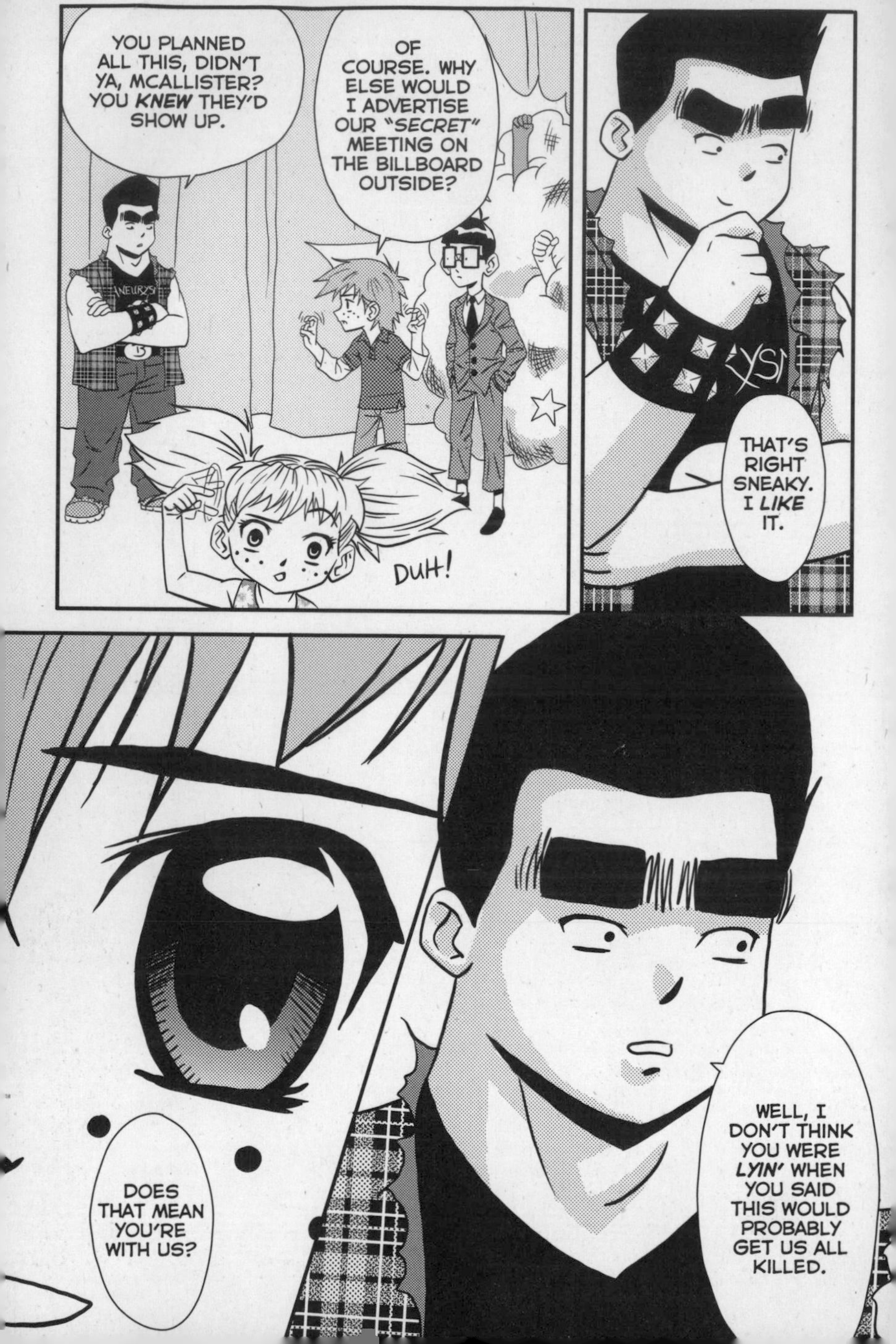
YOU PLANNED ALL THIS, DIDN'T YA, MCALLISTER? YOU *KNEW* THEY'D SHOW UP.
OF COURSE. WHY ELSE WOULD I ADVERTISE OUR *"SECRET"* MEETING ON THE BILLBOARD OUTSIDE?
DUH!
THAT'S RIGHT SNEAKY. I *LIKE* IT.
DOES THAT MEAN YOU'RE WITH US?
WELL, I DON'T THINK YOU WERE *LYIN'* WHEN YOU SAID THIS WOULD PROBABLY GET US ALL KILLED.

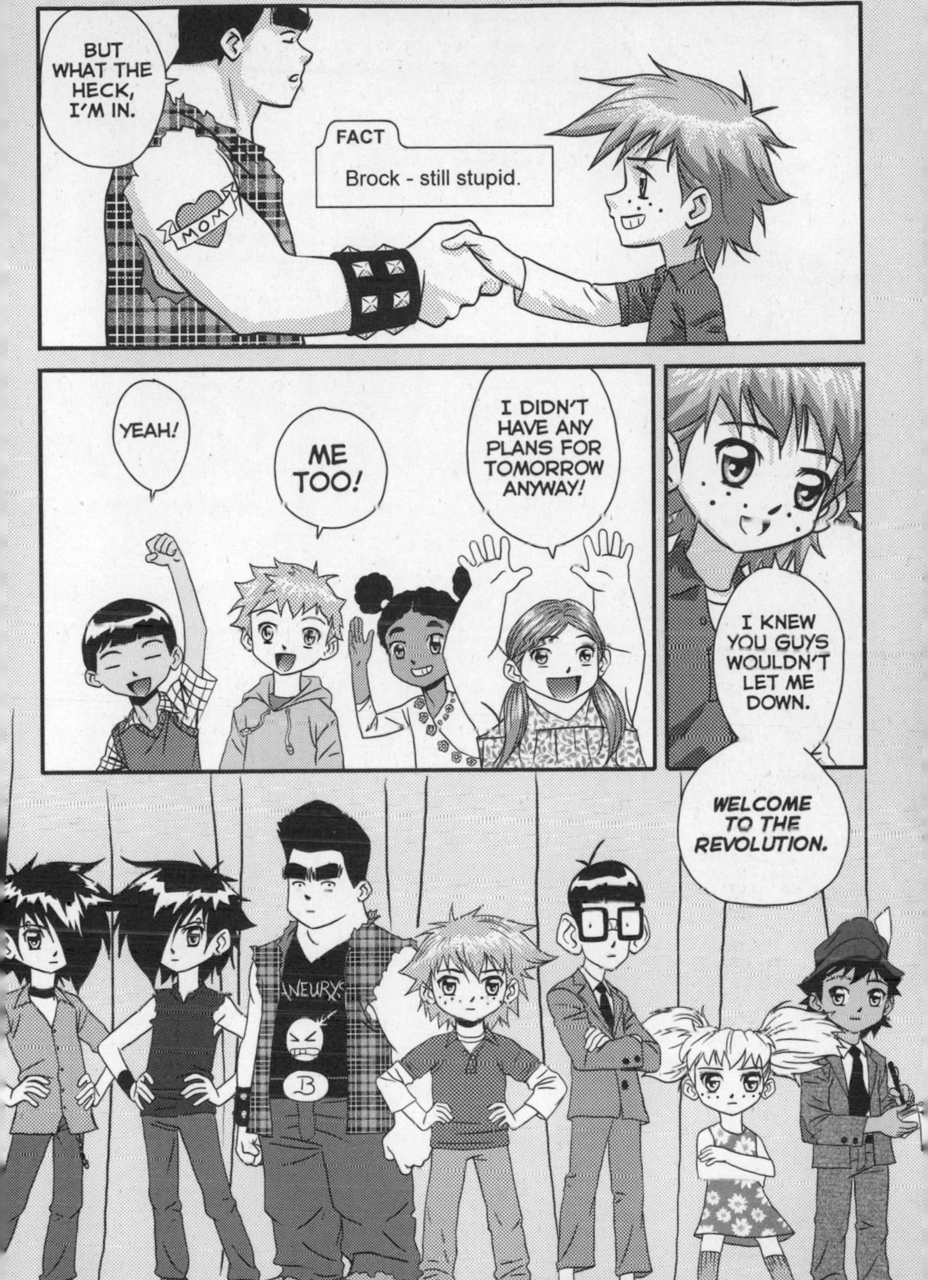
BUT WHAT THE HECK, I'M IN.
FACT
Brock - still stupid.
MOM
YEAH!
ME TOO!
I DIDN'T HAVE ANY PLANS FOR TOMORROW ANYWAY!
I KNEW YOU GUYS WOULDN'T LET ME DOWN.
WELCOME TO THE REVOLUTION.
ANEURYS

CHAPTER 3

"..."

- Yoshida Jiro, legendary ninja warrior. Spoken during the battle of Huntington Square.

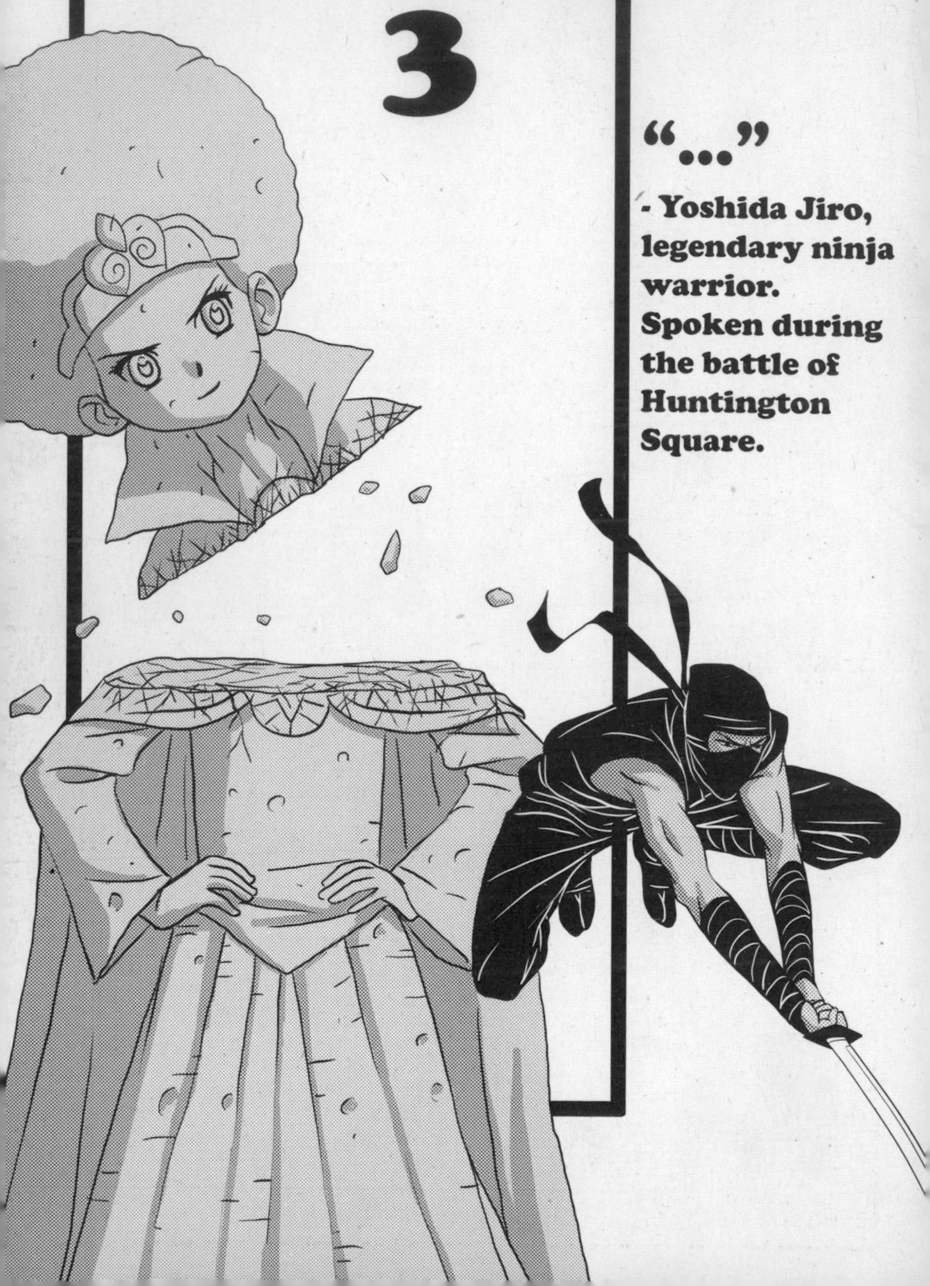

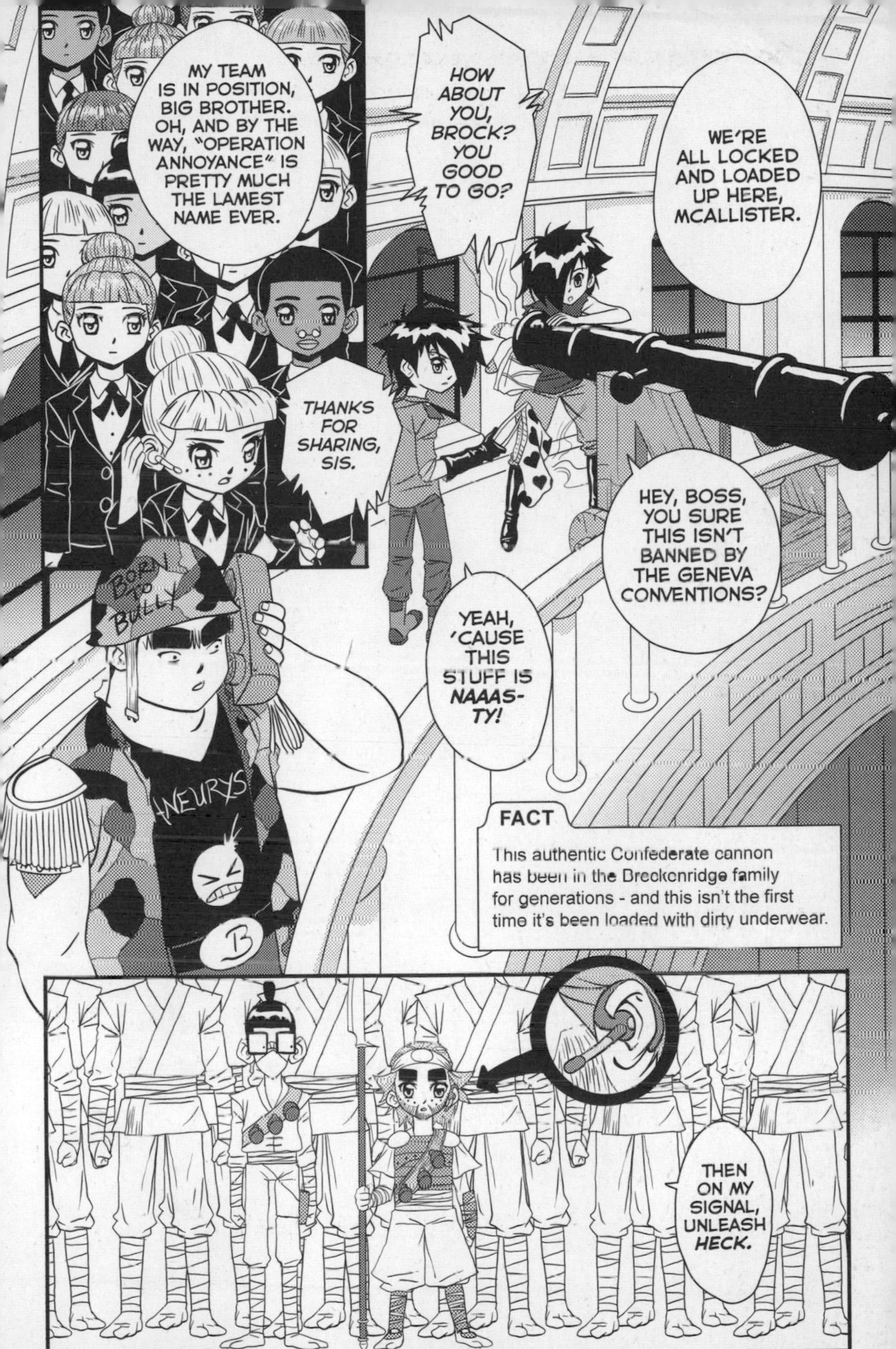
MY TEAM IS IN POSITION, BIG BROTHER. OH, AND BY THE WAY, "OPERATION ANNOYANCE" IS PRETTY MUCH THE LAMEST NAME EVER.
THANKS FOR SHARING, SIS.
HOW ABOUT YOU, BROCK? YOU GOOD TO GO?
WE'RE ALL LOCKED AND LOADED UP HERE, MCALLISTER.
BORN TO BULLY
HEY, BOSS, YOU SURE THIS ISN'T BANNED BY THE GENEVA CONVENTIONS?
YEAH, 'CAUSE THIS STUFF IS *NAAAS-TY!*
FACT
This authentic Confederate cannon has been in the Breckenridge family for generations - and this isn't the first time it's been loaded with dirty underwear.
THEN ON MY SIGNAL, UNLEASH *HECK.*

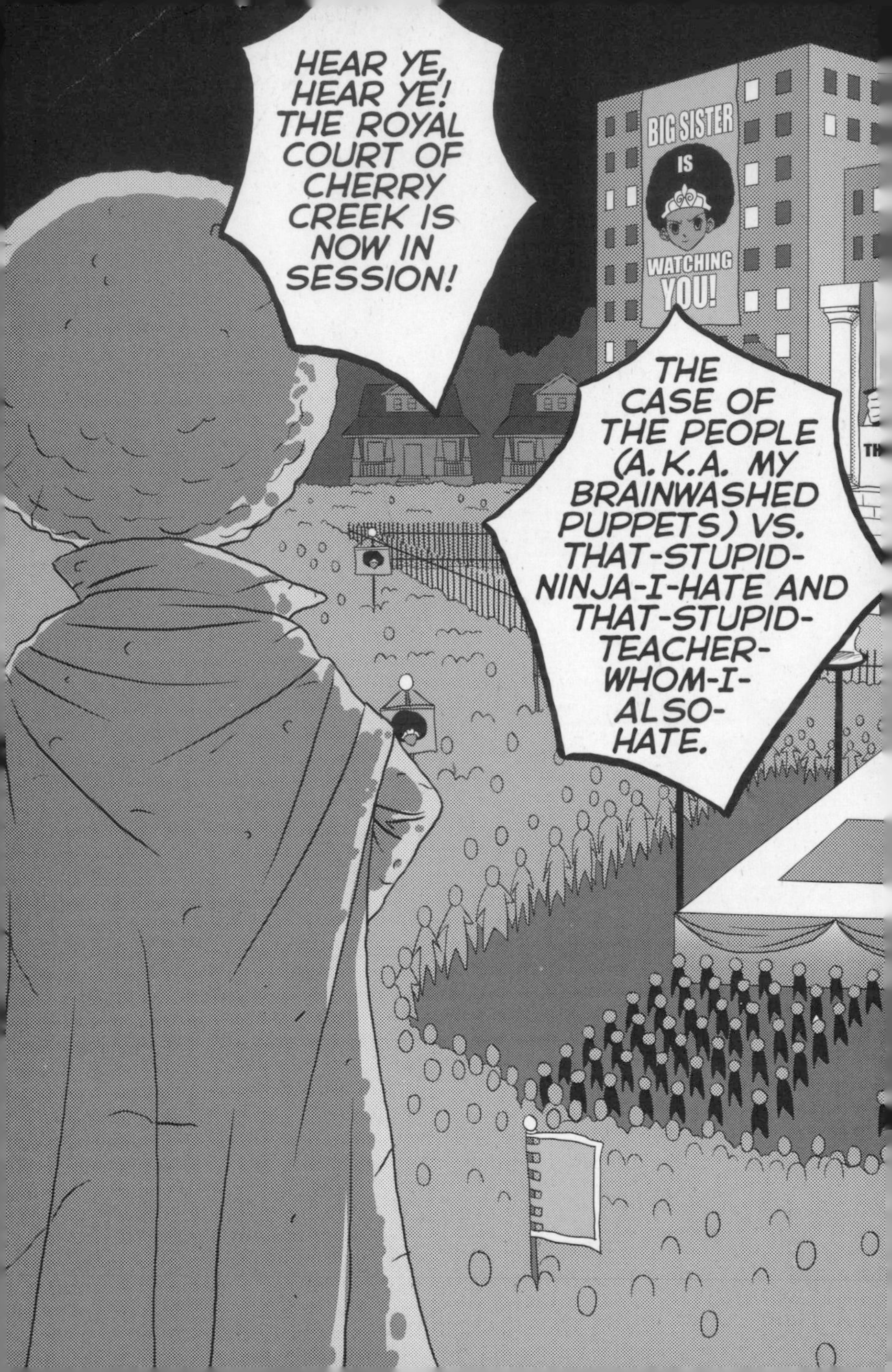
HEAR YE, HEAR YE! THE ROYAL COURT OF CHERRY CREEK IS NOW IN SESSION!
BIG SISTER IS WATCHING YOU!
THE CASE OF THE PEOPLE (A.K.A. MY BRAINWASHED PUPPETS) VS. THAT-STUPID-NINJA-I-HATE AND THAT-STUPID-TEACHER-WHOM-I-ALSO-HATE.

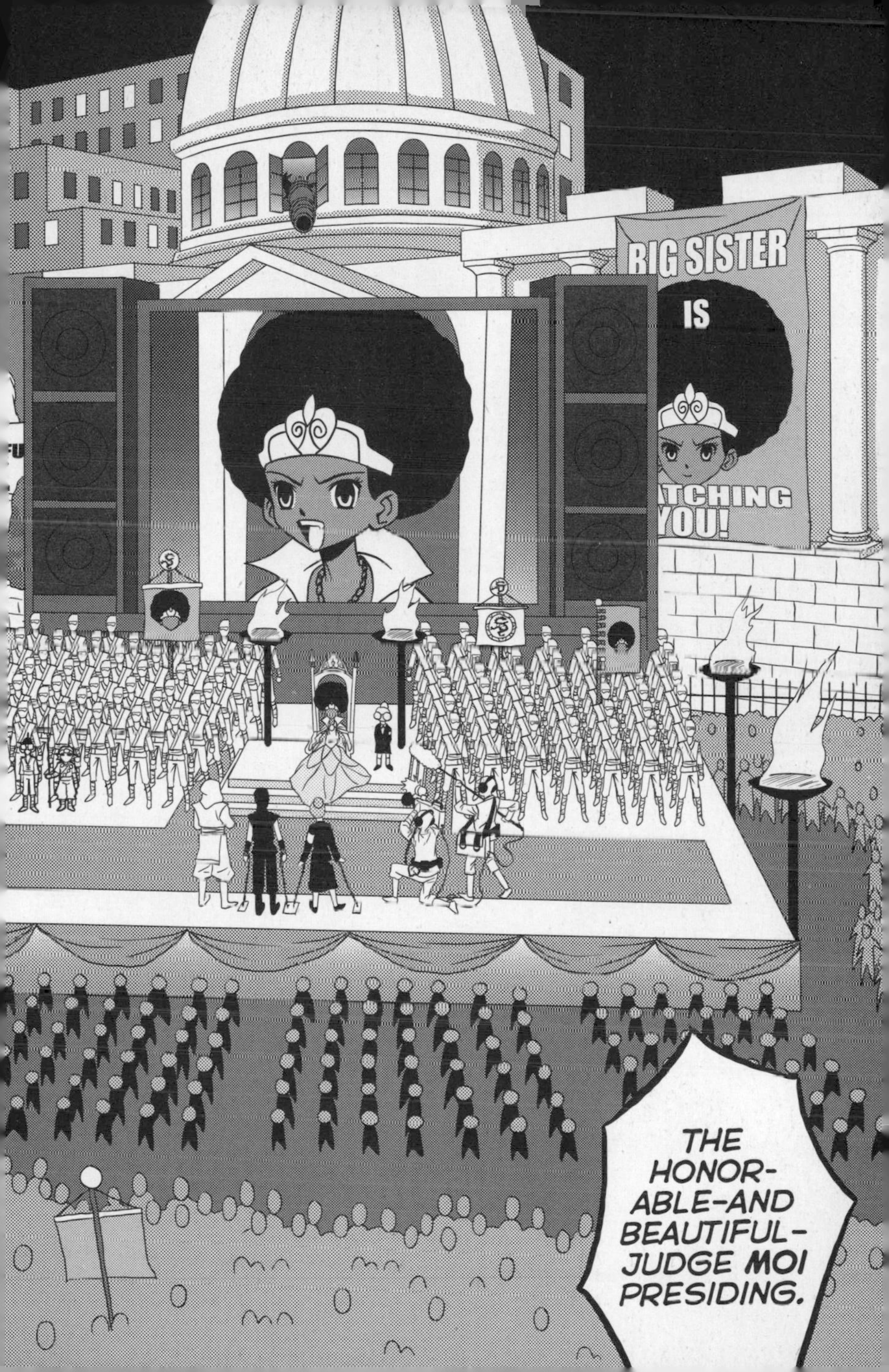
BIG SISTER
IS
ATCHING
YOU!
THE HONOR-ABLE-AND BEAUTIFUL-JUDGE MOI PRESIDING.

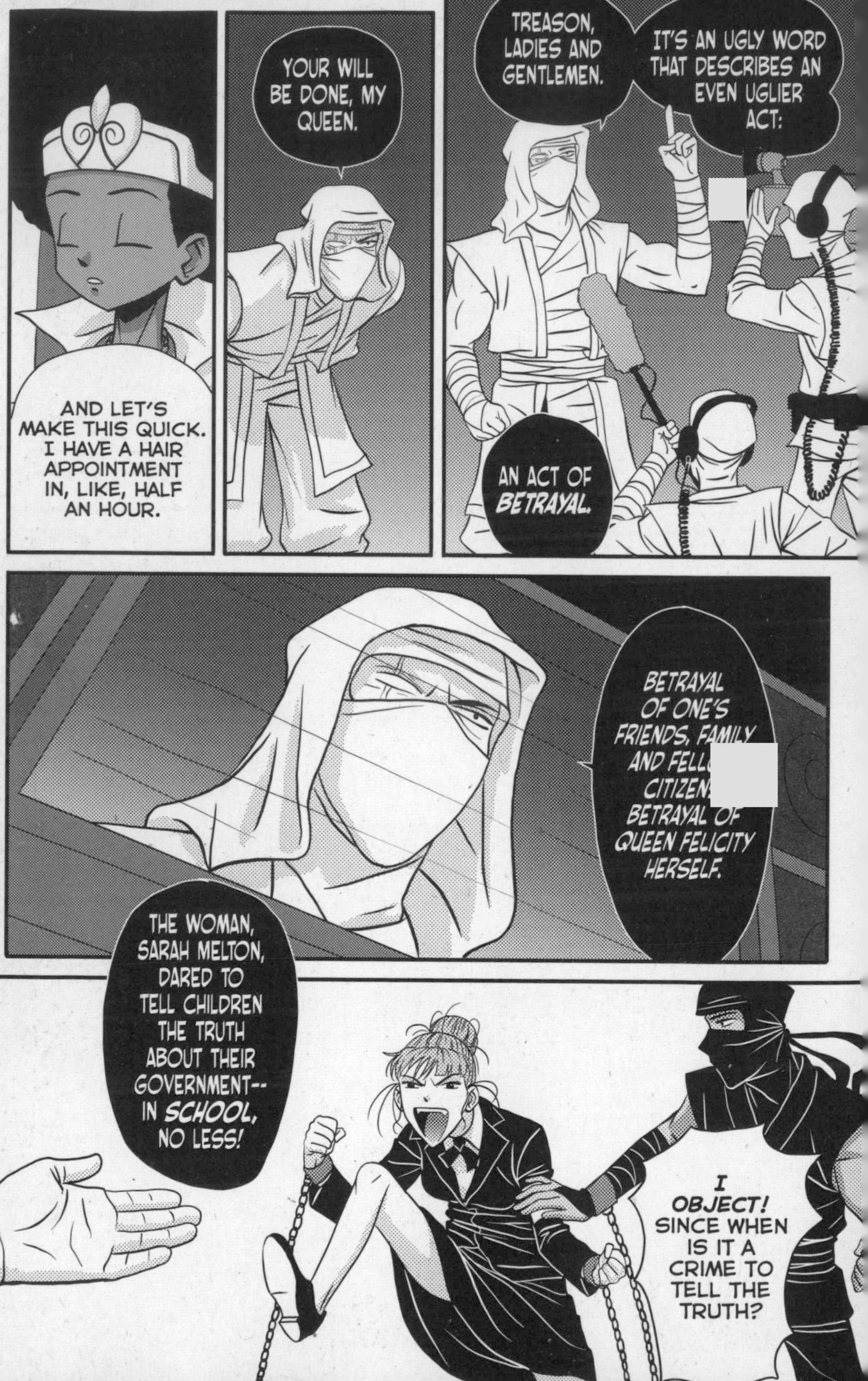
AND LET'S MAKE THIS QUICK. I HAVE A HAIR APPOINTMENT IN, LIKE, HALF AN HOUR.
YOUR WILL BE DONE, MY QUEEN.
TREASON, LADIES AND GENTLEMEN.
IT'S AN UGLY WORD THAT DESCRIBES AN EVEN UGLIER ACT:
AN ACT OF *BETRAYAL.*
BETRAYAL OF ONE'S FRIENDS, FAMILY AND FELL CITIZEN BETRAYAL OF QUEEN FELICITY HERSELF.
THE WOMAN, SARAH MELTON, DARED TO TELL CHILDREN THE TRUTH ABOUT THEIR GOVERNMENT-- IN *SCHOOL,* NO LESS!
I OBJECT! SINCE WHEN IS IT A CRIME TO TELL THE TRUTH?

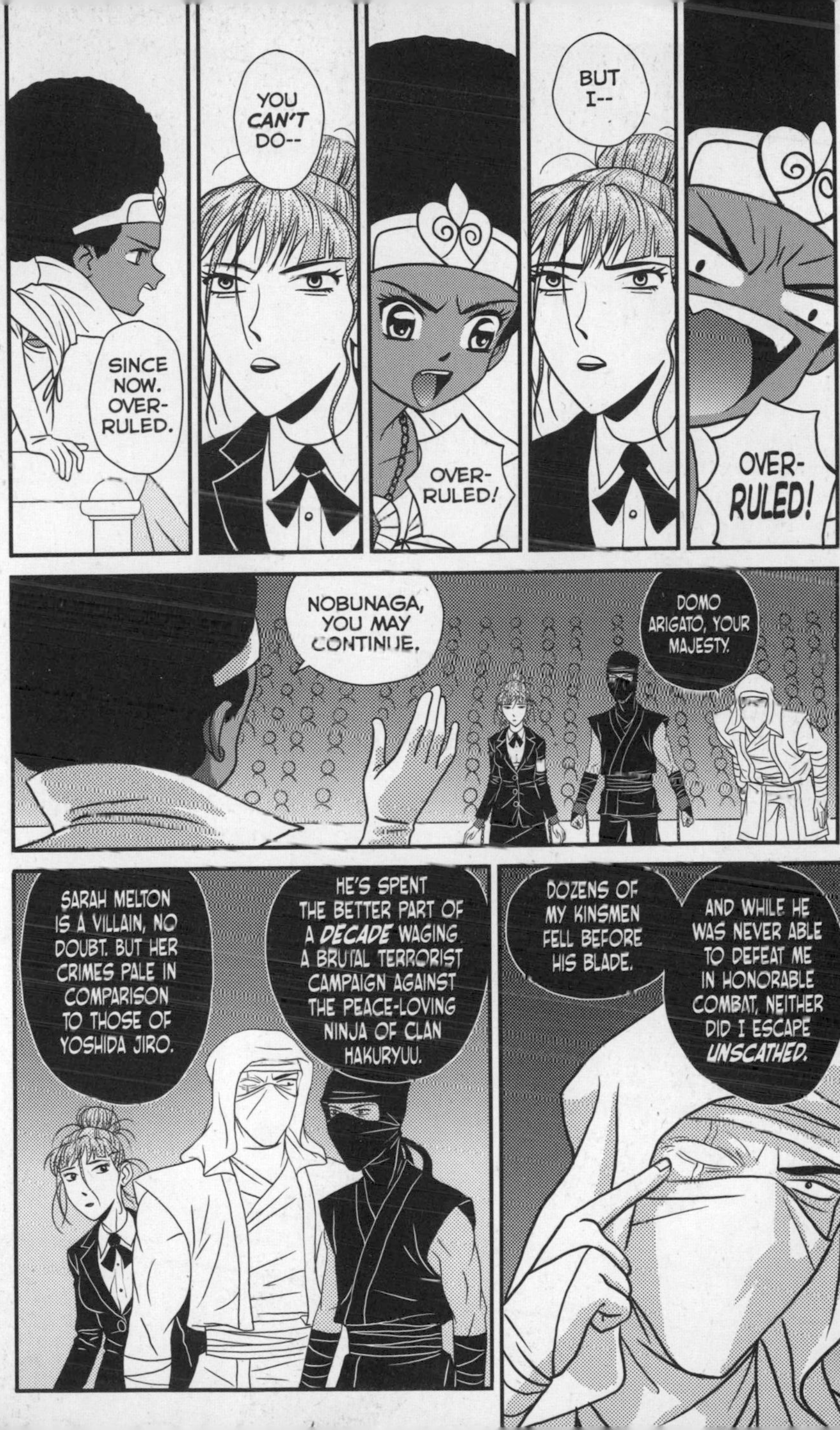
SINCE NOW. OVER-RULED.
YOU CAN'T DO--
OVER-RULED!
BUT I--
OVER-RULED!
NOBUNAGA, YOU MAY CONTINUE.
DOMO ARIGATO, YOUR MAJESTY.
SARAH MELTON IS A VILLAIN, NO DOUBT. BUT HER CRIMES PALE IN COMPARISON TO THOSE OF YOSHIDA JIRO.
HE'S SPENT THE BETTER PART OF A DECADE WAGING A BRUTAL TERRORIST CAMPAIGN AGAINST THE PEACE-LOVING NINJA OF CLAN HAKURYUU.
DOZENS OF MY KINSMEN FELL BEFORE HIS BLADE.
AND WHILE HE WAS NEVER ABLE TO DEFEAT ME IN HONORABLE COMBAT, NEITHER DID I ESCAPE UNSCATHED.

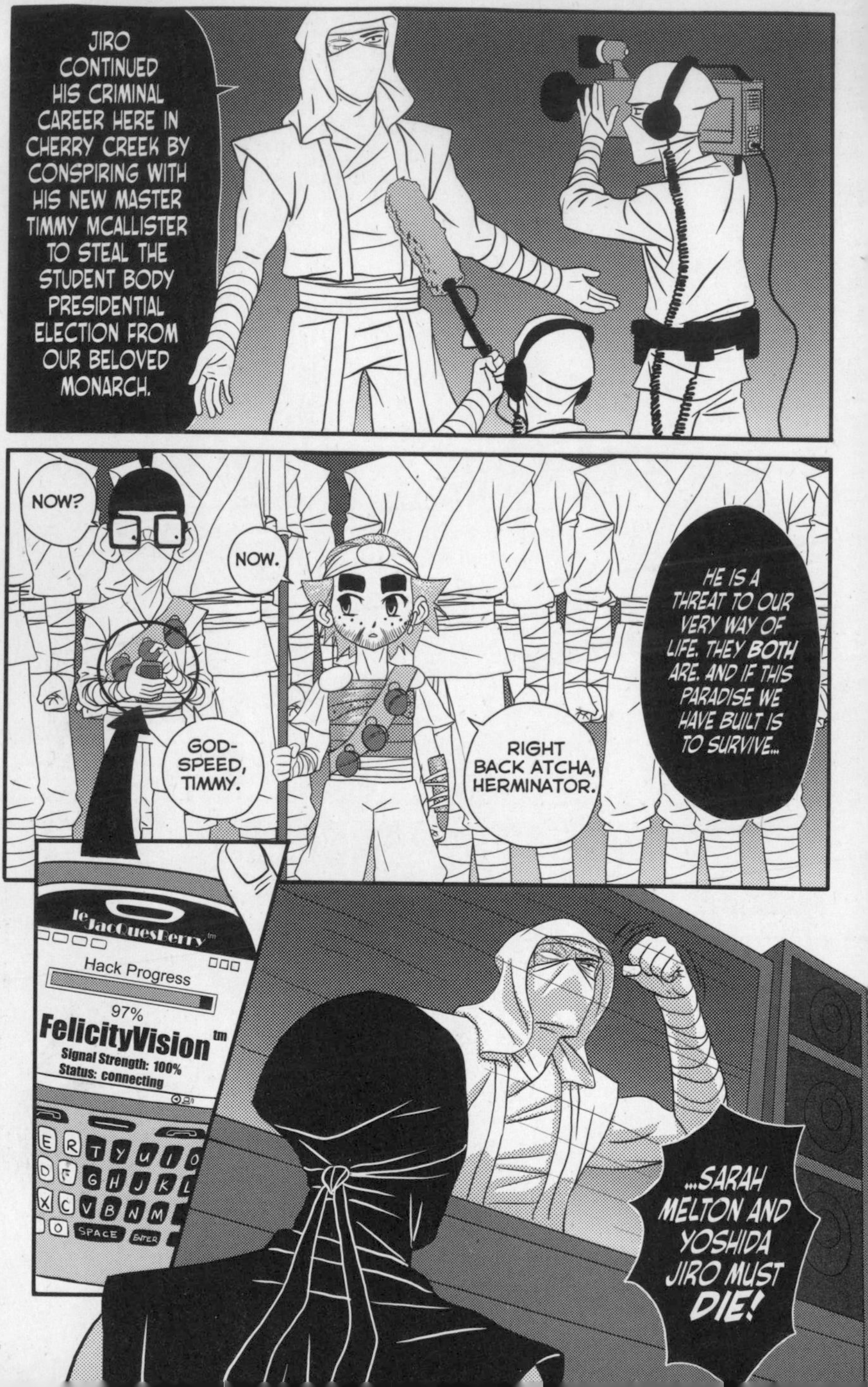
JIRO CONTINUED HIS CRIMINAL CAREER HERE IN CHERRY CREEK BY CONSPIRING WITH HIS NEW MASTER TIMMY MCALLISTER TO STEAL THE STUDENT BODY PRESIDENTIAL ELECTION FROM OUR BELOVED MONARCH.
NOW?
NOW.
GOD-SPEED, TIMMY.
RIGHT BACK ATCHA, HERMINATOR.
HE IS A THREAT TO OUR VERY WAY OF LIFE. THEY BOTH ARE. AND IF THIS PARADISE WE HAVE BUILT IS TO SURVIVE...
leJacQuesBerry tm
Hack Progress
97%
FelicityVision tm
Signal Strength: 100%
Status: connecting
...SARAH MELTON AND YOSHIDA JIRO MUST DIE!

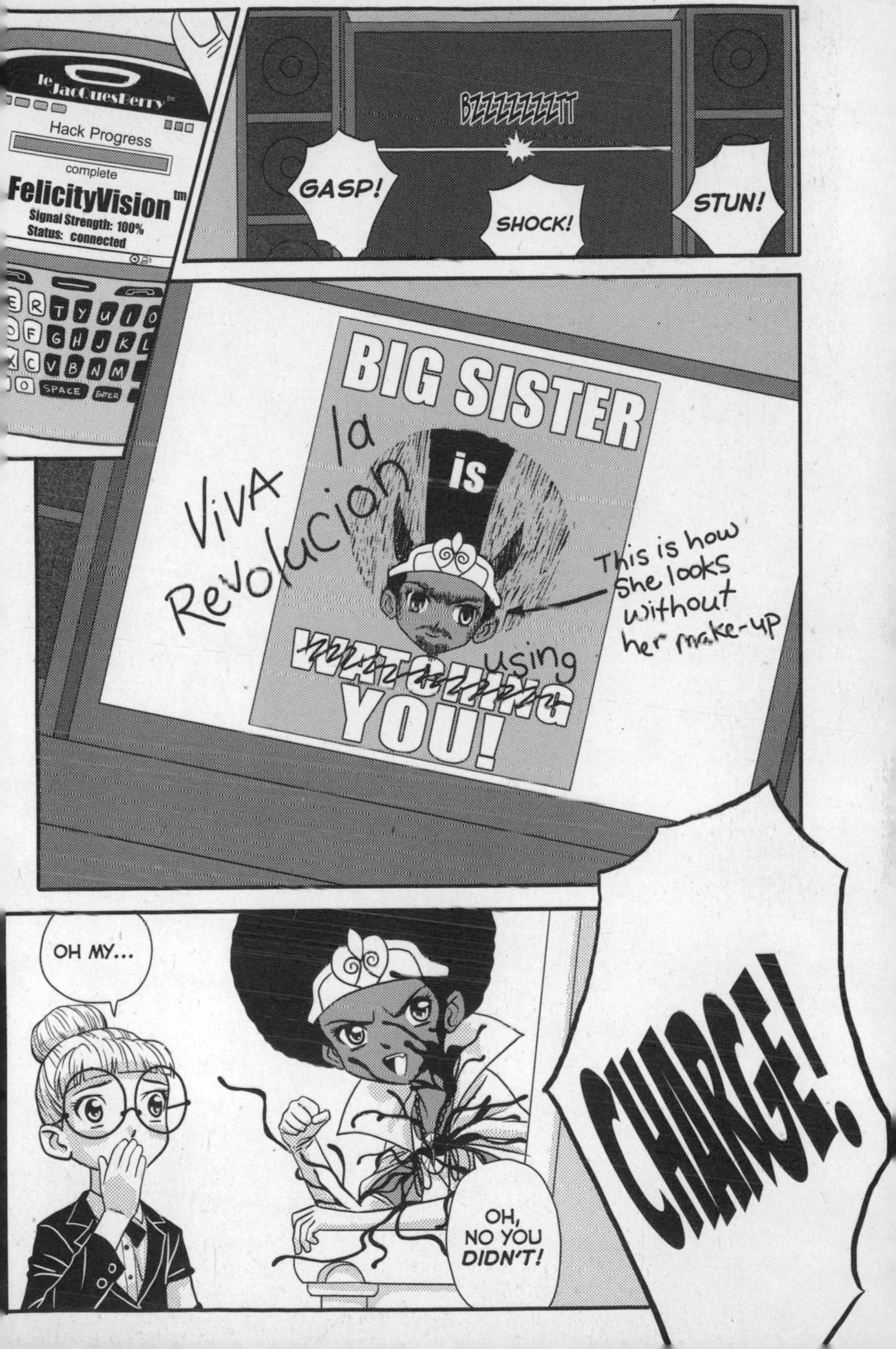

le JacQuesBerry tm
Hack Progress
complete
FelicityVision tm
Signal Strength: 100%
Status: connected
BZZZZZZZZT
GASP!
SHOCK!
STUN!
BIG SISTER is WATCHING using YOU!
Viva la Revolucion
This is how she looks without her make-up
OH MY...
CHARGE!
OH, NO YOU DIDN'T!

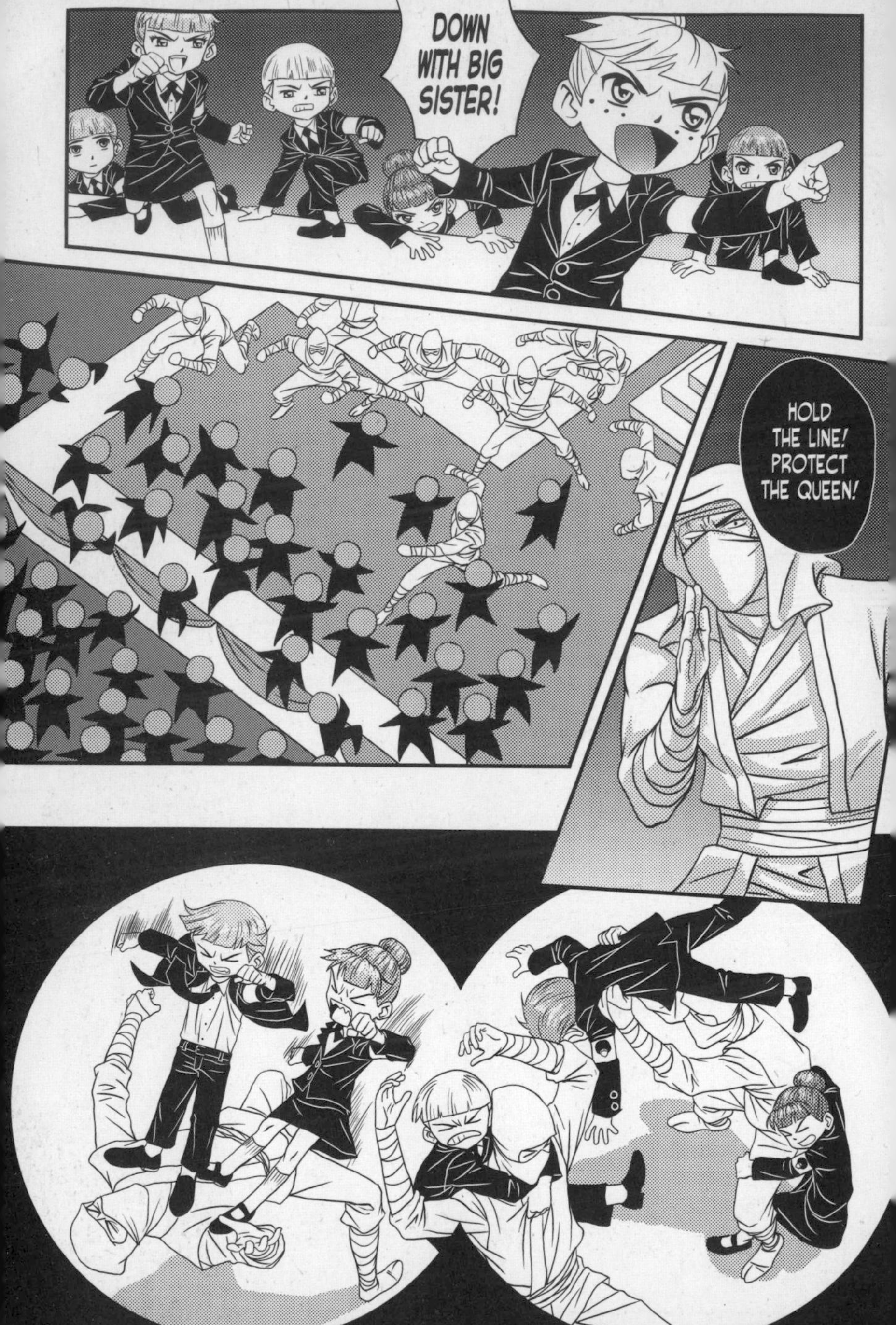
DOWN WITH BIG SISTER!
HOLD THE LINE! PROTECT THE QUEEN!

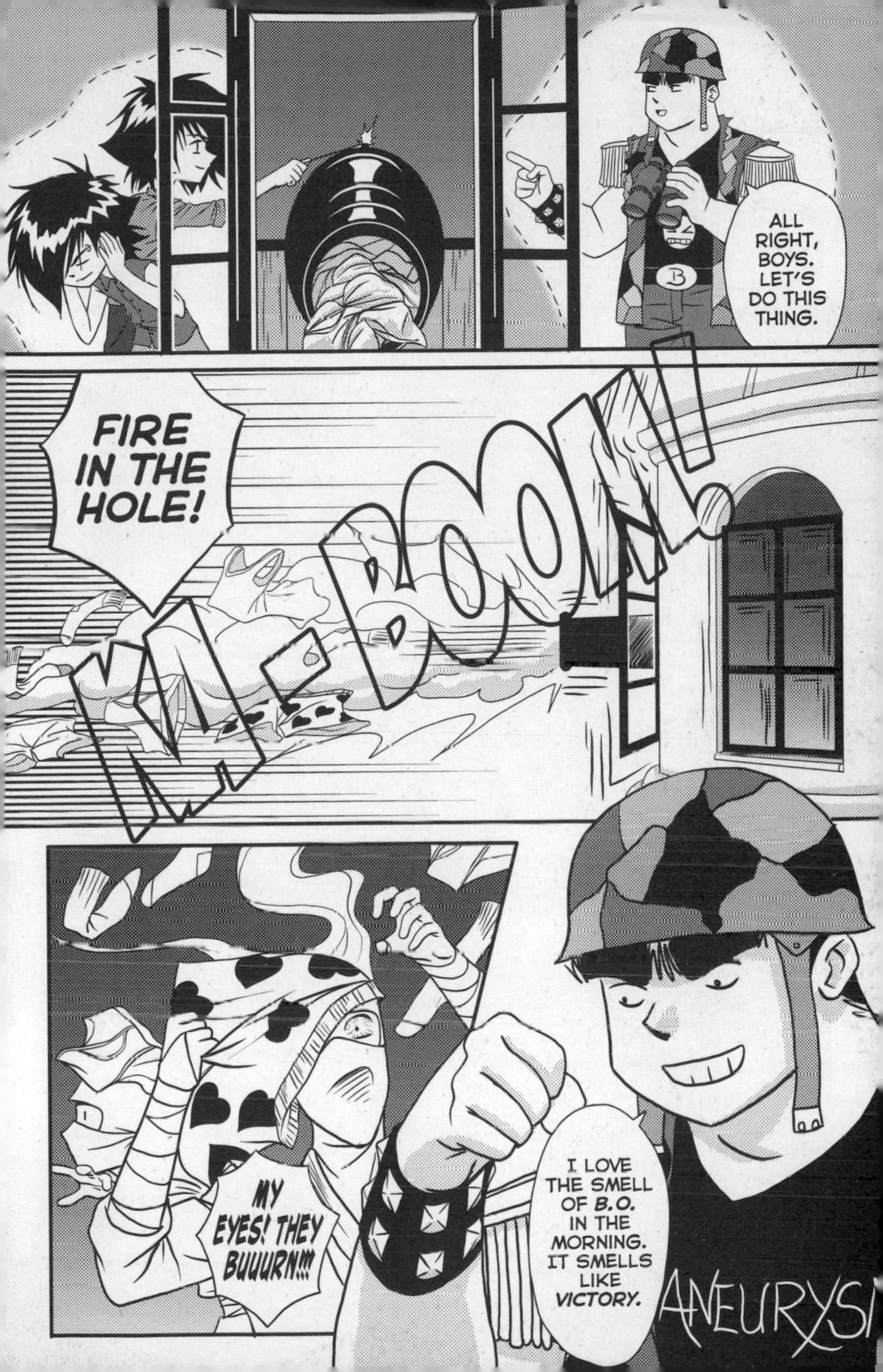
ALL RIGHT, BOYS. LET'S DO THIS THING.
FIRE IN THE HOLE!
KA-BOOM!
I LOVE THE SMELL OF B.O. IN THE MORNING. IT SMELLS LIKE VICTORY.
ANEURYS
MY EYES! THEY BUUURN!!!

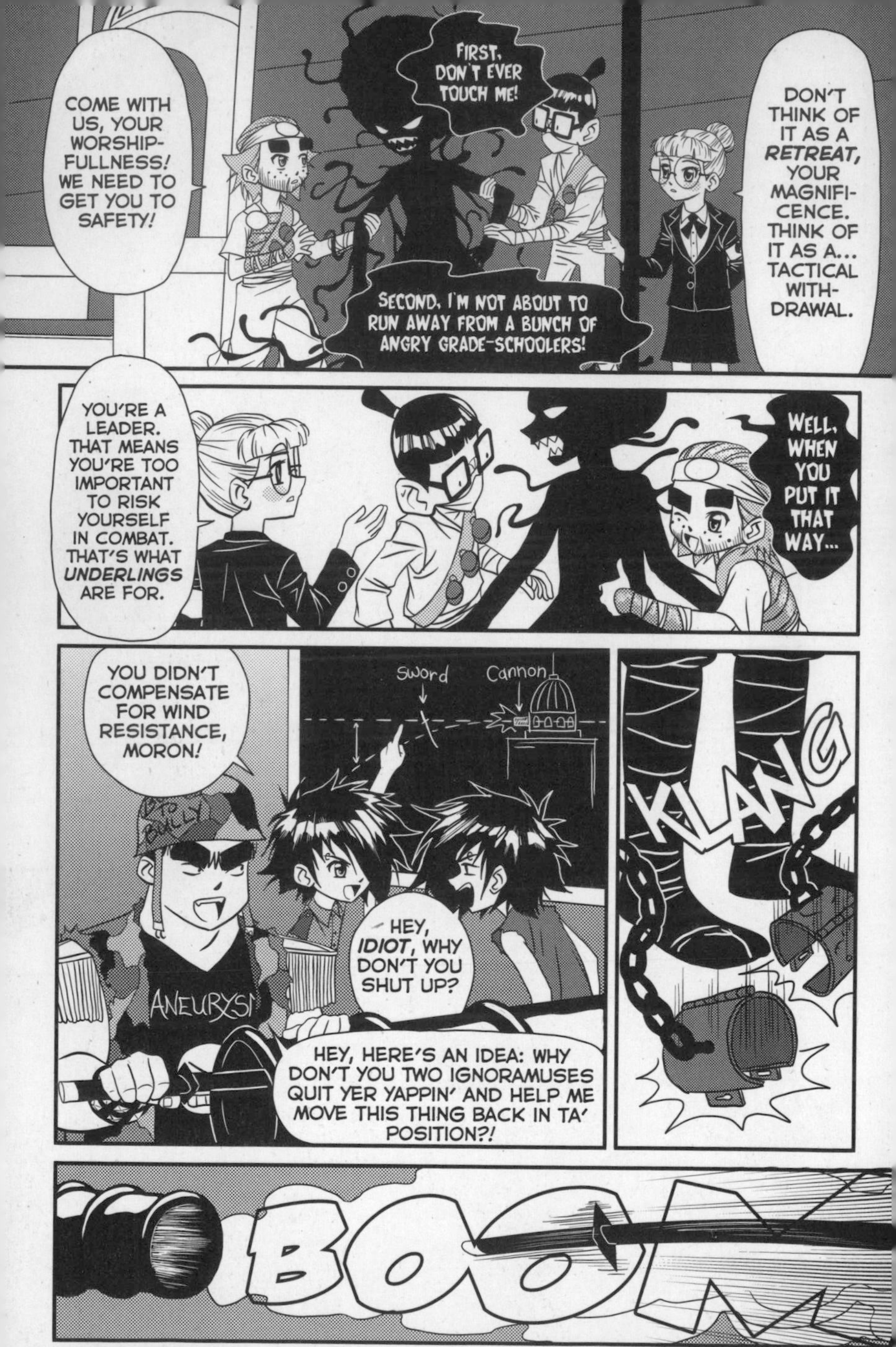
COME WITH US, YOUR WORSHIP-FULLNESS! WE NEED TO GET YOU TO SAFETY!
FIRST, DON'T EVER TOUCH ME!
SECOND, I'M NOT ABOUT TO RUN AWAY FROM A BUNCH OF ANGRY GRADE-SCHOOLERS!
DON'T THINK OF IT AS A *RETREAT*, YOUR MAGNIFI-CENCE. THINK OF IT AS A... TACTICAL WITH-DRAWAL.
YOU'RE A LEADER. THAT MEANS YOU'RE TOO IMPORTANT TO RISK YOURSELF IN COMBAT. THAT'S WHAT *UNDERLINGS* ARE FOR.
WELL, WHEN YOU PUT IT THAT WAY...
YOU DIDN'T COMPENSATE FOR WIND RESISTANCE, MORON!
Sword
Cannon
B.TO BULLY
HEY, *IDIOT*, WHY DON'T YOU SHUT UP?
ANEURYSM
HEY, HERE'S AN IDEA: WHY DON'T YOU TWO IGNORAMUSES QUIT YER YAPPIN' AND HELP ME MOVE THIS THING BACK IN TA' POSITION?!
KLANG
BOOM

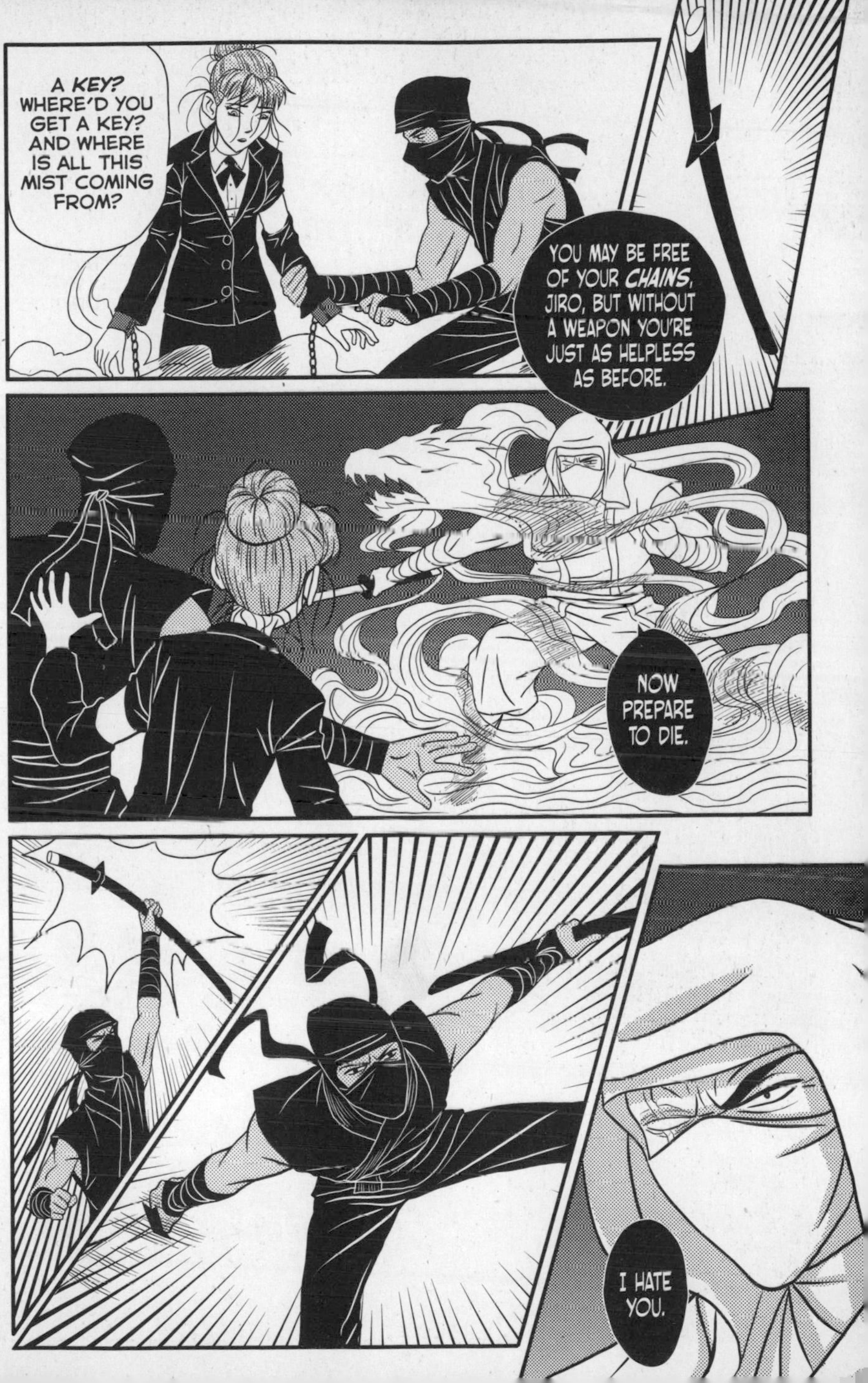
A KEY? WHERE'D YOU GET A KEY? AND WHERE IS ALL THIS MIST COMING FROM?
YOU MAY BE FREE OF YOUR CHAINS, JIRO, BUT WITHOUT A WEAPON YOU'RE JUST AS HELPLESS AS BEFORE.
NOW PREPARE TO DIE.
I HATE YOU.

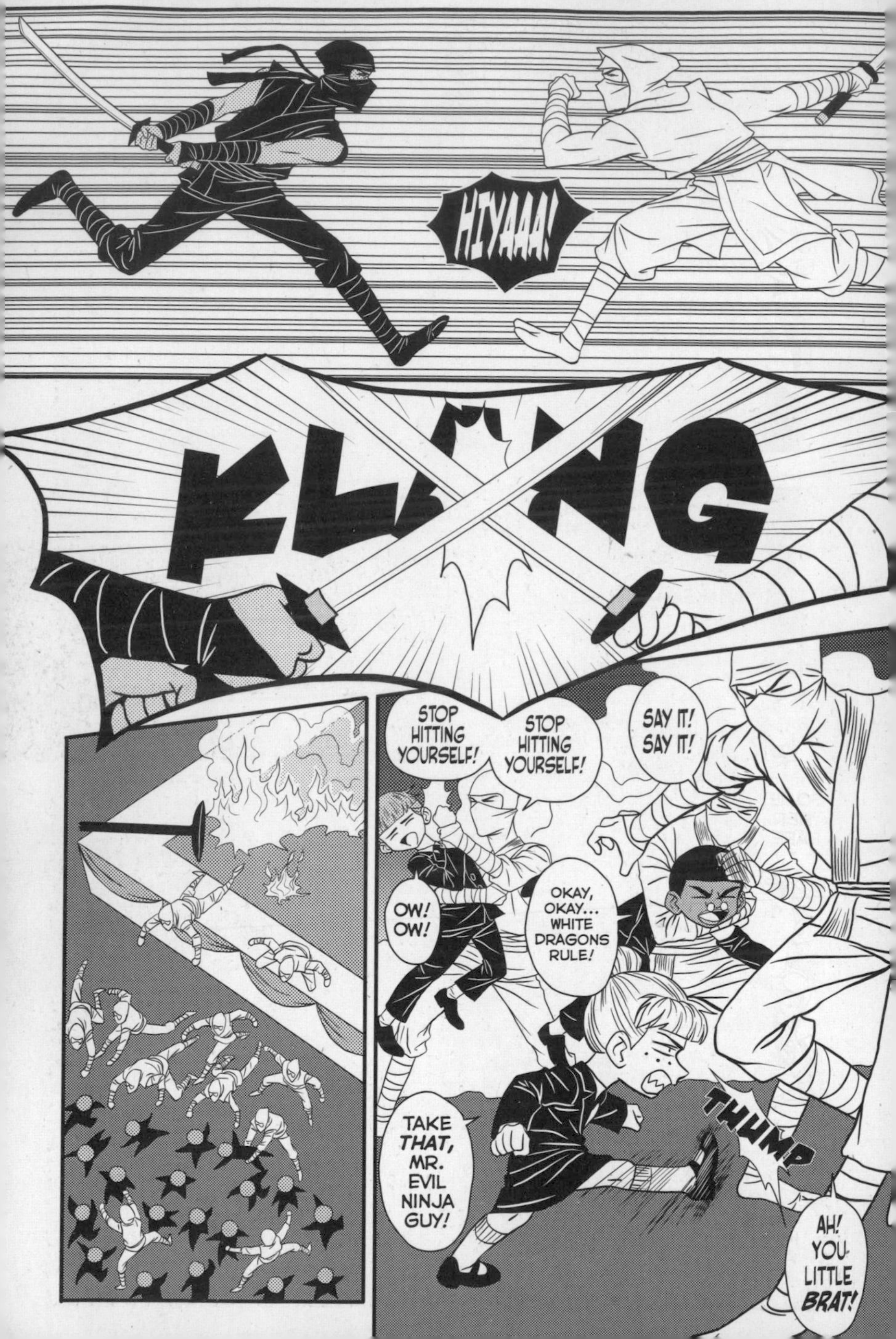
HIYAAA!
KLANG
STOP HITTING YOURSELF!
STOP HITTING YOURSELF!
SAY IT! SAY IT!
OW! OW!
OKAY, OKAY... WHITE DRAGONS RULE!
TAKE *THAT*, MR. EVIL NINJA GUY!
THUMP
AH! YOU LITTLE *BRAT*!

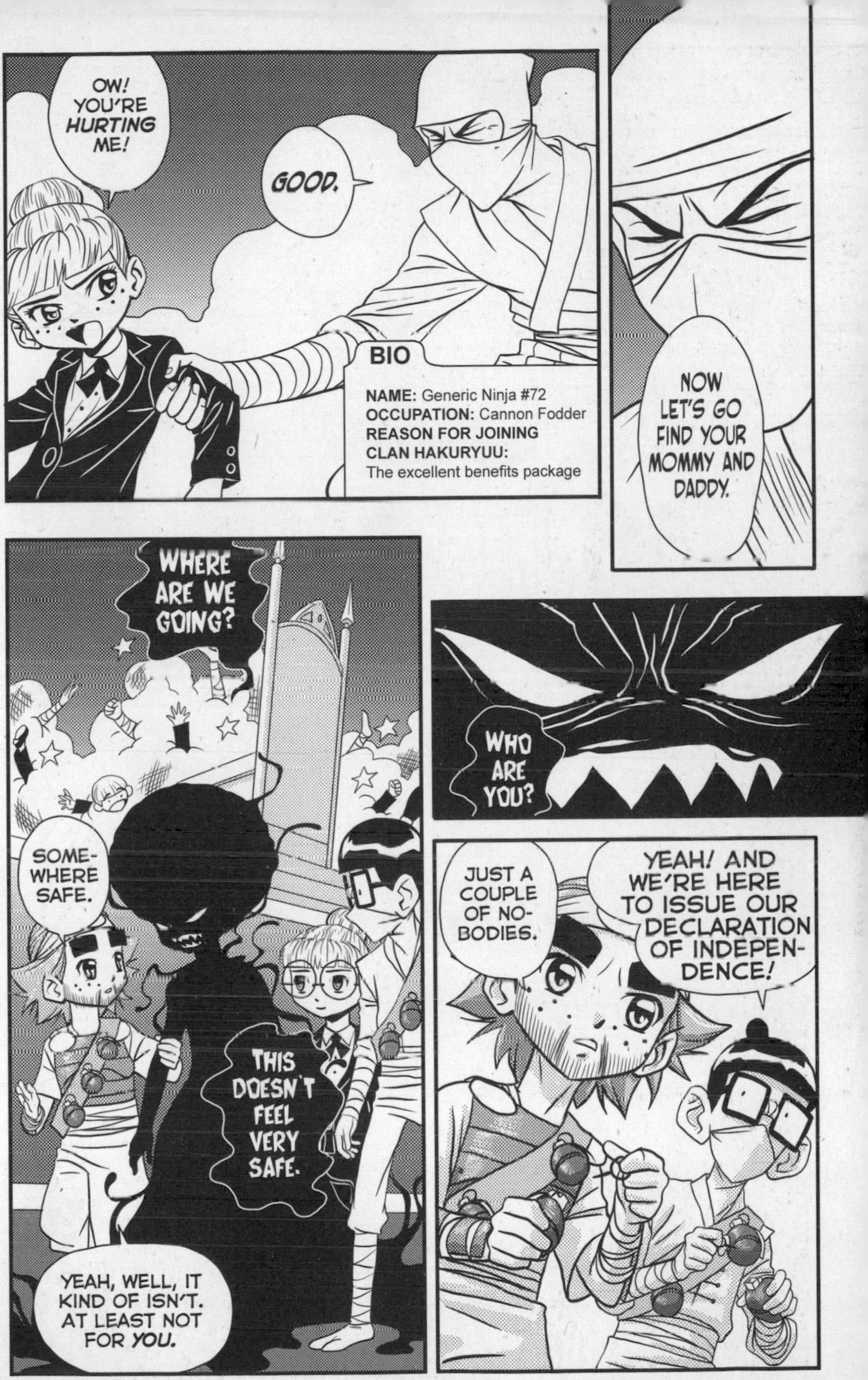
OW! YOU'RE HURTING ME!
GOOD.
BIO
NAME: Generic Ninja #72
OCCUPATION: Cannon Fodder
REASON FOR JOINING CLAN HAKURYUU:
The excellent benefits package
NOW LET'S GO FIND YOUR MOMMY AND DADDY.
WHERE ARE WE GOING?
SOME-WHERE SAFE.
THIS DOESN'T FEEL VERY SAFE.
YEAH, WELL, IT KIND OF ISN'T. AT LEAST NOT FOR YOU.
WHO ARE YOU?
JUST A COUPLE OF NO-BODIES.
YEAH! AND WE'RE HERE TO ISSUE OUR DECLARATION OF INDEPEN-DENCE!

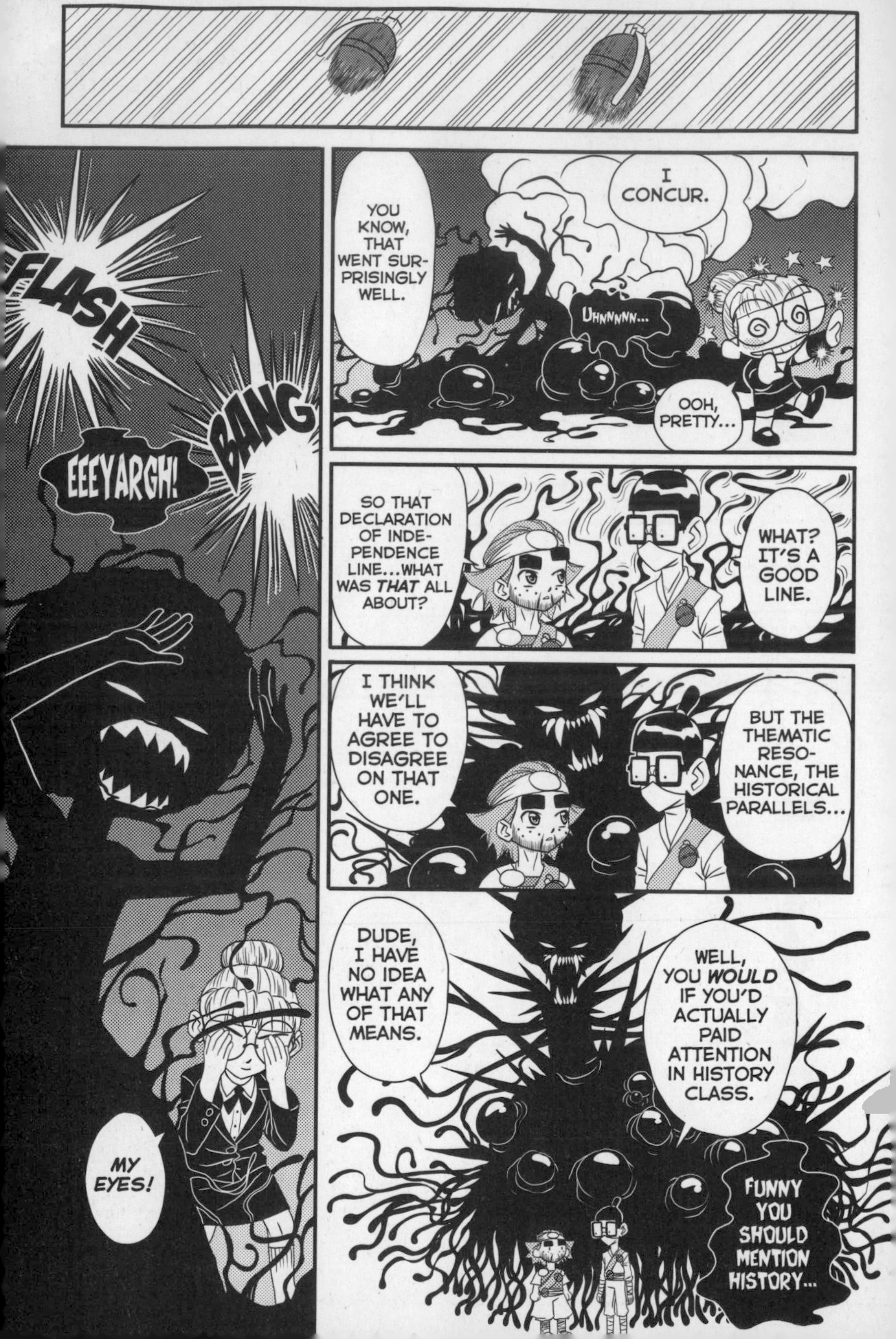
FLASH
BANG
EEEYARGH!
MY EYES!
YOU KNOW, THAT WENT SURPRISINGLY WELL.
I CONCUR.
UHNNNNN...
OOH, PRETTY...
SO THAT DECLARATION OF INDEPENDENCE LINE...WHAT WAS *THAT* ALL ABOUT?
WHAT? IT'S A GOOD LINE.
I THINK WE'LL HAVE TO AGREE TO DISAGREE ON THAT ONE.
BUT THE THEMATIC RESONANCE, THE HISTORICAL PARALLELS...
DUDE, I HAVE NO IDEA WHAT ANY OF THAT MEANS.
WELL, YOU ***WOULD*** IF YOU'D ACTUALLY PAID ATTENTION IN HISTORY CLASS.
FUNNY YOU SHOULD MENTION HISTORY...

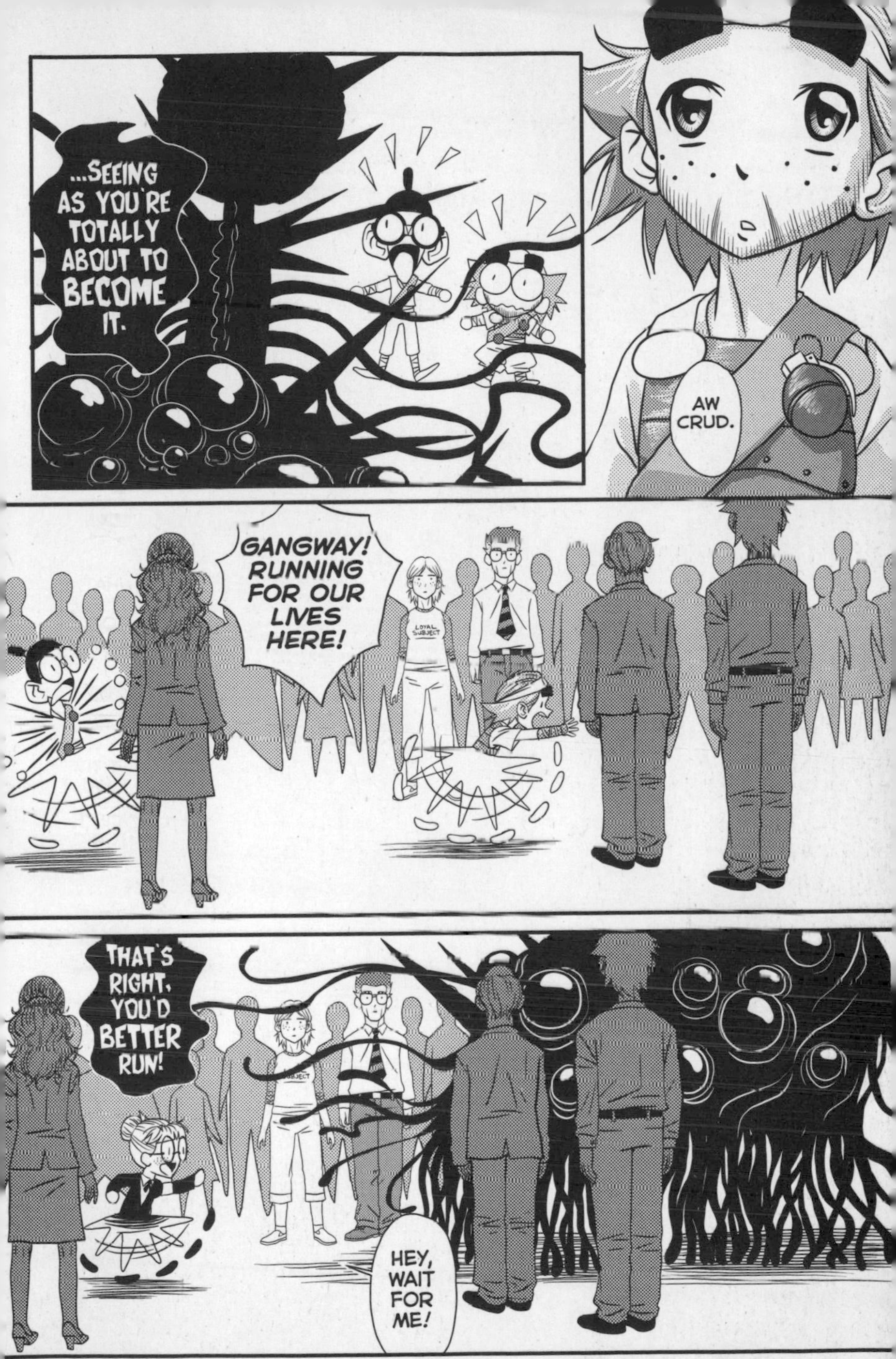
...SEEING AS YOU'RE TOTALLY ABOUT TO BECOME IT.
AW CRUD.
GANGWAY! RUNNING FOR OUR LIVES HERE!
LOYAL SUBJECT
THAT'S RIGHT, YOU'D BETTER RUN!
HEY, WAIT FOR ME!

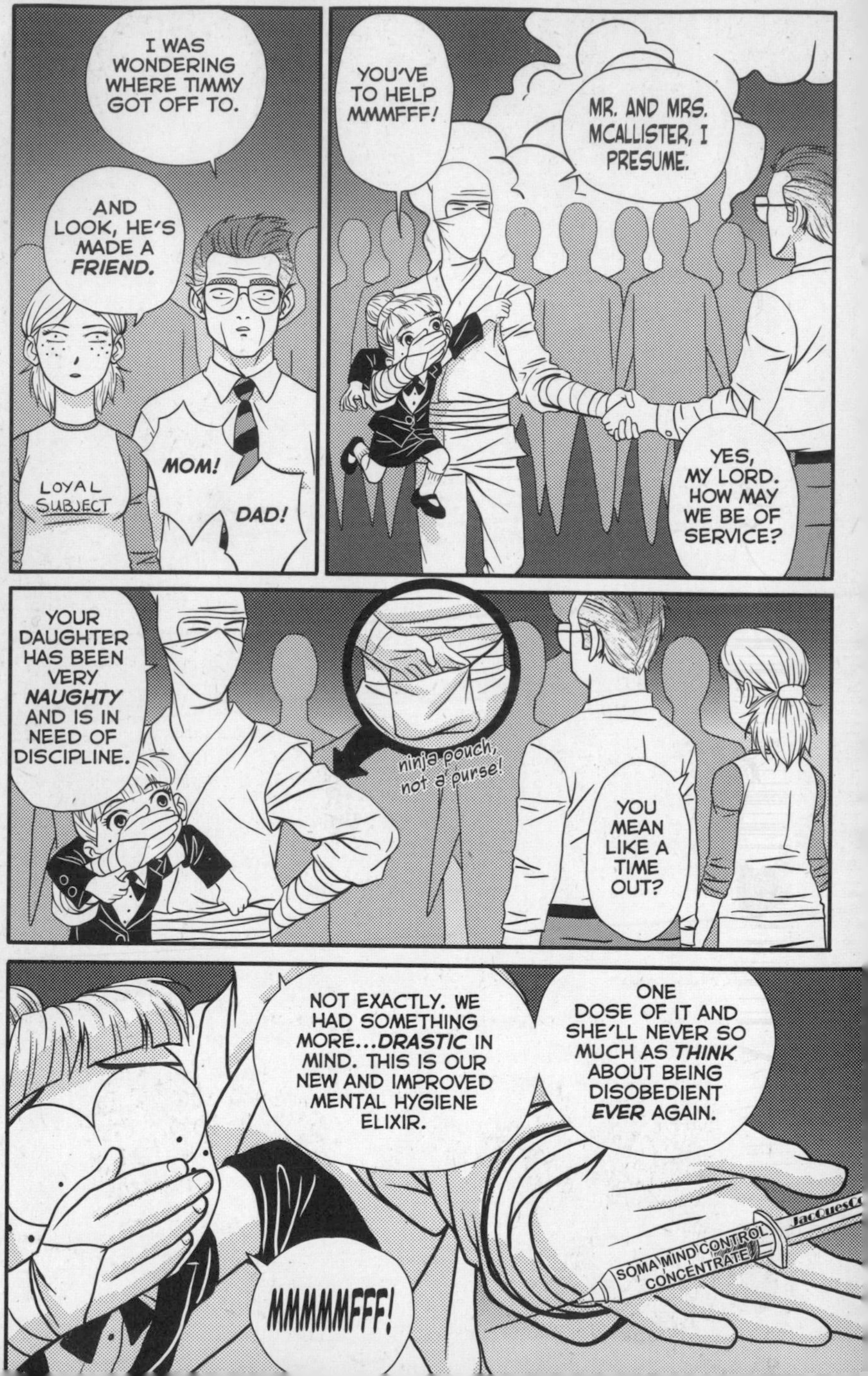
I WAS WONDERING WHERE TIMMY GOT OFF TO.
AND LOOK, HE'S MADE A *FRIEND.*
LOYAL SUBJECT
MOM!
DAD!
YOU'VE TO HELP MMMFFF!
MR. AND MRS. MCALLISTER, I PRESUME.
YES, MY LORD. HOW MAY WE BE OF SERVICE?
YOUR DAUGHTER HAS BEEN VERY *NAUGHTY* AND IS IN NEED OF DISCIPLINE.
ninja pouch, not a purse!
YOU MEAN LIKE A TIME OUT?
NOT EXACTLY. WE HAD SOMETHING MORE...*DRASTIC* IN MIND. THIS IS OUR NEW AND IMPROVED MENTAL HYGIENE ELIXIR.
ONE DOSE OF IT AND SHE'LL NEVER SO MUCH AS *THINK* ABOUT BEING DISOBEDIENT *EVER* AGAIN.
SOMA MIND CONTROL CONCENTRATE
MMMMMFFF!

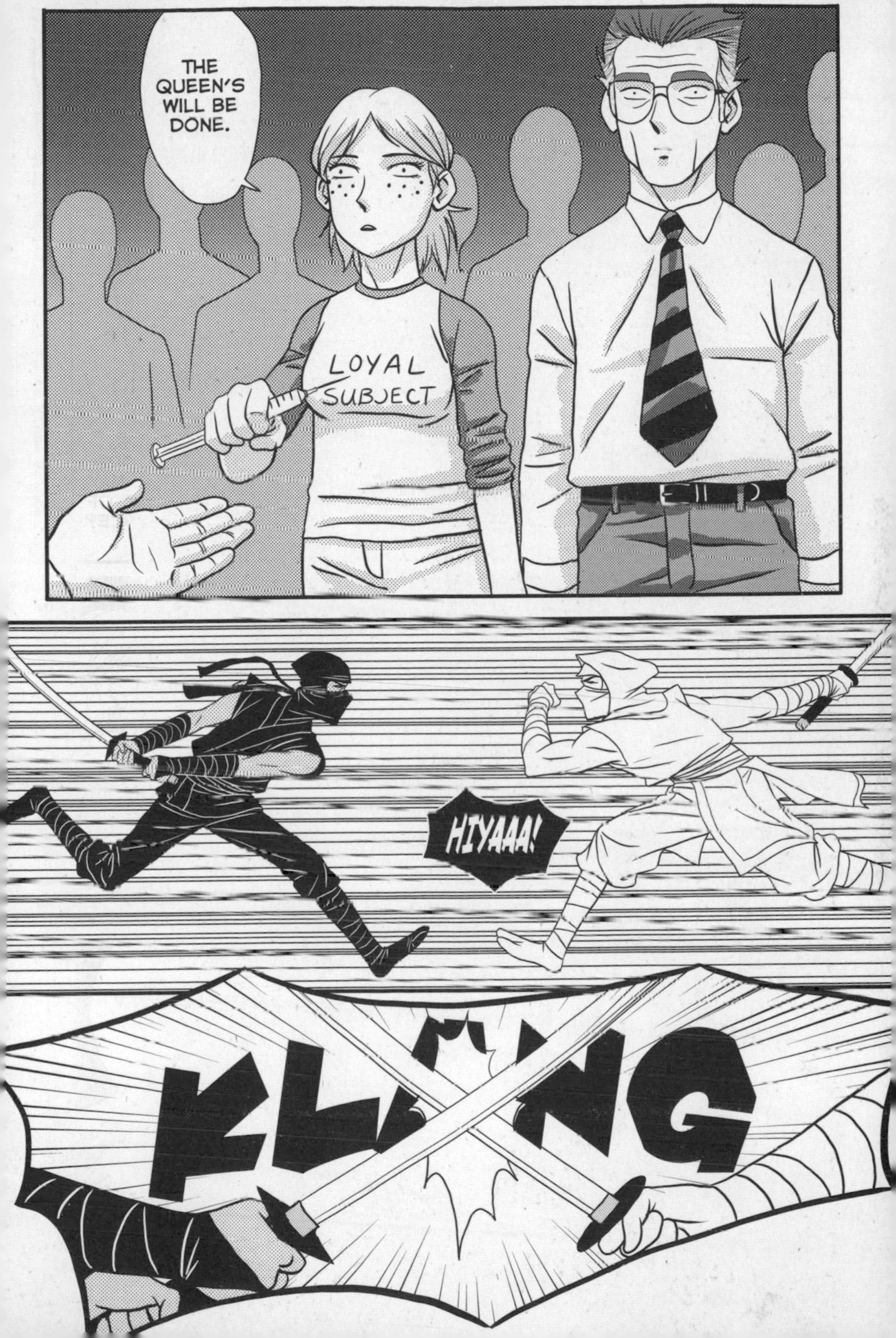
THE QUEEN'S WILL BE DONE.
LOYAL SUBJECT
HIYAAA!
KLANG

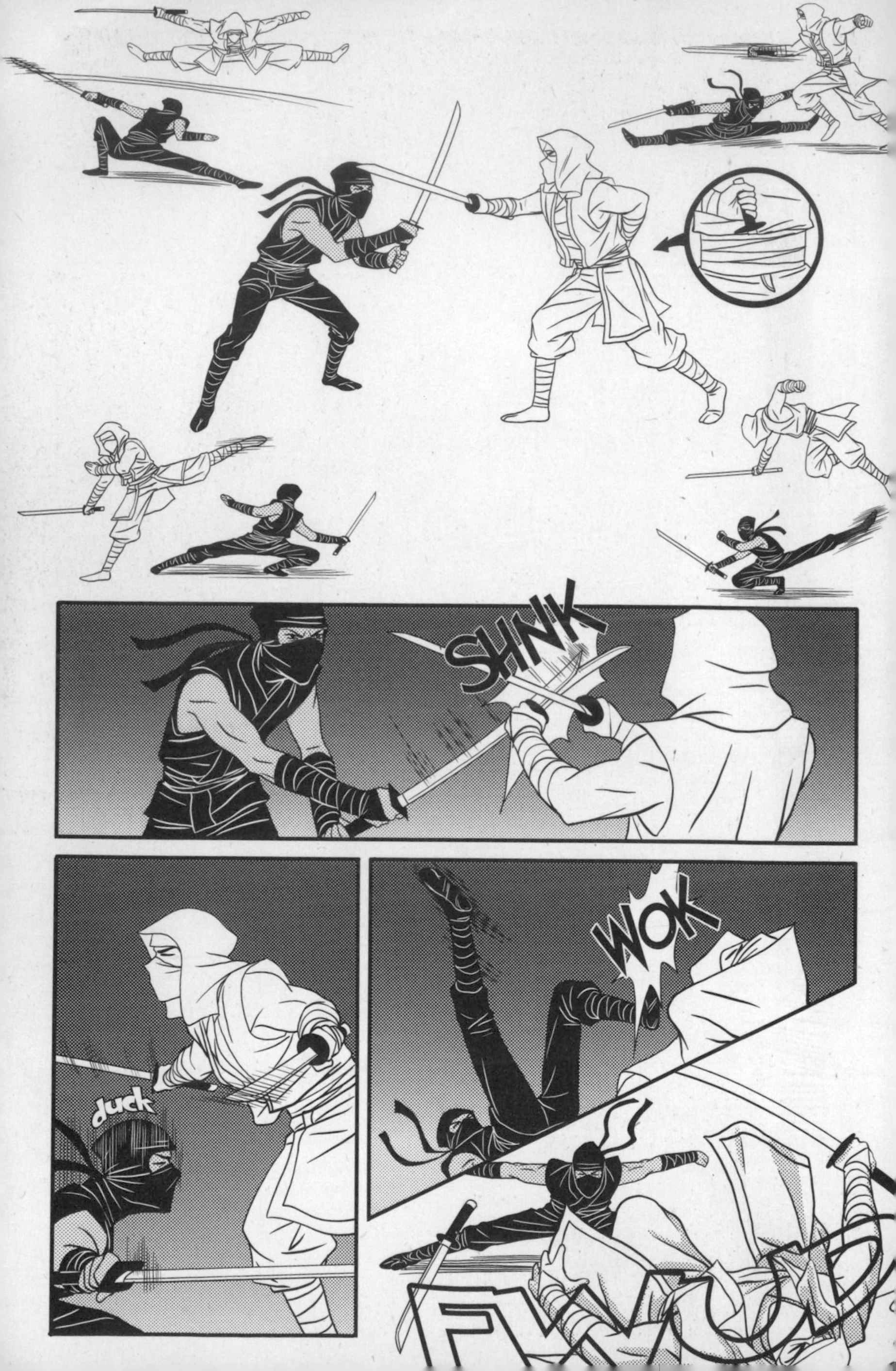
SHNK
WOK
duck

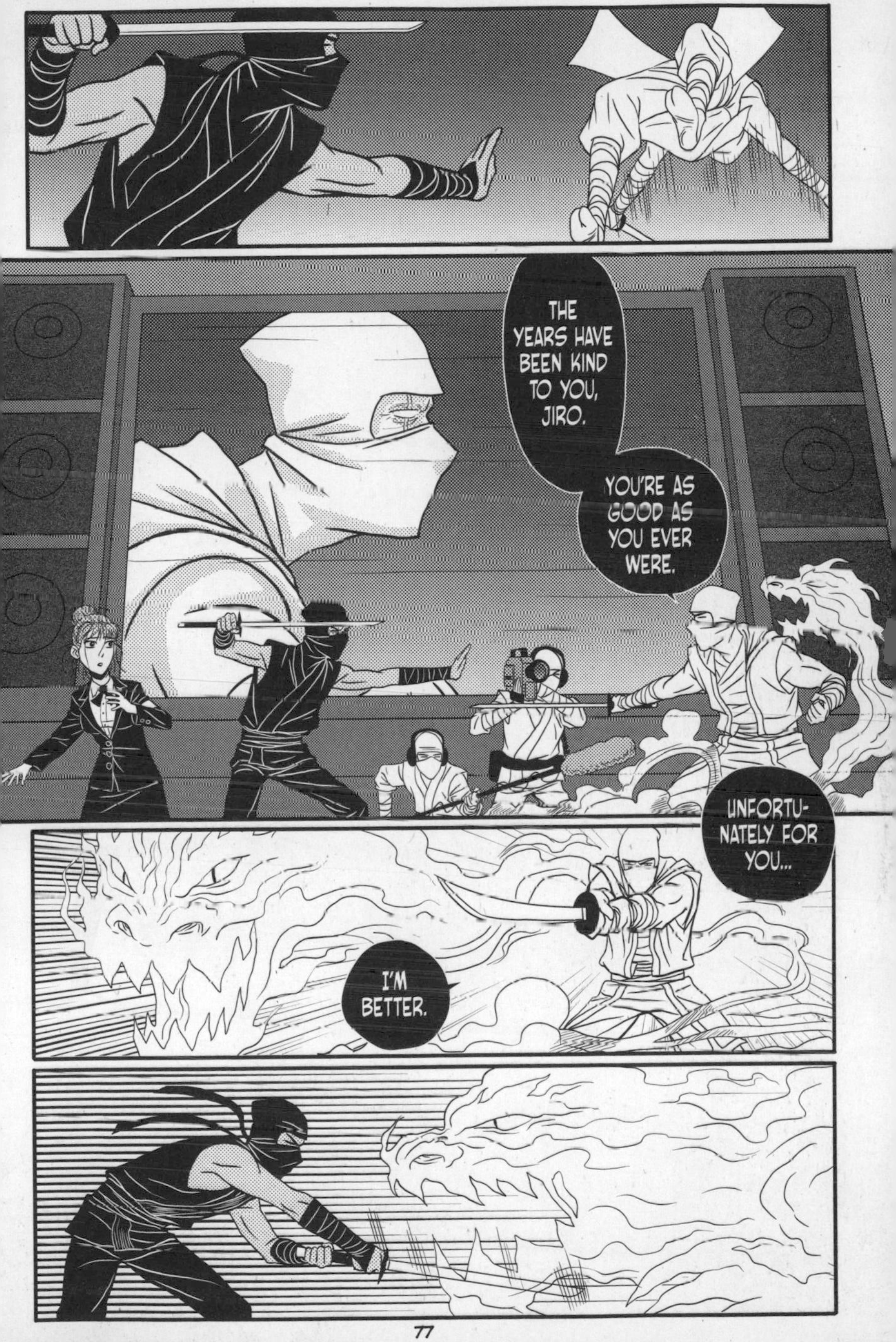
THE YEARS HAVE BEEN KIND TO YOU, JIRO.
YOU'RE AS GOOD AS YOU EVER WERE.
UNFORTUNATELY FOR YOU...
I'M BETTER.

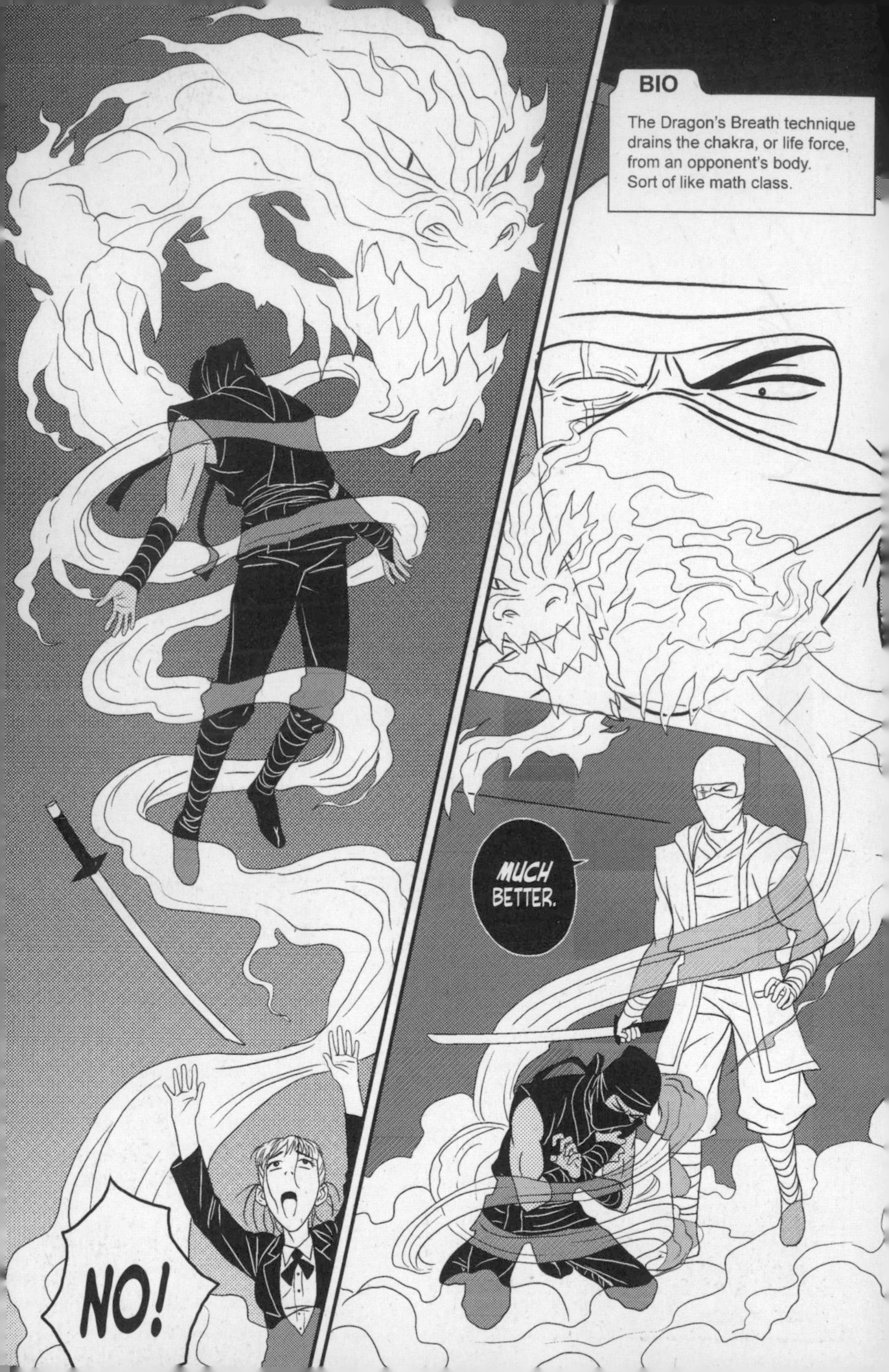
NO!
BIO
The Dragon's Breath technique drains the chakra, or life force, from an opponent's body. Sort of like math class.
MUCH BETTER.

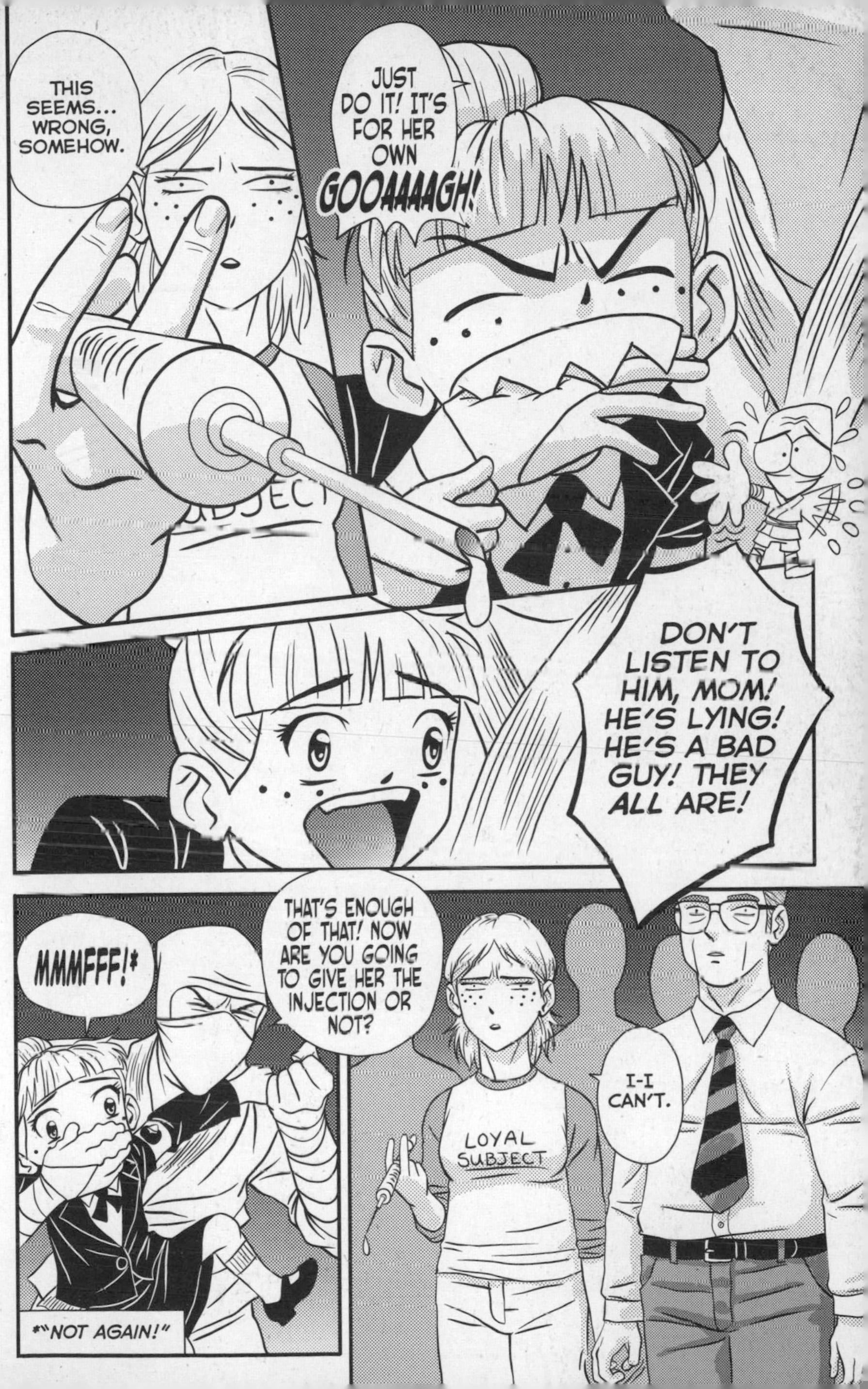
THIS SEEMS... WRONG, SOMEHOW.
JUST DO IT! IT'S FOR HER OWN GOOAAAAGH!
SUBJECT
DON'T LISTEN TO HIM, MOM! HE'S LYING! HE'S A BAD GUY! THEY ALL ARE!
MMMFFF!*
THAT'S ENOUGH OF THAT! NOW ARE YOU GOING TO GIVE HER THE INJECTION OR NOT?
*"NOT AGAIN!"
LOYAL SUBJECT
I-I CAN'T.

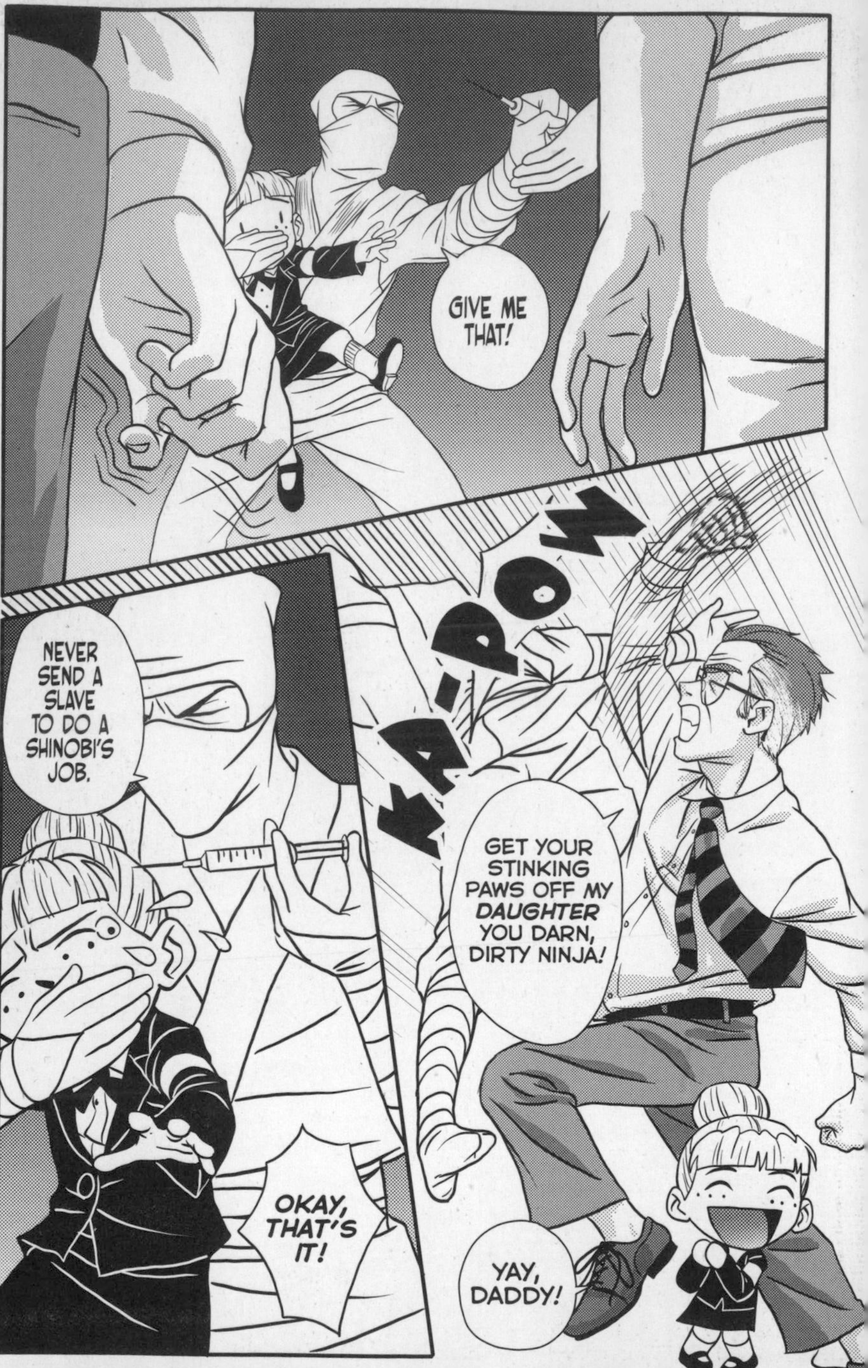
GIVE ME THAT!
NEVER SEND A SLAVE TO DO A SHINOBI'S JOB.
OKAY, THAT'S IT!
KA-POW
GET YOUR STINKING PAWS OFF MY *DAUGHTER* YOU DARN, DIRTY NINJA!
YAY, DADDY!

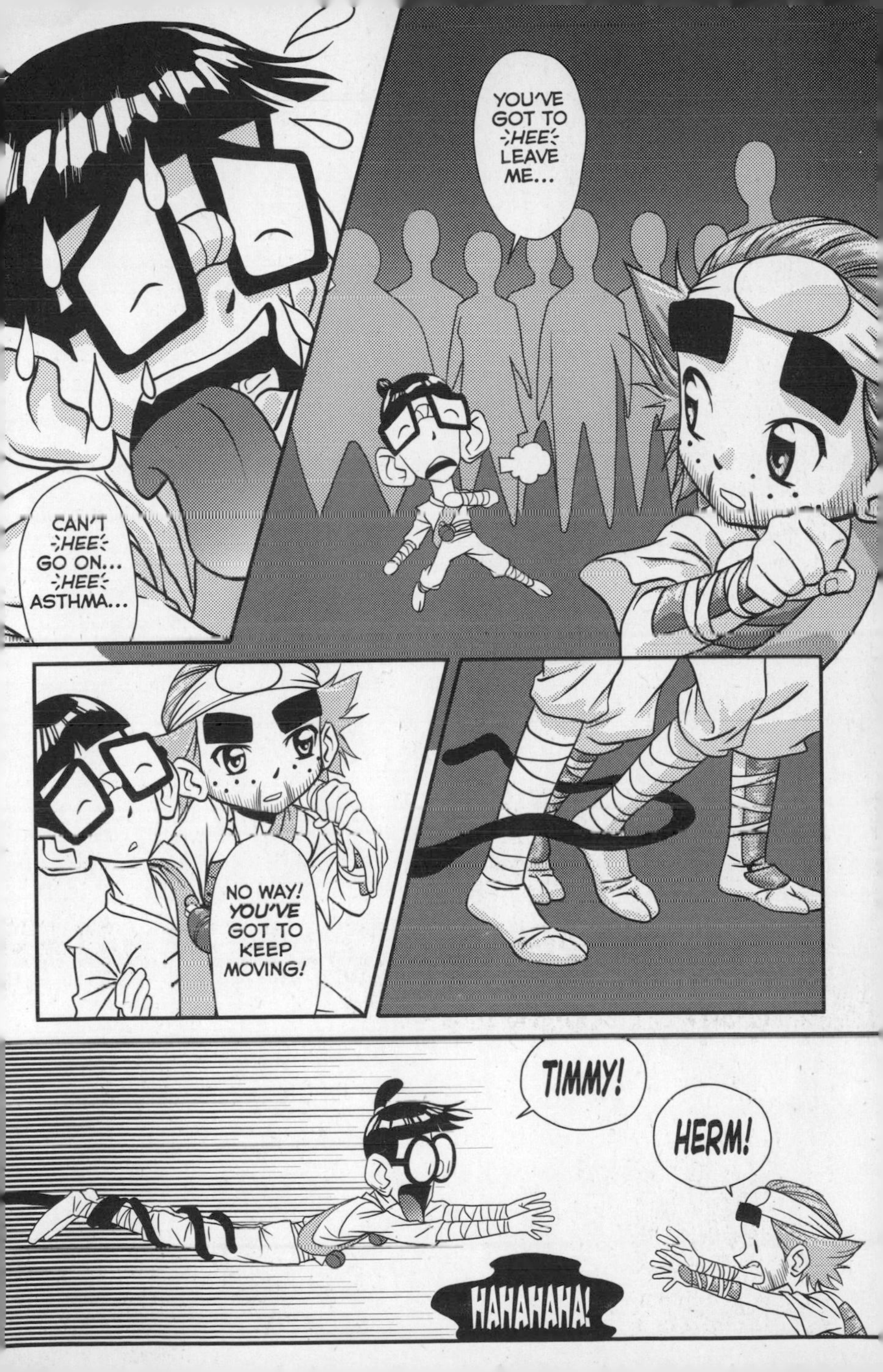
CAN'T -HEE- GO ON... -HEE- ASTHMA...
YOU'VE GOT TO -HEE- LEAVE ME...
NO WAY! YOU'VE GOT TO KEEP MOVING!
TIMMY!
HERM!
HAHAHAHA!

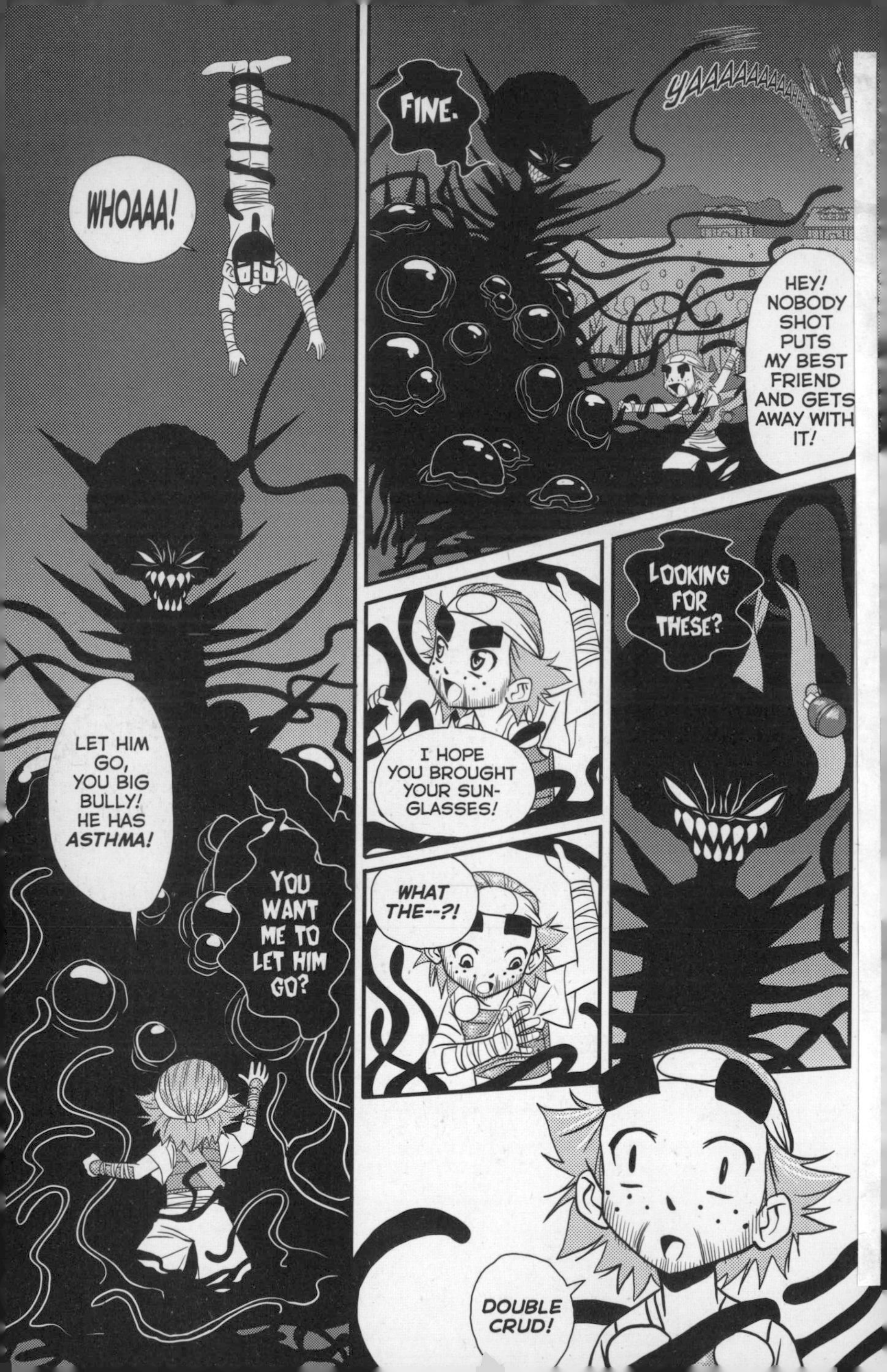
WHOAAA!
LET HIM GO, YOU BIG BULLY! HE HAS ASTHMA!
YOU WANT ME TO LET HIM GO?
FINE.
YAAAAAAAAAAHHH
HEY! NOBODY SHOT PUTS MY BEST FRIEND AND GETS AWAY WITH IT!
I HOPE YOU BROUGHT YOUR SUN-GLASSES!
WHAT THE--?!
LOOKING FOR THESE?
DOUBLE CRUD!

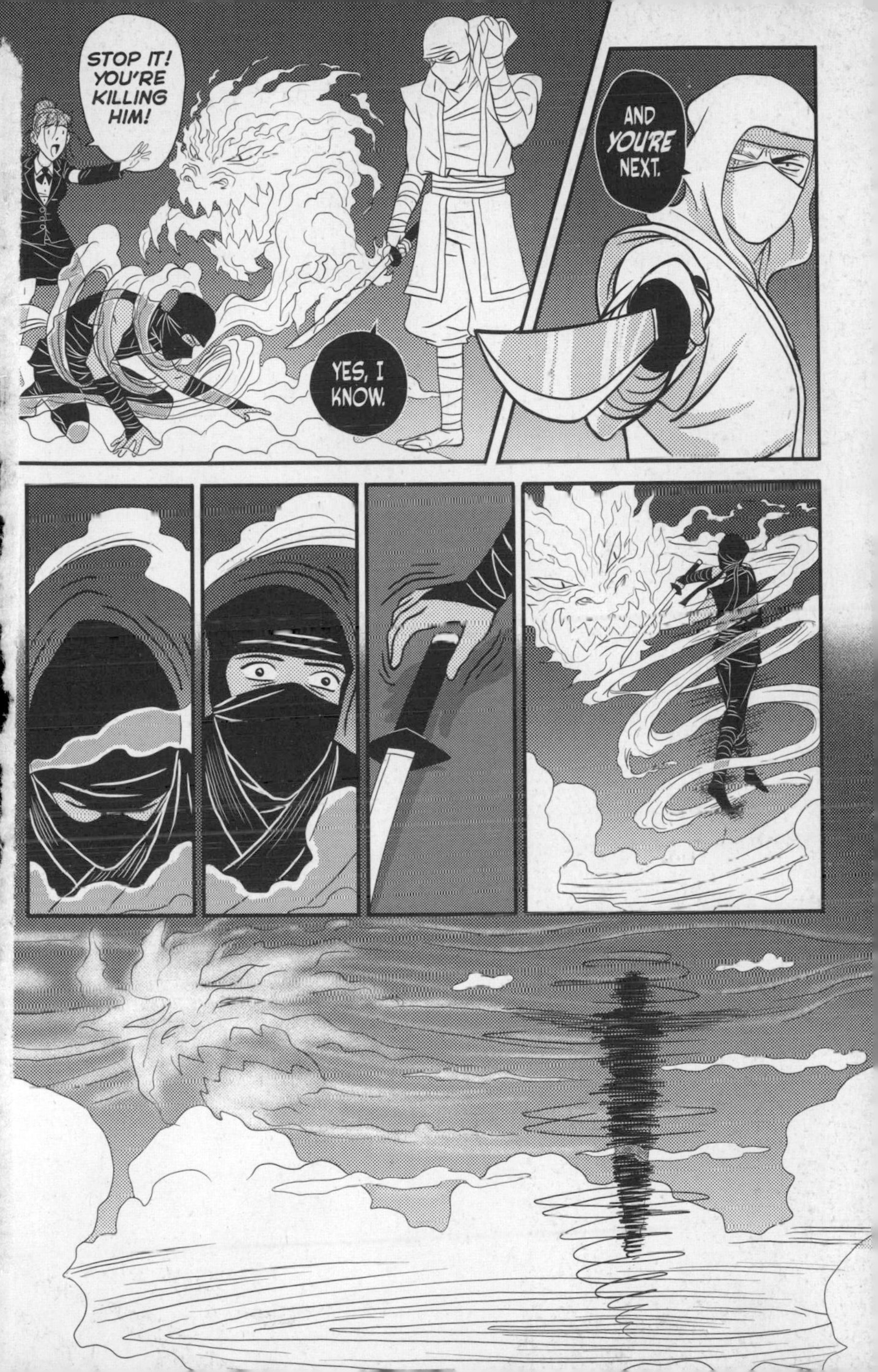
STOP IT! YOU'RE KILLING HIM!
YES, I KNOW.
AND YOU'RE NEXT.

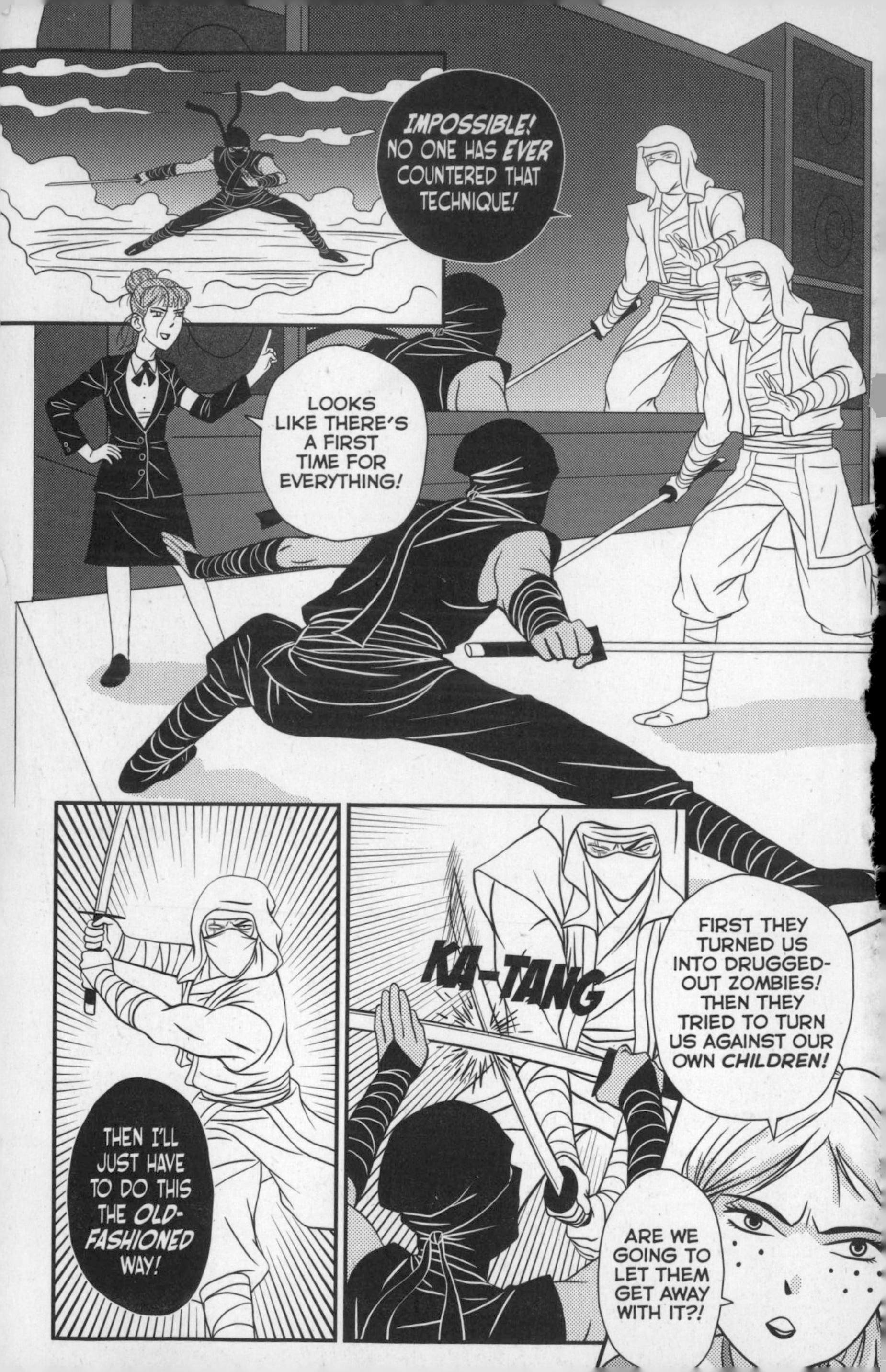
IMPOSSIBLE! NO ONE HAS EVER COUNTERED THAT TECHNIQUE!
LOOKS LIKE THERE'S A FIRST TIME FOR EVERYTHING!
THEN I'LL JUST HAVE TO DO THIS THE OLD-FASHIONED WAY!
KA-TANG
FIRST THEY TURNED US INTO DRUGGED-OUT ZOMBIES! THEN THEY TRIED TO TURN US AGAINST OUR OWN CHILDREN!
ARE WE GOING TO LET THEM GET AWAY WITH IT?!

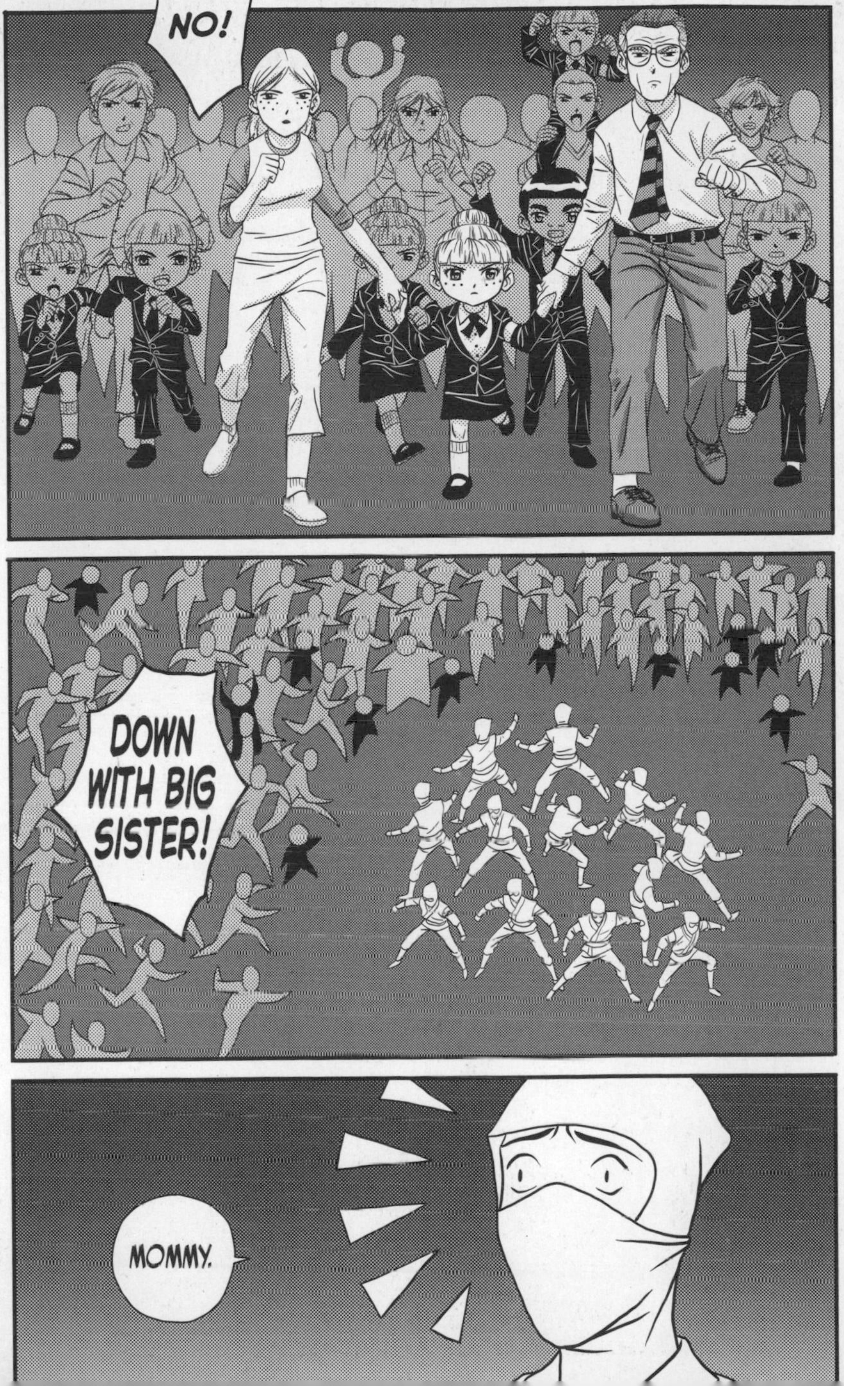
NO!
DOWN WITH BIG SISTER!
MOMMY.

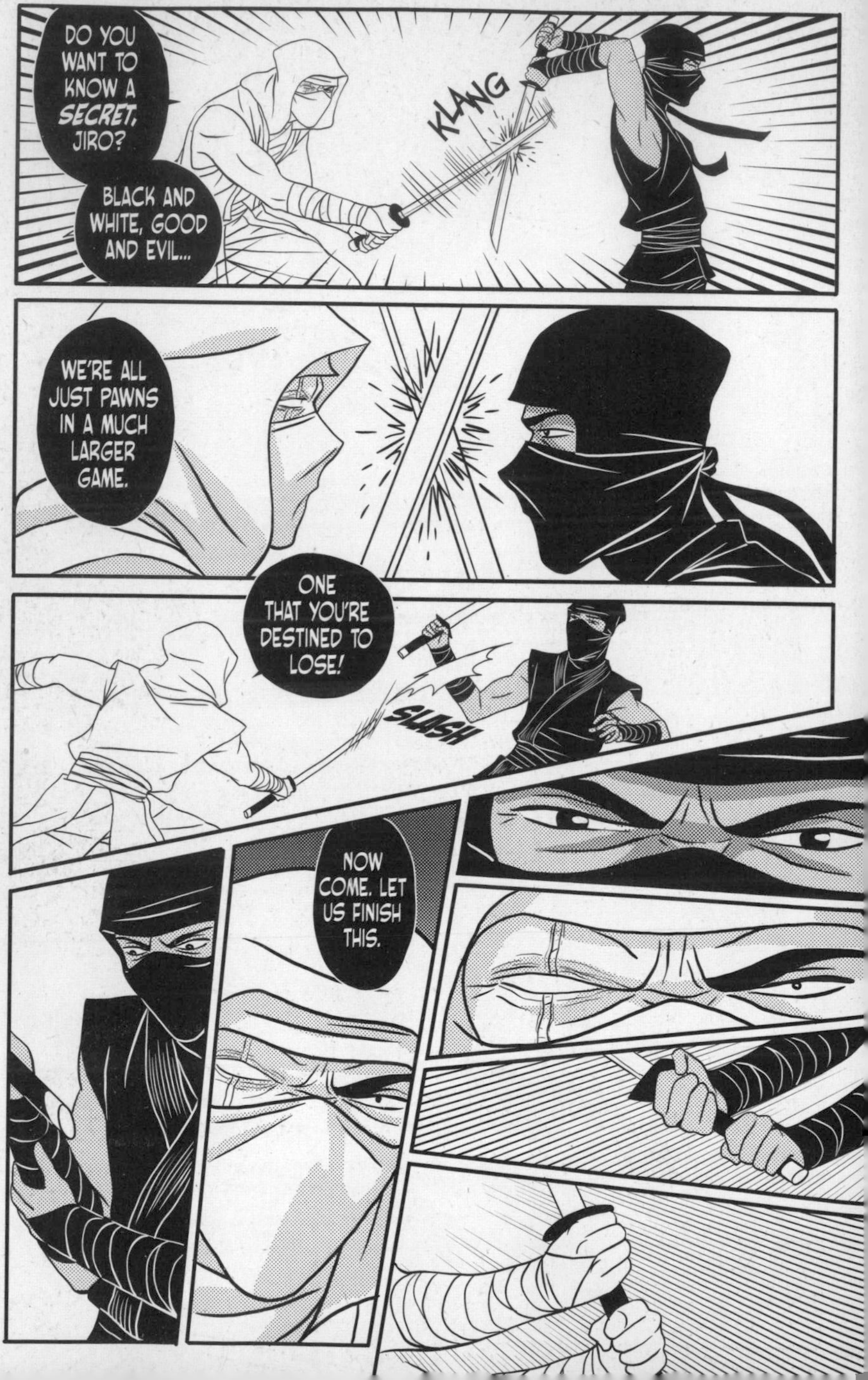
DO YOU WANT TO KNOW A *SECRET,* JIRO?
BLACK AND WHITE, GOOD AND EVIL...
KLANG
WE'RE ALL JUST PAWNS IN A MUCH LARGER GAME.
ONE THAT YOU'RE DESTINED TO LOSE!
SLASH
NOW COME. LET US FINISH THIS.

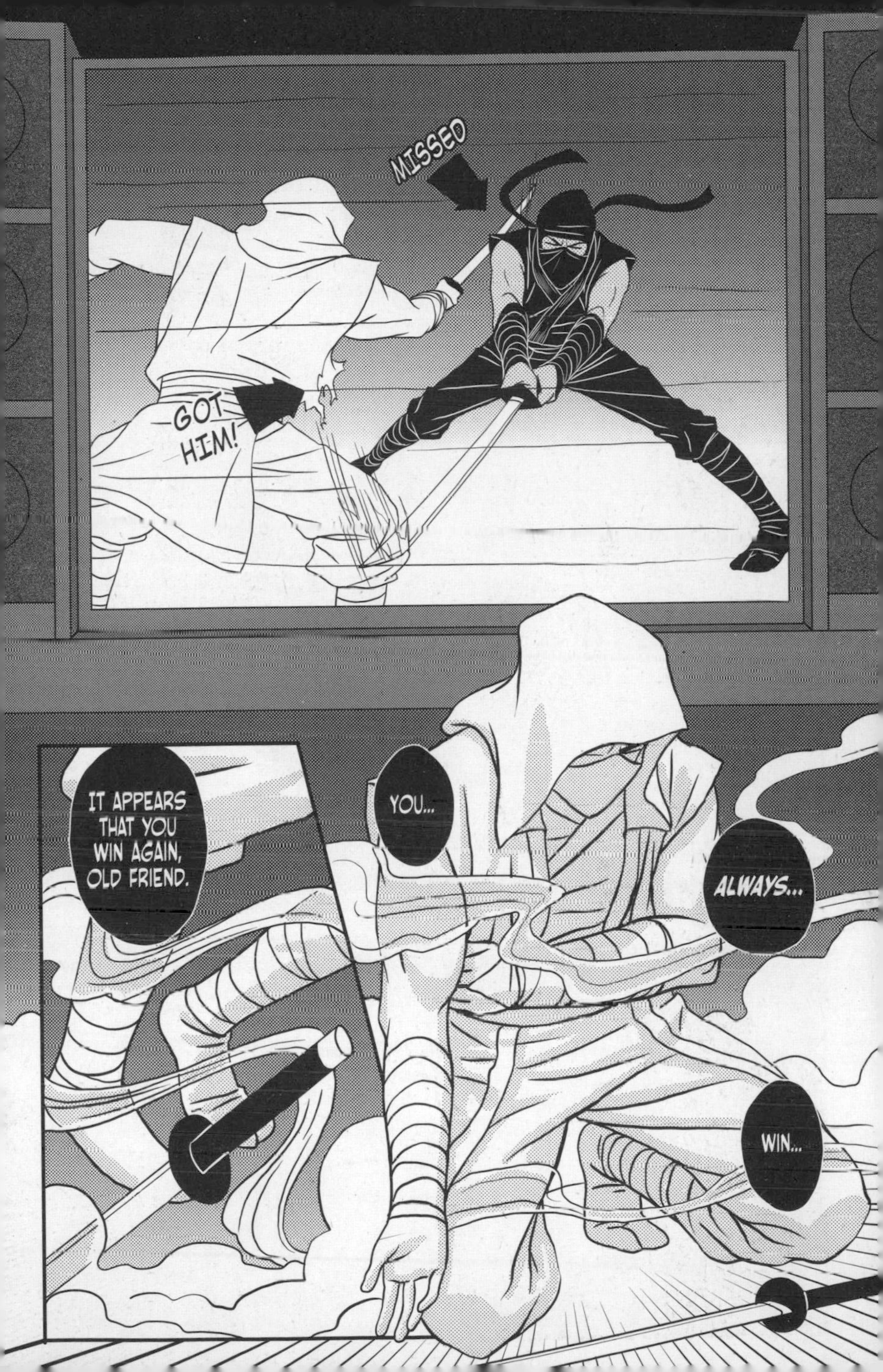
MISSED
GOT HIM!
IT APPEARS THAT YOU WIN AGAIN, OLD FRIEND.
YOU...
ALWAYS...
WIN...

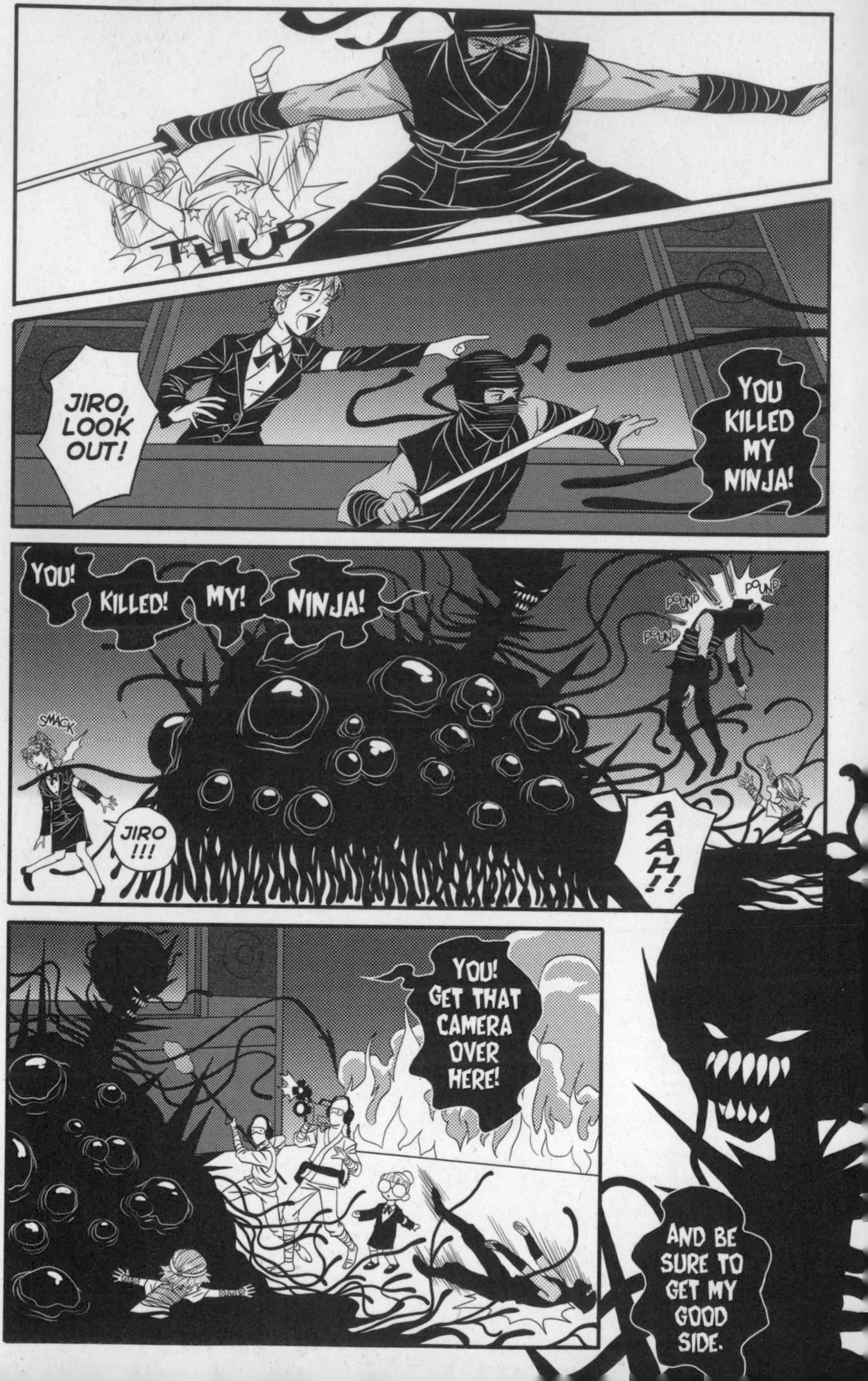
THUD
JIRO, LOOK OUT!
YOU KILLED MY NINJA!
YOU!
KILLED!
MY!
NINJA!
POUND
POUND
POUND
SMACK
JIRO !!!
AAAH!!
YOU! GET THAT CAMERA OVER HERE!
AND BE SURE TO GET MY GOOD SIDE.

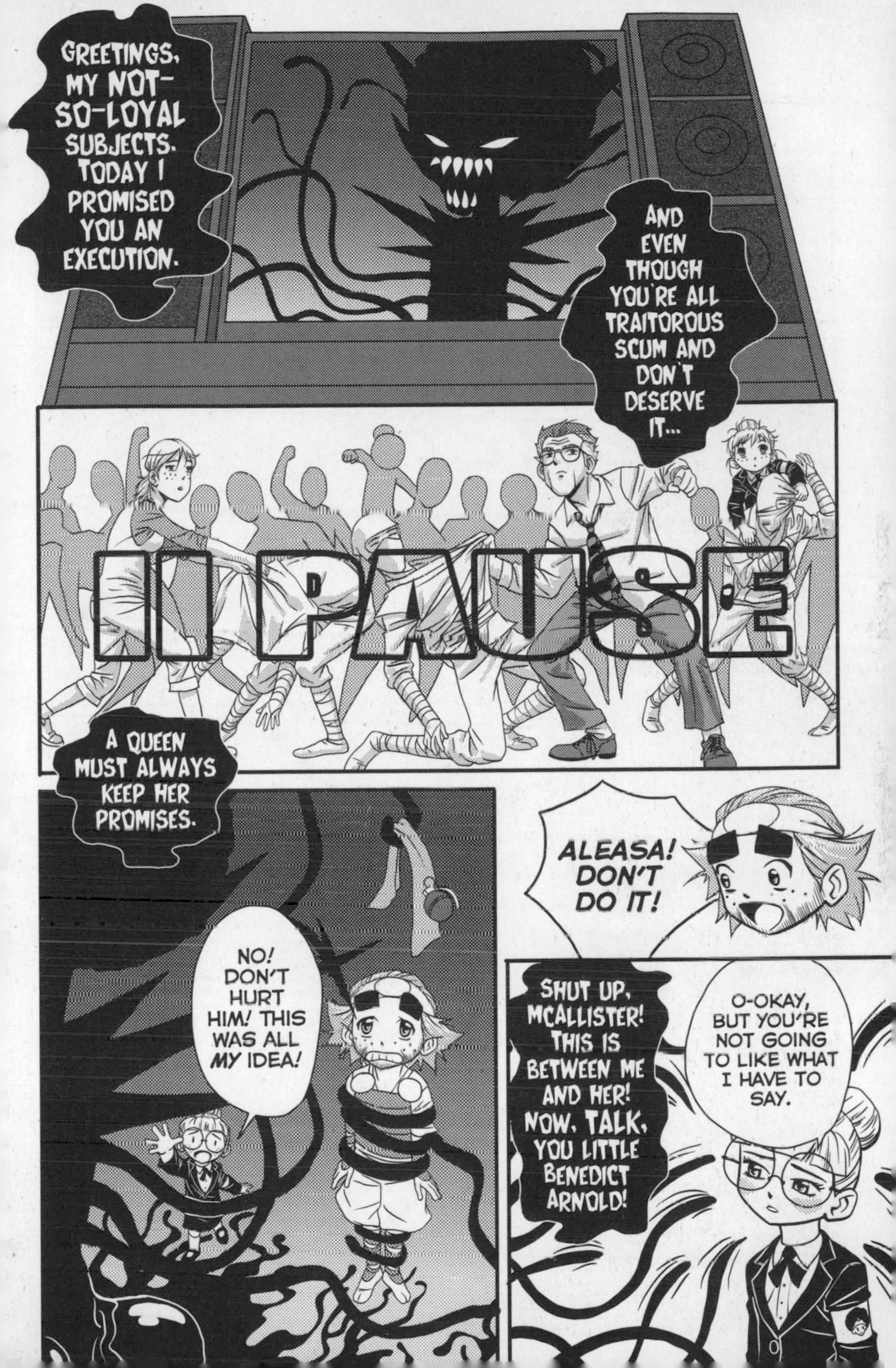
GREETINGS, MY NOT-SO-LOYAL SUBJECTS. TODAY I PROMISED YOU AN EXECUTION.
AND EVEN THOUGH YOU'RE ALL TRAITOROUS SCUM AND DON'T DESERVE IT...
II PAUSE
A QUEEN MUST ALWAYS KEEP HER PROMISES.
NO! DON'T HURT HIM! THIS WAS ALL MY IDEA!
ALEASA! DON'T DO IT!
SHUT UP, MCALLISTER! THIS IS BETWEEN ME AND HER! NOW, TALK, YOU LITTLE BENEDICT ARNOLD!
O-OKAY, BUT YOU'RE NOT GOING TO LIKE WHAT I HAVE TO SAY.

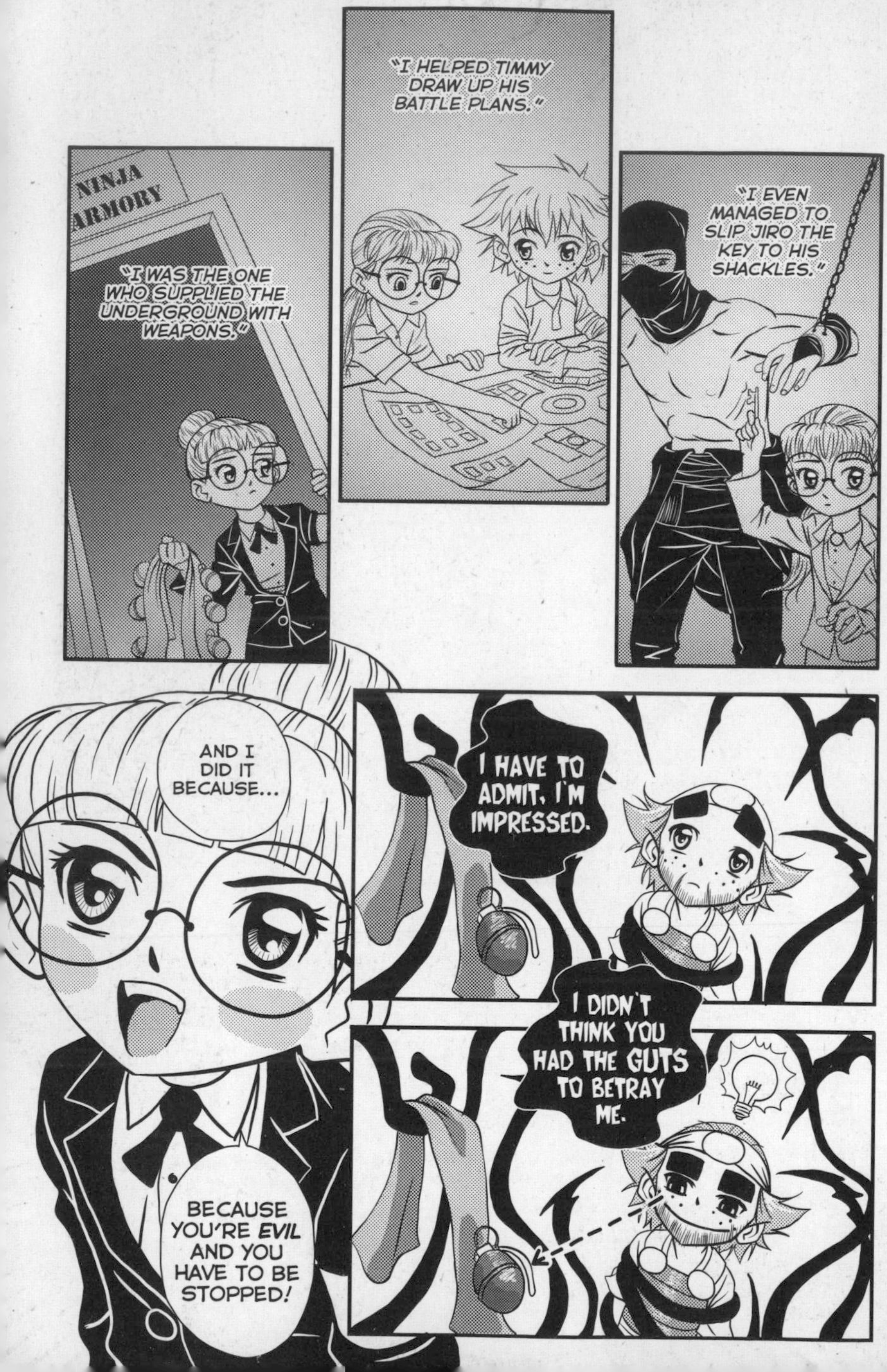
NINJA ARMORY
"I WAS THE ONE WHO SUPPLIED THE UNDERGROUND WITH WEAPONS."
"I HELPED TIMMY DRAW UP HIS BATTLE PLANS."
"I EVEN MANAGED TO SLIP JIRO THE KEY TO HIS SHACKLES."
AND I DID IT BECAUSE...
BECAUSE YOU'RE *EVIL* AND YOU HAVE TO BE STOPPED!
I HAVE TO ADMIT, I'M IMPRESSED.
I DIDN'T THINK YOU HAD THE GUTS TO BETRAY ME.

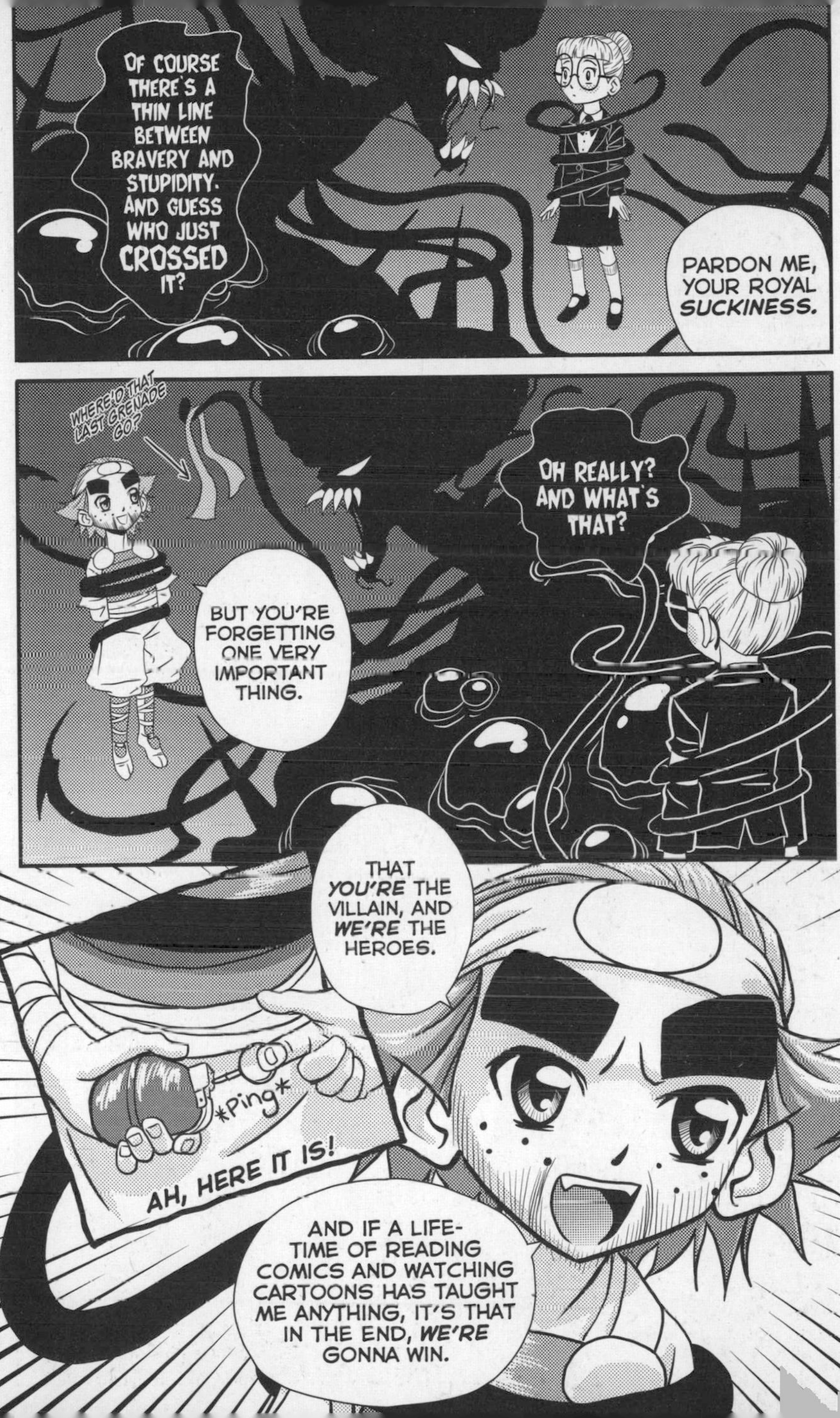
OF COURSE THERE'S A THIN LINE BETWEEN BRAVERY AND STUPIDITY. AND GUESS WHO JUST CROSSED IT?
PARDON ME, YOUR ROYAL SUCKINESS.
WHERE'D THAT LAST GRENADE GO?
BUT YOU'RE FORGETTING ONE VERY IMPORTANT THING.
OH REALLY? AND WHAT'S THAT?
THAT YOU'RE THE VILLAIN, AND WE'RE THE HEROES.
Ping
AH, HERE IT IS!
AND IF A LIFE-TIME OF READING COMICS AND WATCHING CARTOONS HAS TAUGHT ME ANYTHING, IT'S THAT IN THE END, WE'RE GONNA WIN.

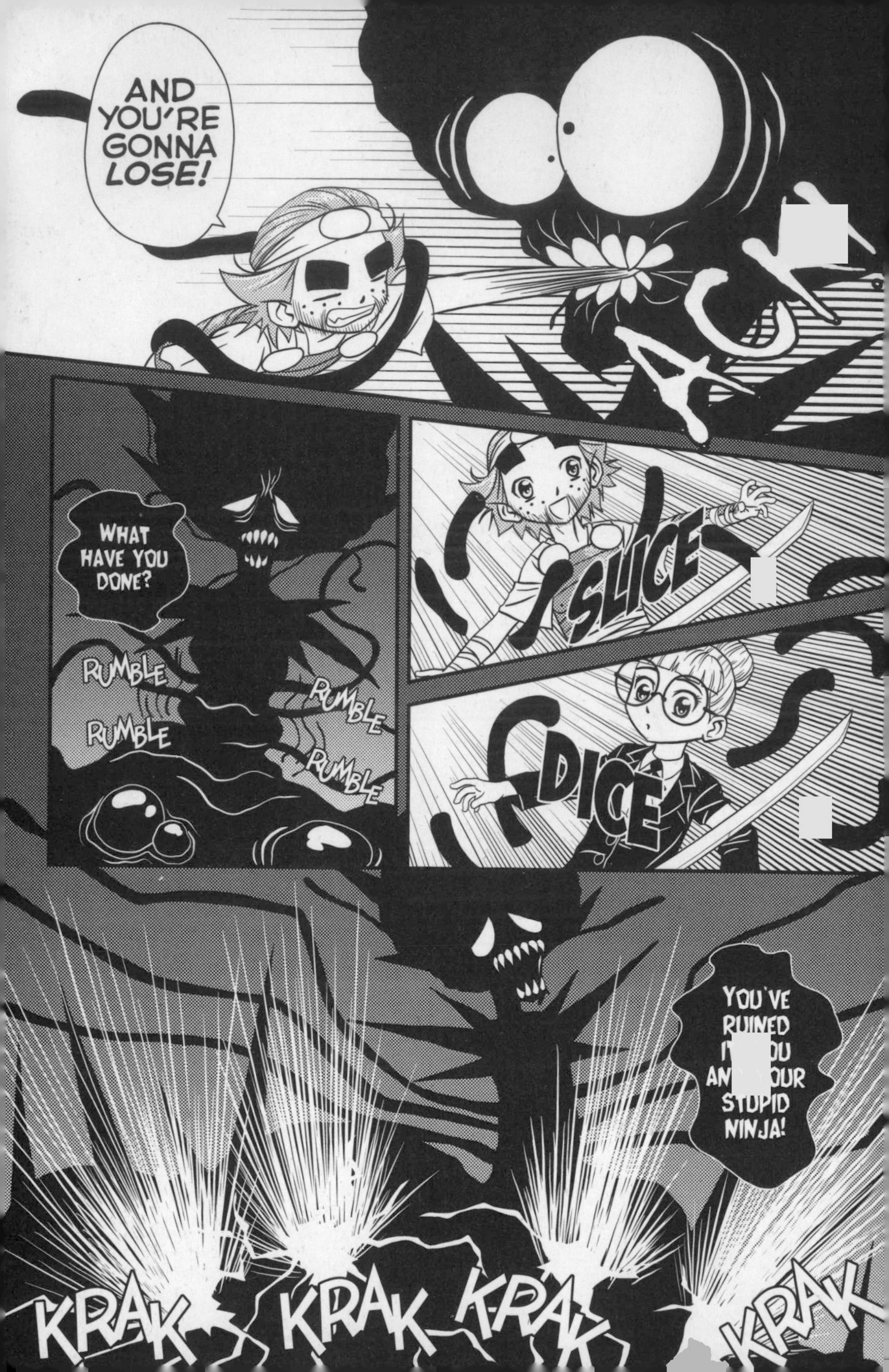
AND YOU'RE GONNA LOSE!
ACK
WHAT HAVE YOU DONE?
RUMBLE
RUMBLE
RUMBLE
RUMBLE
SLICE
DICE
YOU'VE RUINED
STUPID NINJA!
KRAK KRAK KRAK KRAK

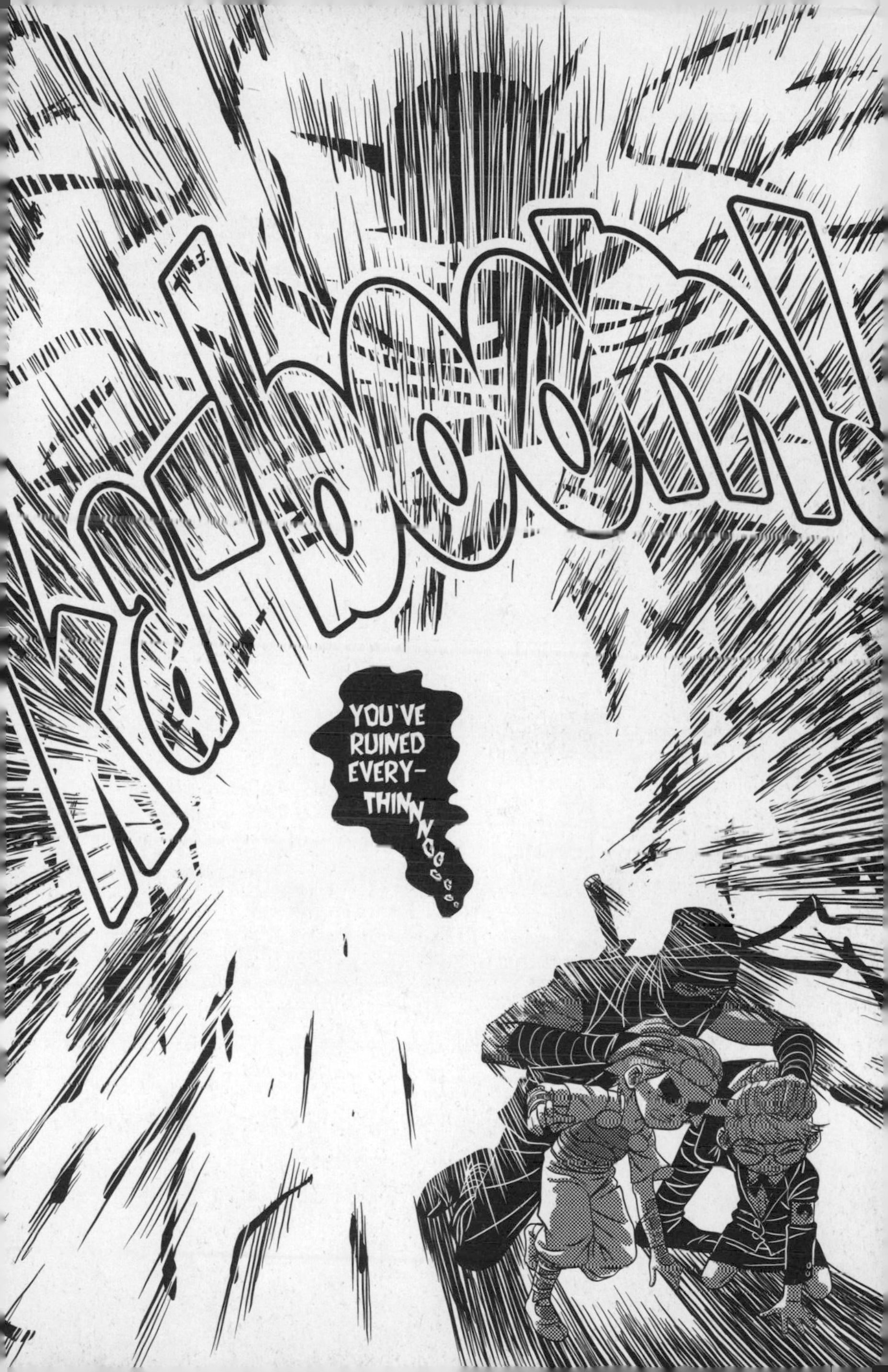
KABOOM!
YOU'VE RUINED EVERY-THINNNGGG...

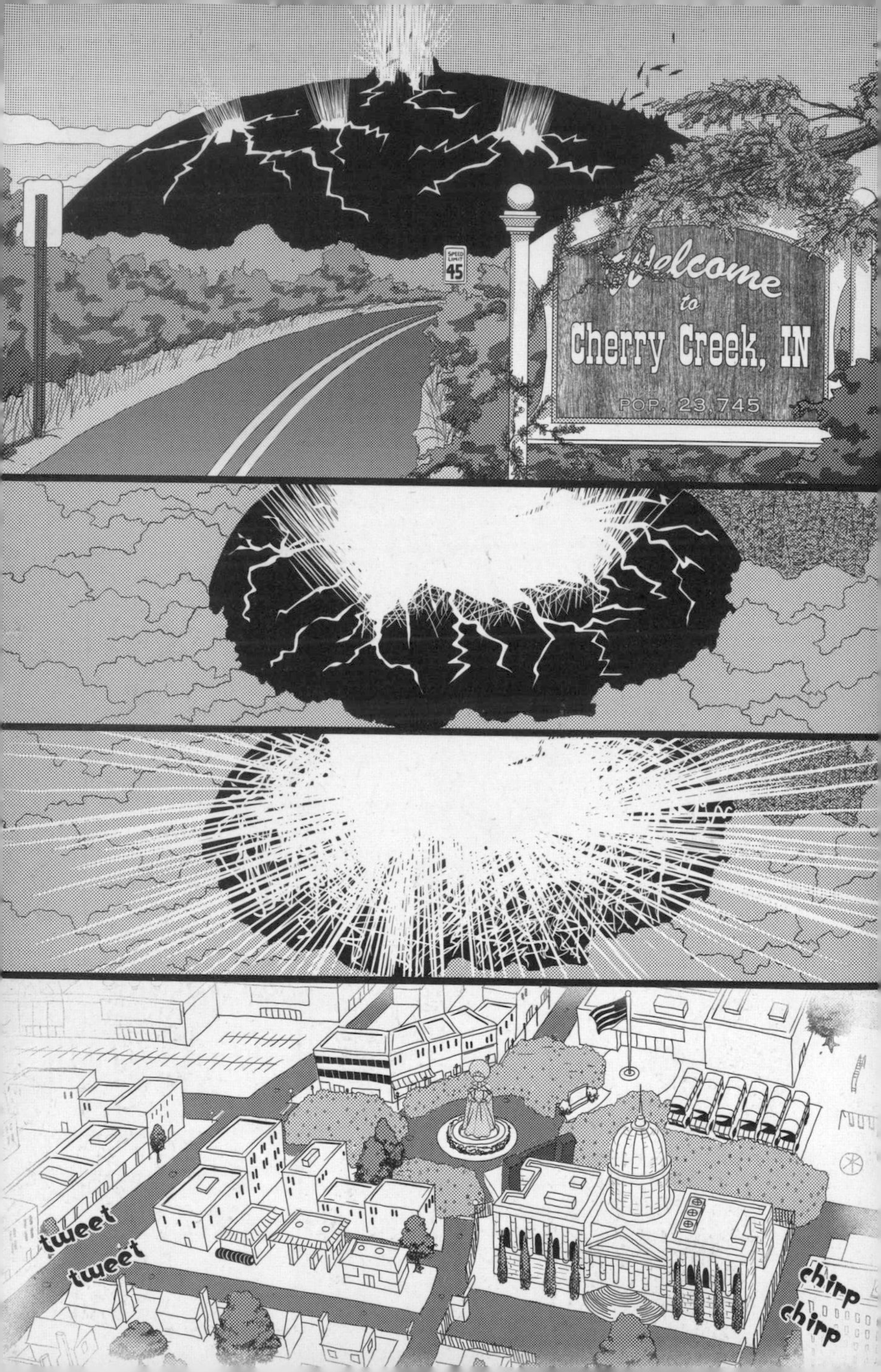
SPEED LIMIT 45
Welcome to Cherry Creek, IN
POP. 23,745
tweet
tweet
chirp
chirp

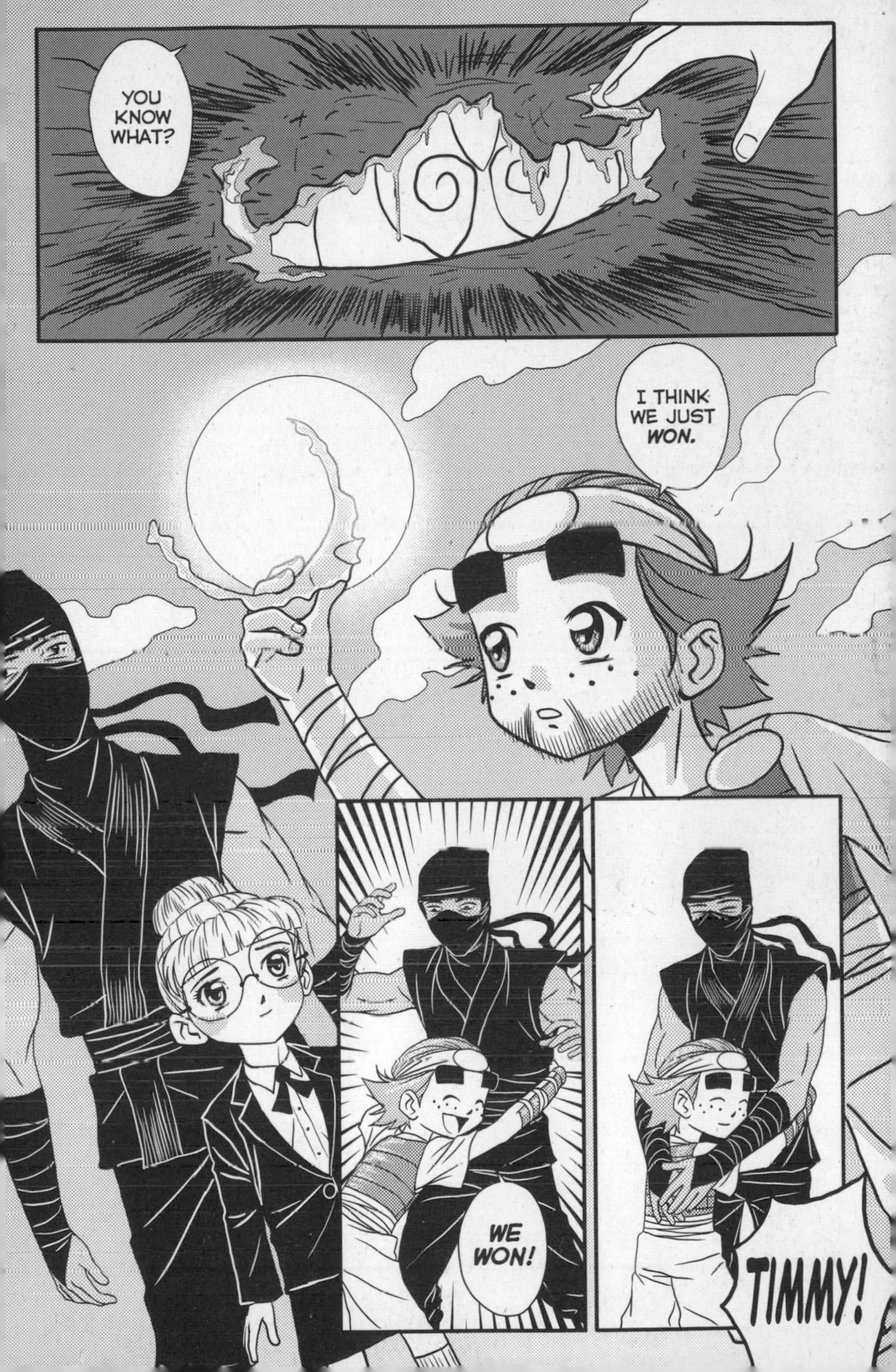
YOU KNOW WHAT?
I THINK WE JUST WON.
WE WON!
TIMMY!

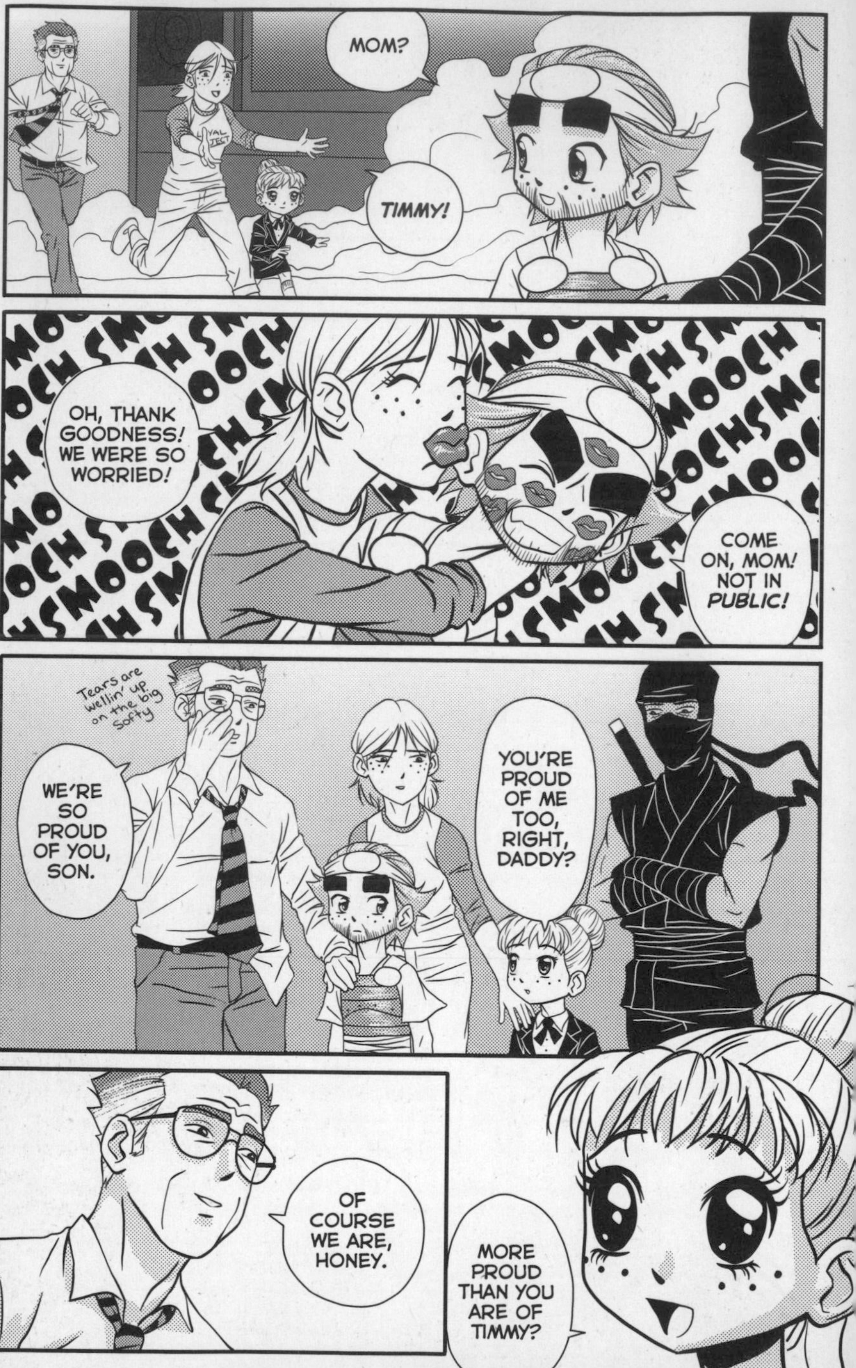
MOM?
TIMMY!
OH, THANK GOODNESS! WE WERE SO WORRIED!
SMOOCH SMOOCH SMOOCH
COME ON, MOM! NOT IN PUBLIC!
Tears are wellin' up on the big softy
WE'RE SO PROUD OF YOU, SON.
YOU'RE PROUD OF ME TOO, RIGHT, DADDY?
OF COURSE WE ARE, HONEY.
MORE PROUD THAN YOU ARE OF TIMMY?

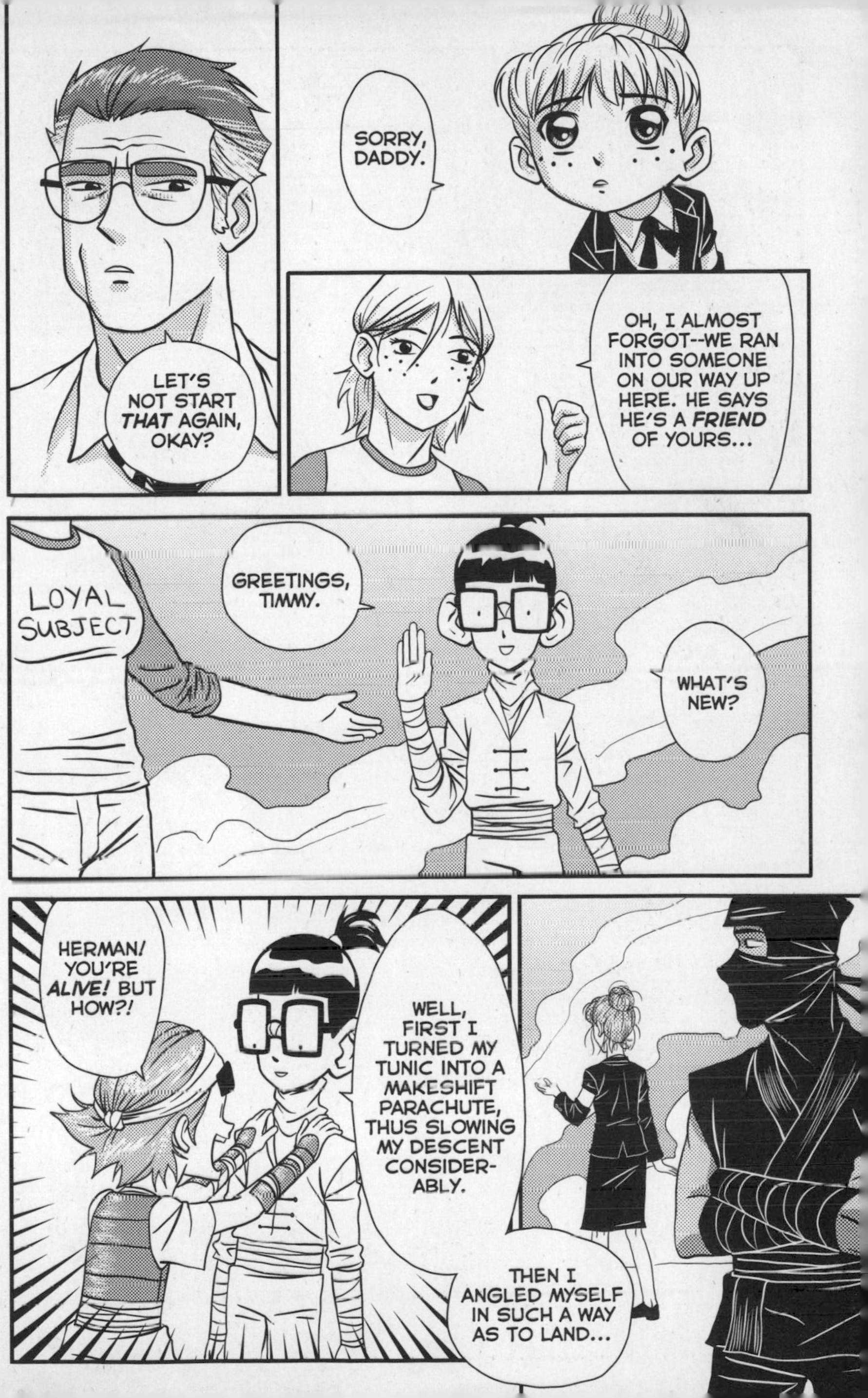
SORRY, DADDY.
LET'S NOT START *THAT* AGAIN, OKAY?
OH, I ALMOST FORGOT--WE RAN INTO SOMEONE ON OUR WAY UP HERE. HE SAYS HE'S A *FRIEND* OF YOURS...
LOYAL SUBJECT
GREETINGS, TIMMY.
WHAT'S NEW?
HERMAN! YOU'RE *ALIVE!* BUT HOW?!
WELL, FIRST I TURNED MY TUNIC INTO A MAKESHIFT PARACHUTE, THUS SLOWING MY DESCENT CONSIDER-ABLY.
THEN I ANGLED MYSELF IN SUCH A WAY AS TO LAND...

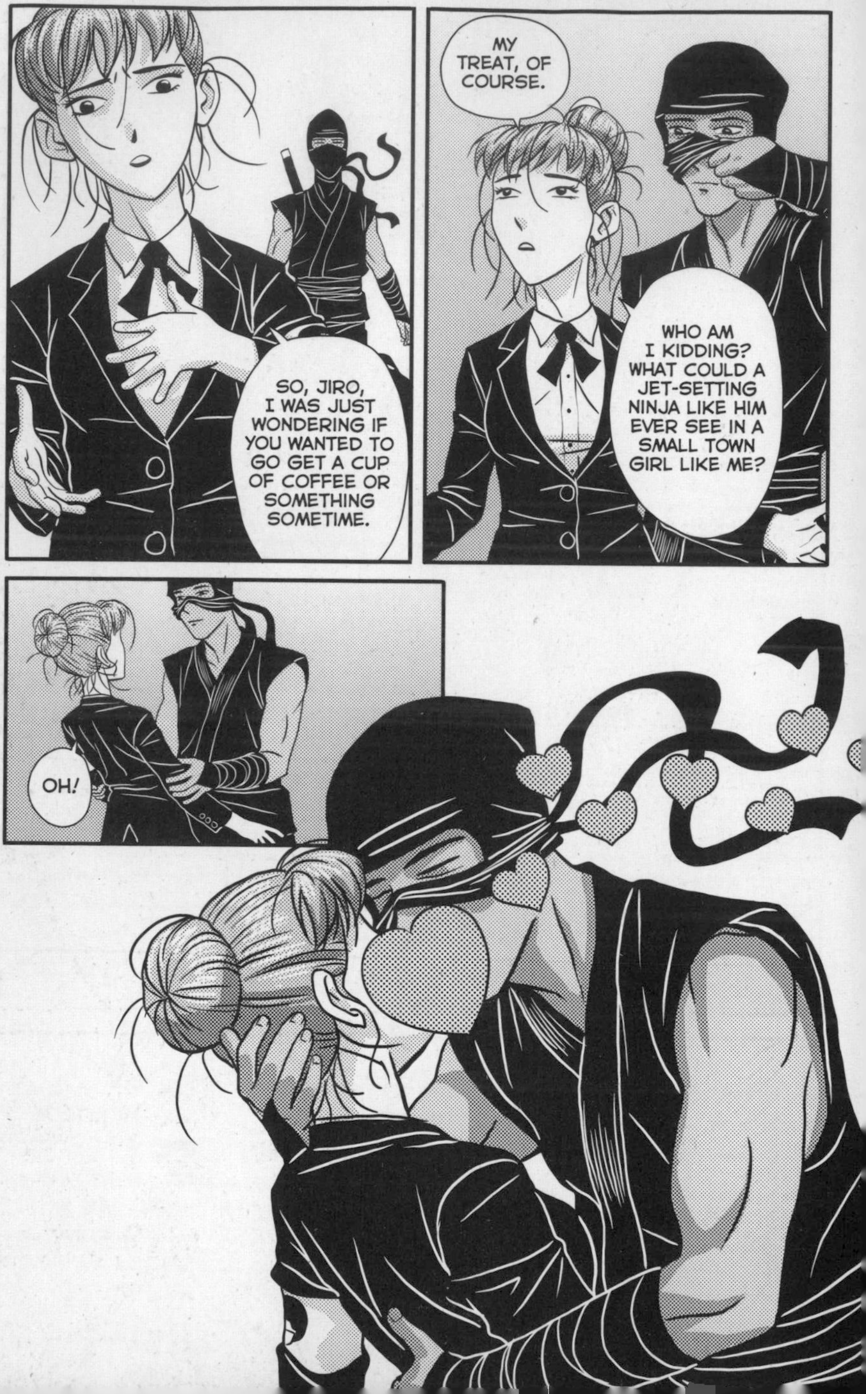
SO, JIRO, I WAS JUST WONDERING IF YOU WANTED TO GO GET A CUP OF COFFEE OR SOMETHING SOMETIME.
MY TREAT, OF COURSE.
WHO AM I KIDDING? WHAT COULD A JET-SETTING NINJA LIKE HIM EVER SEE IN A SMALL TOWN GIRL LIKE ME?
OH!

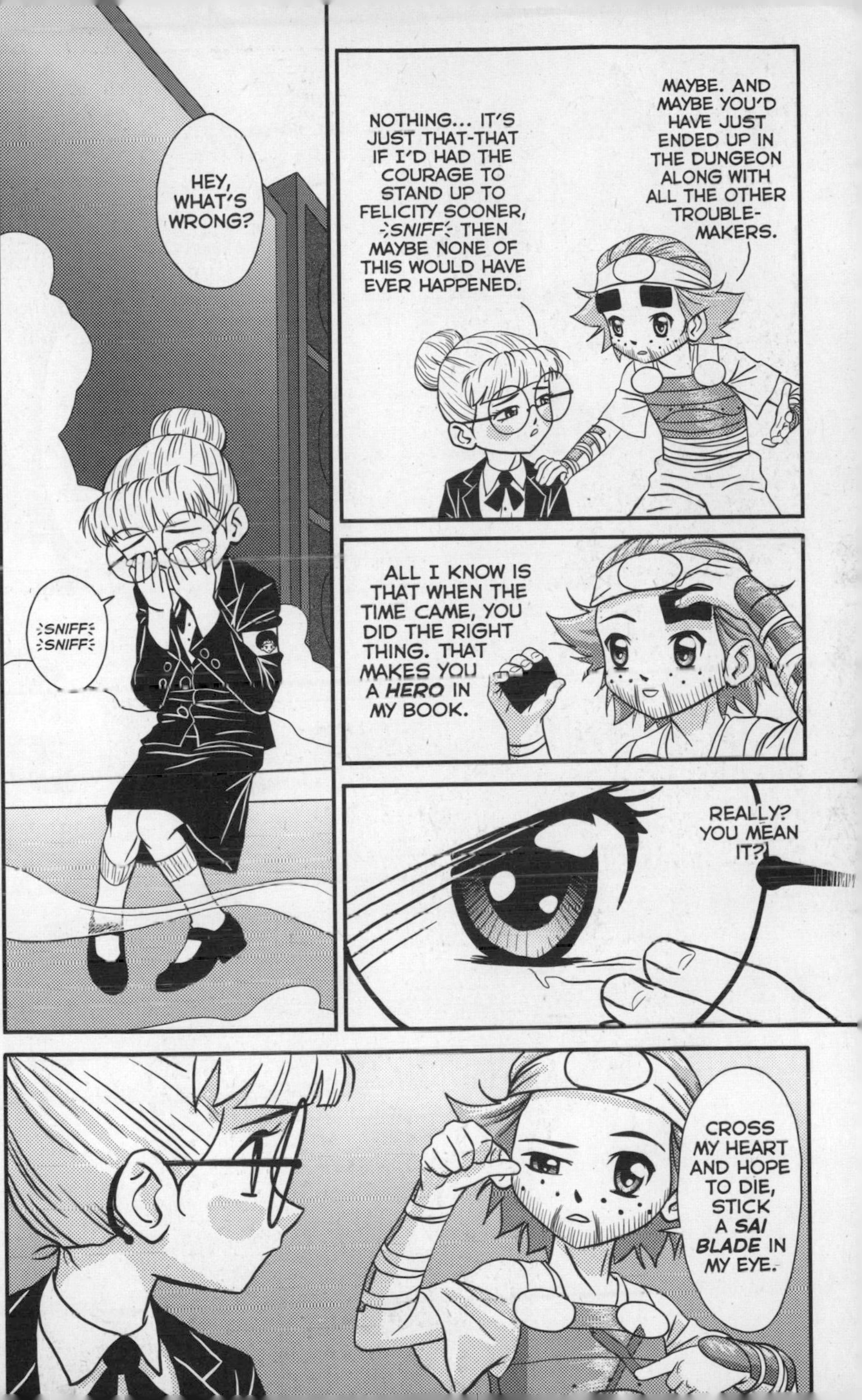
HEY, WHAT'S WRONG?
⁏SNIFF⁏ ⁏SNIFF⁏
NOTHING... IT'S JUST THAT-THAT IF I'D HAD THE COURAGE TO STAND UP TO FELICITY SOONER, ⁏SNIFF⁏ THEN MAYBE NONE OF THIS WOULD HAVE EVER HAPPENED.
MAYBE. AND MAYBE YOU'D HAVE JUST ENDED UP IN THE DUNGEON ALONG WITH ALL THE OTHER TROUBLE-MAKERS.
ALL I KNOW IS THAT WHEN THE TIME CAME, YOU DID THE RIGHT THING. THAT MAKES YOU A *HERO* IN MY BOOK.
REALLY? YOU MEAN IT?
CROSS MY HEART AND HOPE TO DIE, STICK A *SAI BLADE* IN MY EYE.

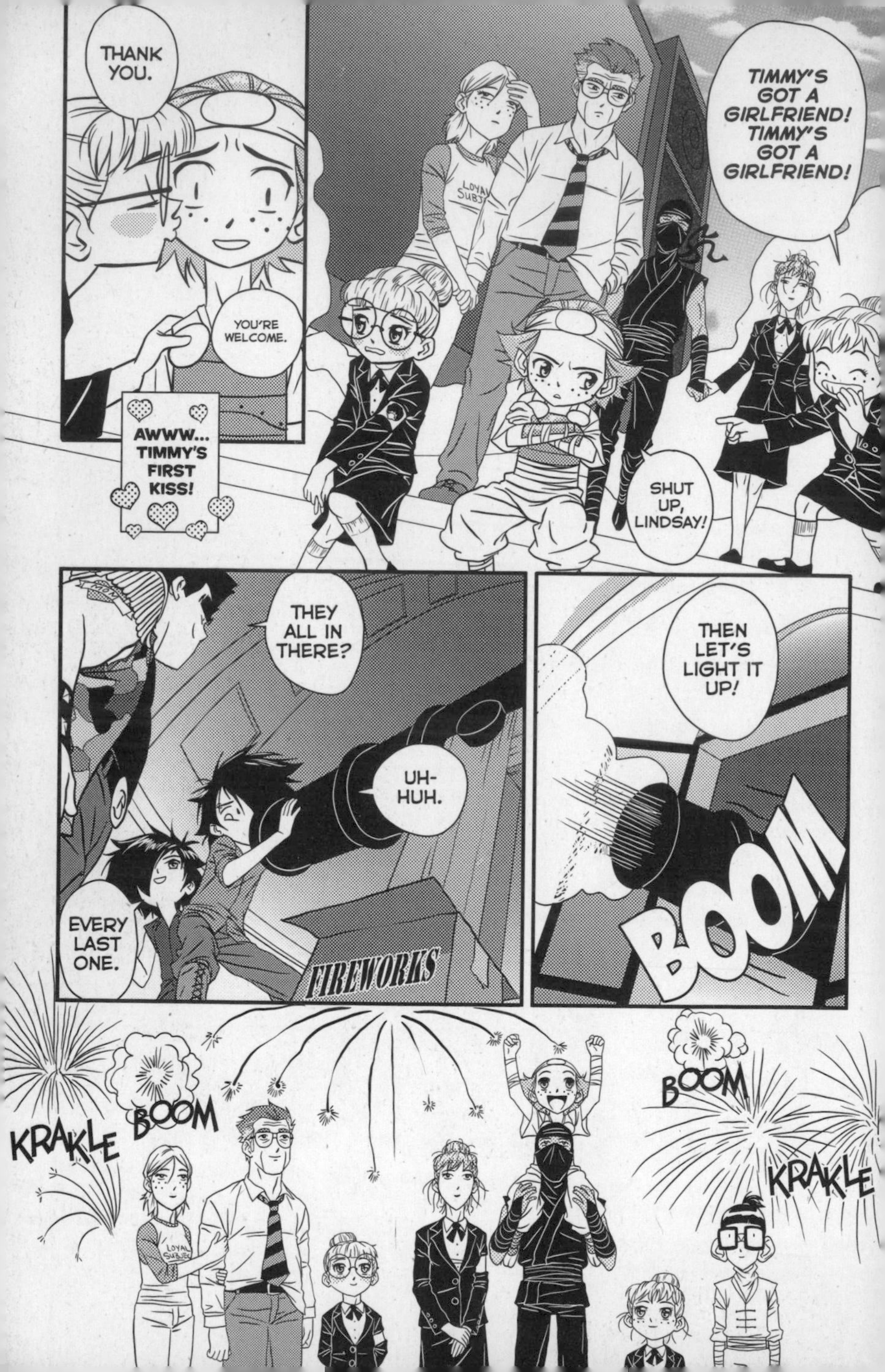
THANK YOU.
YOU'RE WELCOME.
AWWW... TIMMY'S FIRST KISS!
LOYAL SUBJ
TIMMY'S GOT A GIRLFRIEND! TIMMY'S GOT A GIRLFRIEND!
SHUT UP, LINDSAY!
THEY ALL IN THERE?
UH-HUH.
EVERY LAST ONE.
FIREWORKS
THEN LET'S LIGHT IT UP!
BOOM
KRAKLE
BOOM
BOOM
KRAKLE

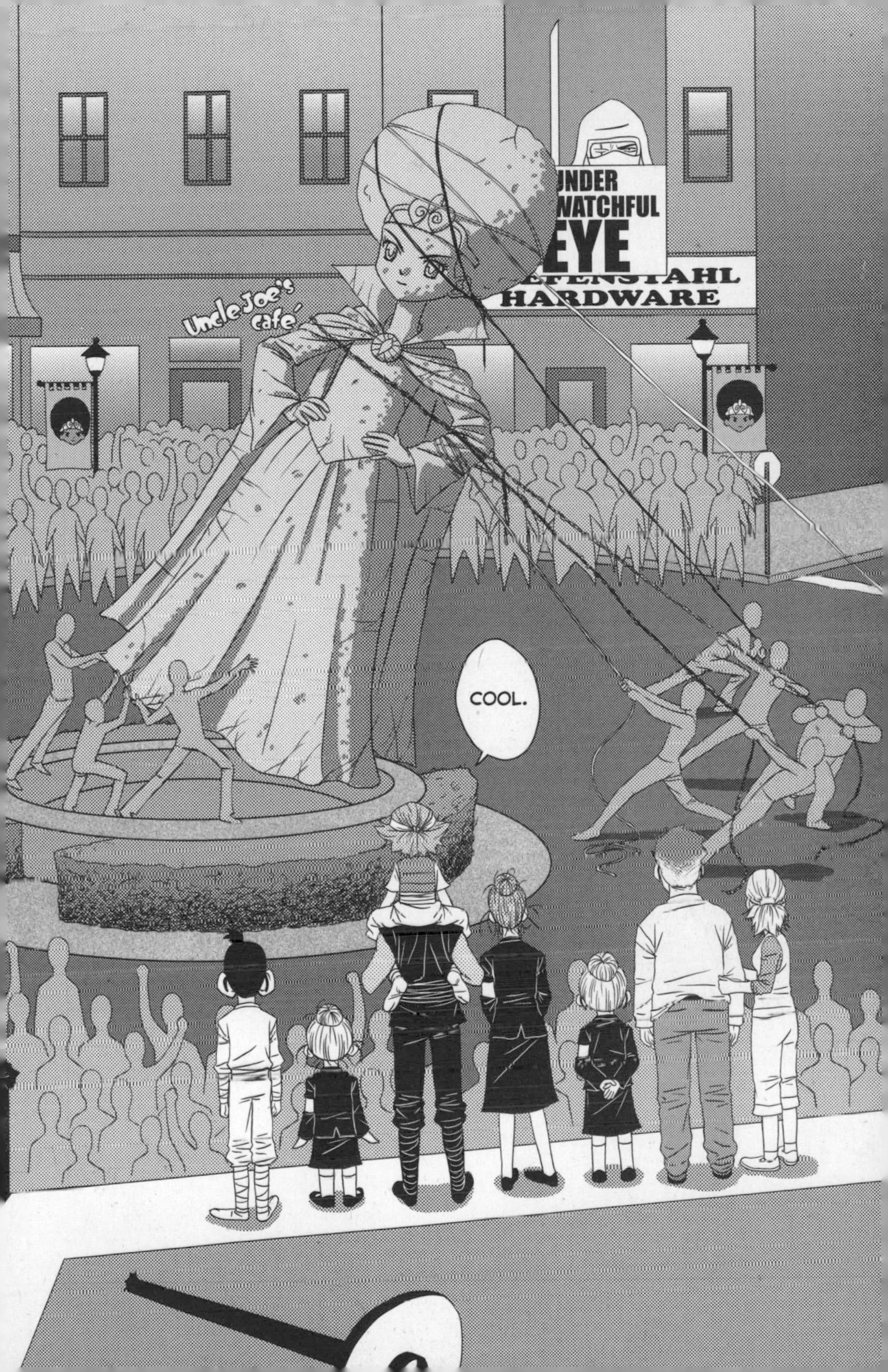
UNDER
WATCHFUL
EYE
HARDWARE
Uncle Joe's café
COOL.

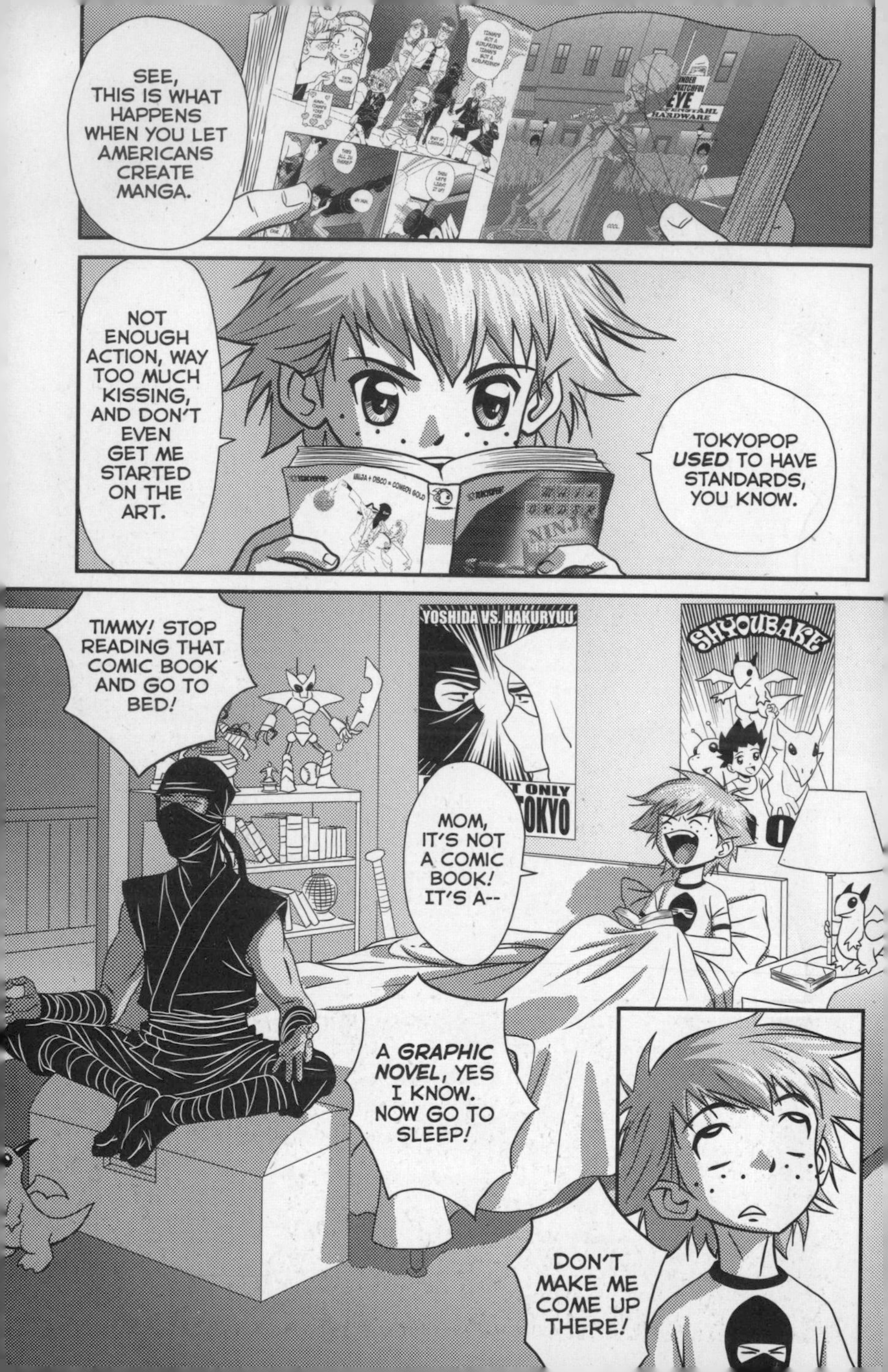
SEE, THIS IS WHAT HAPPENS WHEN YOU LET AMERICANS CREATE MANGA.
NOT ENOUGH ACTION, WAY TOO MUCH KISSING, AND DON'T EVEN GET ME STARTED ON THE ART.
TOKYOPOP *USED* TO HAVE STANDARDS, YOU KNOW.
TIMMY! STOP READING THAT COMIC BOOK AND GO TO BED!
YOSHIDA VS. HAKURYUU
SHYOUBAKE
MOM, IT'S NOT A COMIC BOOK! IT'S A--
A *GRAPHIC NOVEL*, YES I KNOW. NOW GO TO SLEEP!
DON'T MAKE ME COME UP THERE!

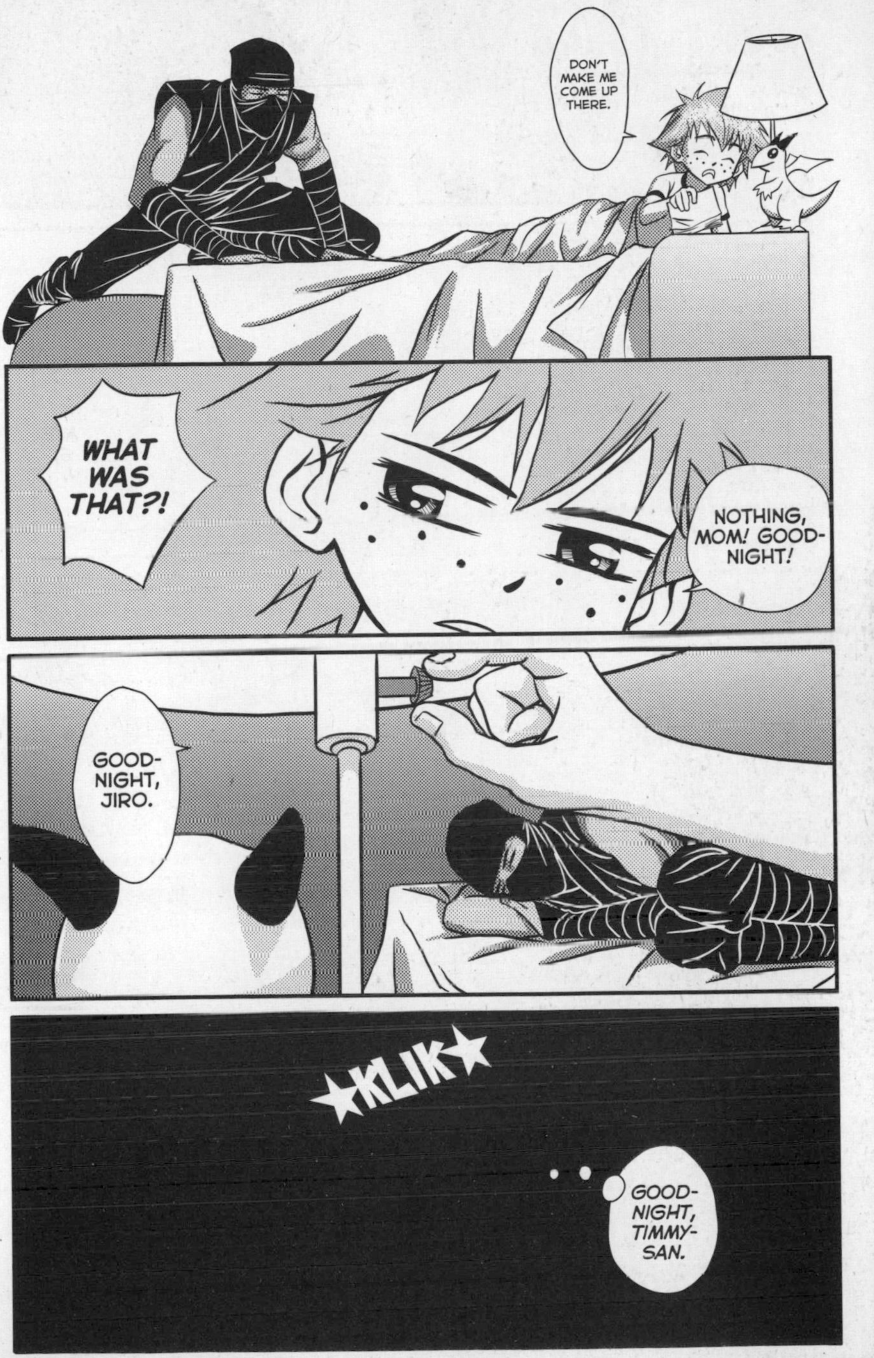
DON'T MAKE ME COME UP THERE.
WHAT WAS THAT?!
NOTHING, MOM! GOOD-NIGHT!
GOOD-NIGHT, JIRO.
★KLIK★
GOOD-NIGHT, TIMMY-SAN.

NINJAZ N DA HOOD

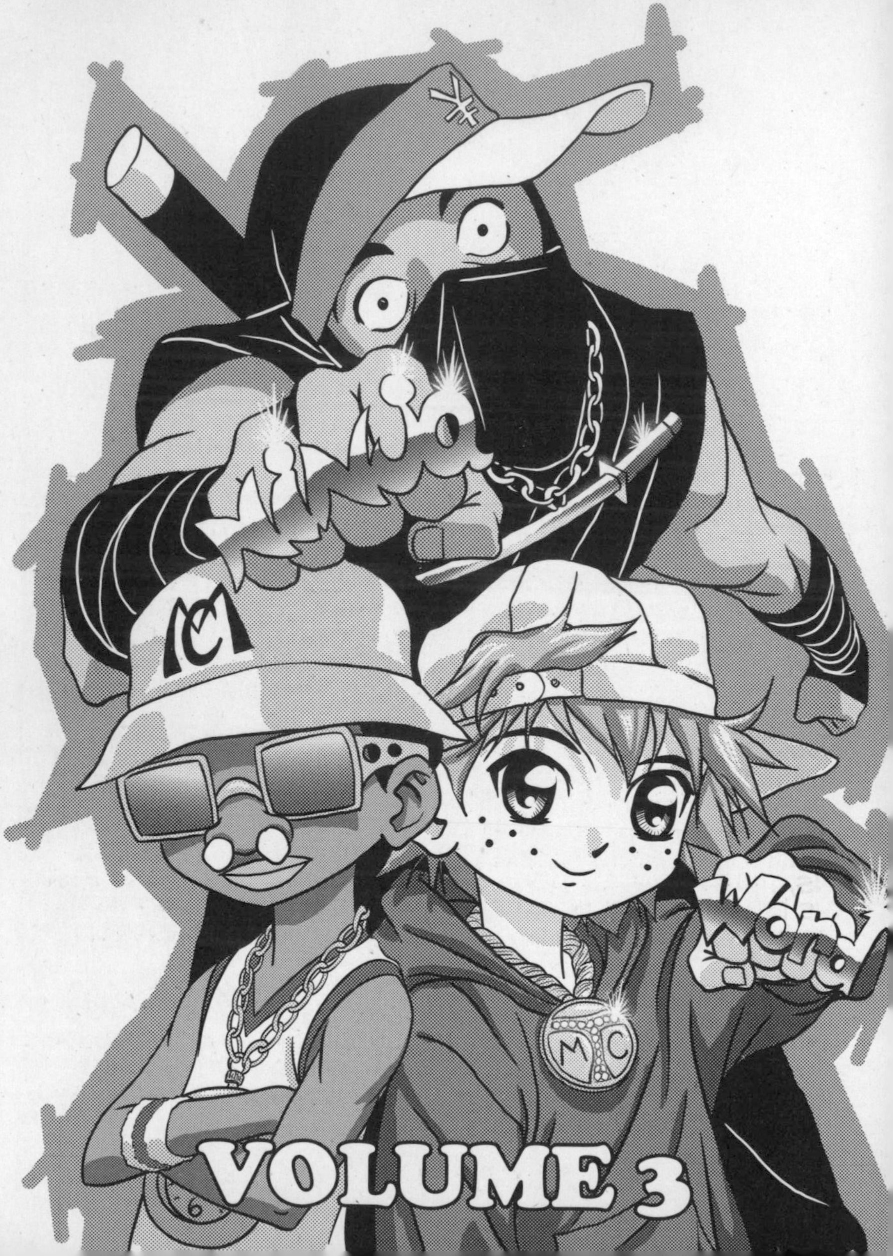

VOLUME 3

VOL. 3 PREVIEW

SEVERAL WEEKS HAVE PASSED SINCE THE CLIMACTIC
EVENTS OF *MAIL ORDER NINJA BOOK TWO: TIMMY STRIKES BACK*,
AND THINGS ARE FINALLY STARTING TO RETURN TO NORMAL.
THE TOWN HAS BEEN REBUILT, FELICITY HAS BEEN DEPOSED
AND NOW LIES COMATOSE IN A HOSPITAL BED, WHILE THE
WARRIORS OF THE WHITE DRAGON CLAN--SAVE FOR THE DEVIOUS
HAKURYUU MITSUHIDE AND HIS BRUTISH COUSIN GOEMON--
HAVE ALL BEEN DEFEATED. OF COURSE, IN CHERRY CREEK,
NORMAL IS SYNONYMOUS WITH BORING. AND THAT'S WHY
TIMMY AND JIRO ARE TAKING A LITTLE ROAD TRIP.

OUR DYNAMIC DUO JETS OFF TO SUNNY SAN DIEGO WHERE
THEY'LL BE THE GUESTS OF HONOR AT THE WORLD'S LARGEST
NINJA CONVENTION, THE 25TH ANNUAL SHINOBICON. ONLY ONE
GROUP OF DISGRUNTLED OTAKU COMES NOT TO PRAISE TIMMY
BUT TO BURY HIM. CALLING THEMSELVES THE SEVEN DEADLY
FANS, THEY'VE MADE A DEAL WITH THE DREAD DEMON DRALTHOR
THE DOOMBRINGER IN ORDER TO GAIN THE POWER THEY NEED
TO DESTROY OUR PLUCKY YOUNG HERO ONCE AND FOR ALL.

WILL JIRO BE ABLE TO DEFEAT SEVEN SUPERNATURALLY
SOUPED-UP PSYCHOS? IS NOBUNAGA REALLY DEAD? IS TIMMY
GOING TO TURN INTO A BIG JERK NOW THAT HE'S ALL FAMOUS
AND STUFF? THE ANSWERS TO ALL THESE QUESTIONS AND
MORE CAN BE FOUND IN THE NEXT HIP-HOPTACULAR VOLUME
OF MAIL ORDER NINJA...

NINJAZ 'N DA HOOD!

JOSHUA ELDER IS THE HANDSOME AND BRILLIANT WRITER OF *MAIL ORDER NINJA*, WHICH HE'S PRETTY SURE HAS BEEN ACCLAIMED BY SOME CRITIC, SOMEWHERE. A GRADUATE OF NORTHWESTERN UNIVERSITY WITH A DEGREE IN FILM, JOSHUA CURRENTLY RESIDES IN THE QUAINT, LITTLE MIDWESTERN TOWN OF CHICAGO, ILLINOIS.

FUN FACTS

- JOSHUA HAS BEEN HIT IN THE HEAD WITH A BASEBALL BAT-- TWICE!

- JOSHUA WAS A HIGHLY VALUED MEMBER OF HIS HIGH SCHOOL'S MATH AND SPEECH TEAMS.

- BUT JOSHUA ALSO PLAYED FOOTBALL, SO HE ISN'T A TOTAL DORK.

- BUT HE ALSO PLAYED *DUNGEONS & DRAGONS*. SO YEAH, HE KIND OF IS A TOTAL DORK.

ERICH OWEN

HEY, EVERYBODY! THANK YOU FOR READING THIS CRAZY CREATION OF OURS. I HOPE YOU ENJOYED IT, CUZ WE ENJOYED CREATING IT. WELL, WITHOUT FURTHER ADO, HERE IS MY BIO:

I WAS BORN AND GREW UP IN MICHIGAN. I AM A SELF TAUGHT ILLUSTRATOR AND GOT MY FIRST FREELANCE JOB IN '97. IN 2000, AFTER WORKING AS A DIGITAL RETOUCH ARTIST, I TAUGHT MYSELF FLASH AND GOT A JOB IN CALIFORNIA WITH A DOT COM COMPANY AS A FLASH CHARACTER ANIMATOR. WHEN THE DOT COM CRASH HIT, I STARTED FREELANCING AGAIN. SINCE THEN I HAVE WORKED ON VIDEO GAME CONCEPT ART, COMIC STRIPS, CHILDREN'S COMICS, AND VARIOUS OTHER ILLUSTRATION PROJECTS. I HAVE ALSO WORKED WITH VIPER COMICS AND ARCANA STUDIO. RIGHT NOW, I AM WORKING ON A FEW PROJECTS, TWO OF WHICH ARE FOR TOKYOPOP, AND ALSO GEARING UP TO BEGIN ON M.O.N. VOL. 3 AT THE FIRST OF THE YEAR. CURRENTLY, I LIVE IN NASHVILLE, TN WITH MY LOVELY WIFE AND TWO BEAUTIFUL CHILDREN AND OUR HAMSTER.

DISNEY · SQUARESOFT

KINGDOM HEARTS

TOKYOPOP

**THE QUEST TO SAVE THE WORLD
CONTINUES IN THE BEST-SELLING
MANGA FROM TOKYOPOP!**

AVAILABLE WHEREVER BOOKS ARE SOLD.

www.TOKYOPOP.com

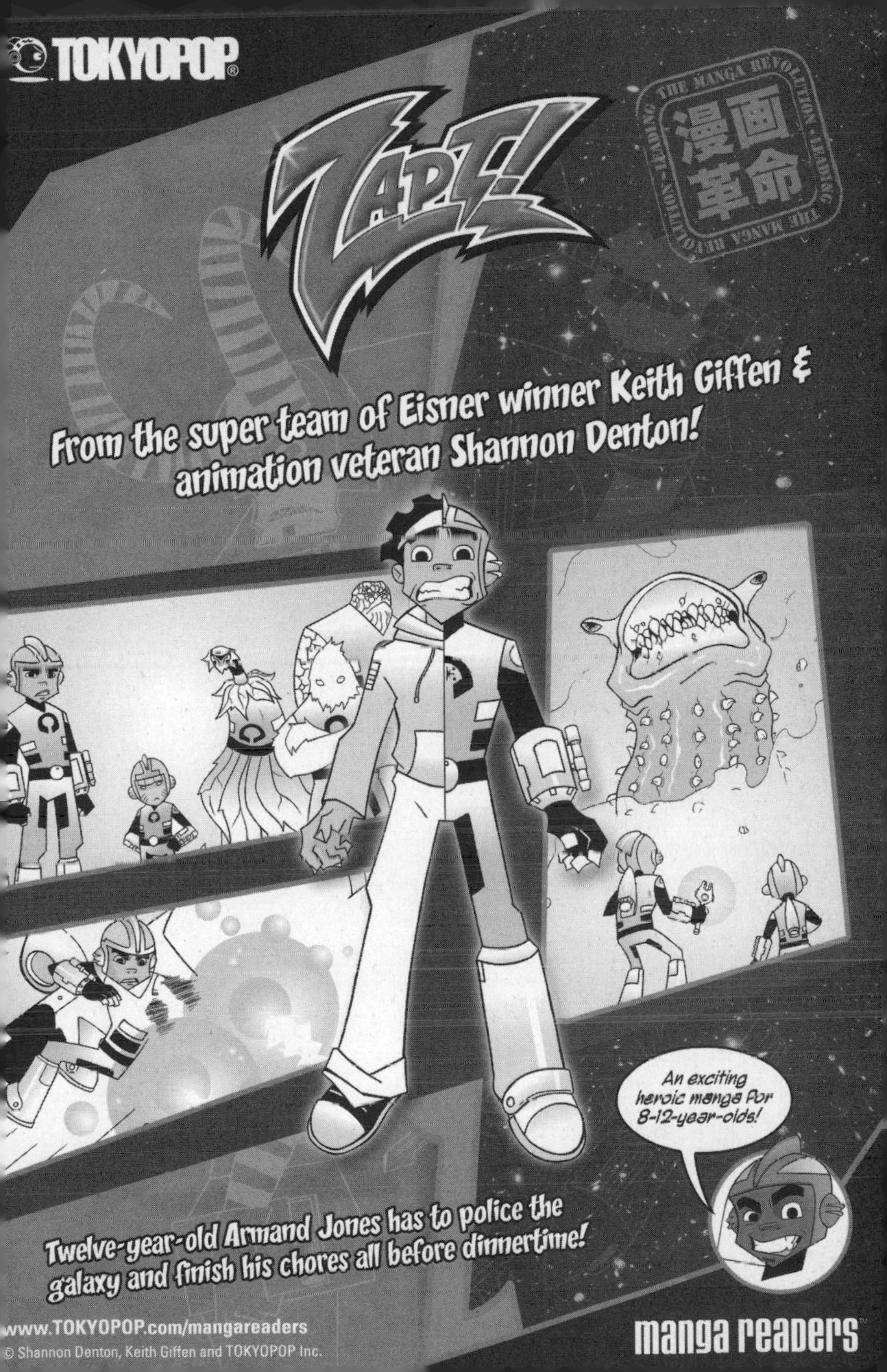
TOKYOPOP
ZAP!
THE MANGA REVOLUTION · LEADING
漫画革命
From the super team of Eisner winner Keith Giffen &
animation veteran Shannon Denton!
An exciting heroic manga for 8-12-year-olds!
Twelve-year-old Armand Jones has to police the galaxy and finish his chores all before dinnertime!
www.TOKYOPOP.com/mangareaders
© Shannon Denton, Keith Giffen and TOKYOPOP Inc.
manga readers

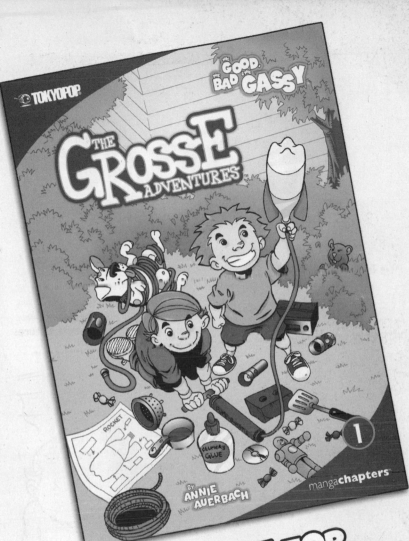

PERFECT FOR
8-10 year olds!
ENJOYABLE
for everyone!